Skies of Steel

The Ether Chronicles

by Zoë Archer
Skies of Steel
Skies of Fire

by Nico Rosso
Nights of Steel
Night of Fire

Skies of Steel

THE ETHER CHRONICLES

ZOË ARCHER

RT ·14

AVONIMPULSE
An Imprint of HarperCollinsPublishers

Excerpt from *The Forbidden Lady* copyright © 2002, 2012 by
Kerrelyn Sparks.

Excerpt from *Turn to Darkness* copyright © 2012 by Tina
Wainscott.

EPub Edition OCTOBER 2012 ISBN: 9780062109156

Print Edition ISBN: 9780062218155

10 9 8 7 6 5 4 3 2 1

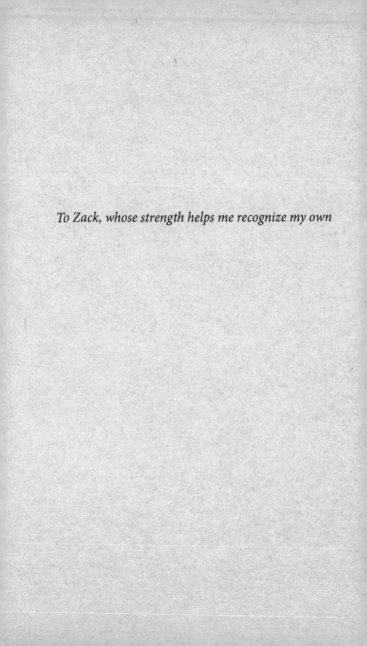

To Zack, whose strength helps me recognize my own

Acknowledgments

Special thanks to Susan Crangle, Jane Johnson, and Adriana Baranello, for their language expertise.

Chapter One

Palermo, Sicily

DAPHNE CARLISLE DUCKED as a mechanical arm soared past. It narrowly missed her head and smashed on the wall behind her. Pieces of rusted metal flew everywhere, landing in her hair and scattering on the floor. Someone gave a coarse laugh. Angry shouts ensued, followed by the sounds of fisticuffs and wooden furniture shattering.

Assuredly, this isn't the Accademia.

Straightening, Daphne picked the bits of metal and gearworks from her hair. She tugged on her short, fitted jacket and smoothed out her skirts. This tavern might be the gathering spot for thieves, miscreants, and scoundrels, but she needn't look as though she was one of their number. Her mission necessitated appearing as respectable and honest as possible. She couldn't fail. The stakes were far too high.

She scanned the smoke-filled room. The fight had subsided, or at least the participants had grown bored of their brawl. Men—and some women—of every nation huddled around tables, their hands possessively wrapped around mugs and greasy wine glasses. One group gambled using a clockwork game of chance, others used old-fashioned playing cards. An automaton with a concertina honked out what might be music, but it had to have been years since the mechanized musician had been serviced. It missed every fifth note.

"Looking for someone, *bella*?" someone slurred at her in Italian.

She raised an eyebrow at the poorly groomed man staggering toward her. Stains covered his clothing, and his hair hung in greasy strands over his collar. Wine dribbled from the rim of his cup and onto his worn shoes.

"You've found him," the man added with a leer. He stood far too close. Fumes of many varieties wafted off of him.

"If I'm in need of a lesson in bad hygiene," she answered, also in Italian, "I know precisely who to call upon."

The man blinked at her, then slowly realized he'd been insulted. "Hey, now, I'm only being friendly." He reached for her.

She knocked his hand back. "I've got more than enough friends."

He fumbled for her again. "I—"

Moving as quickly as her skirts would allow, Daphne

hooked her foot behind his ankle, then tugged. He stumbled backward, landing with a thud in a nearby chair. An expression of bafflement crossed his face, as though he couldn't quite understand how he'd wound up sitting.

"Truly, *signore*," she said, shaking out her skirts once more, "there are plenty of women here who will find your . . . charms . . . alluring. I'm not one of them."

Before he could form a rejoinder, Daphne moved on. She hadn't time to waste with drunkards and fools.

Pressing further into the tavern, she saw that it stretched out in a labyrinth of rooms.

Now I know how Theseus felt.

Except the creature she sought wasn't a bull-headed monster, but another kind of hybrid. One that the Ancients would most definitely have found equally fantastic. She had no ball of string to help find her way out of this place, and it struck her again how very alone she was in this endeavor.

She dodged more groping hands and impertinent questions, all the while conscious of how out of place she had to look. Palermo, and this tavern in particular, served as the gathering place for the seafaring criminals of the western Mediterranean. Part of the Mechanized War was being fought in the sky using airships, but seafaring battles were still common, and the war had destabilized the seas, leaving them ripe for infestation by pirates and smugglers. Not since the days of the wild Spanish Main had the oceans been so perilous.

Which was precisely why Daphne needed to travel in the sky, and why she'd come to this place.

But the man she sought was nowhere to be found. She cursed under her breath.

He *had* to be here. His airship, *Bielyi Voron*, had been spotted nearby. Through the judicious use of bribery, she had learned that he frequented this tavern. If he wasn't here, she would have to come up with a whole new plan, but that would take costly time. Every hour, every day that passed meant the danger only increased.

She walked past another room, then halted abruptly when she heard a deep voice inside the chamber speaking in Russian. Cautiously, she peered around the doorway. A man sat in a booth against the far wall. The man she sought. Of that she had no doubt.

Captain Mikhail Mikhailovich Denisov. Rogue Man O' War.

Like most people, Daphne had heard of the Man O' Wars, but she'd never seen one in person. Not until this moment. Newspaper reports and even cinemagraphs could not fully do justice to this amalgam of man and machine. The telumium implants that all Man O' Wars possessed gave them incredible might and speed, and heightened senses. Those same implants also created a symbiotic relationship between Man O' Wars and their airships. They both captained and powered these airborne vessels. The implants fed off of and engendered the Man O' Wars' natural strength of will and courage.

Even standing at the far end of the room, Daphne felt Denisov's energy—invisible, silent waves of power that resonated in her very bones. As a scholar, she found the phenomenon fascinating. As a woman, she was . . . troubled.

Hard angles comprised his face: a boldly square jaw, high cheekbones, a decidedly Slavic nose. The slightly almond shape of his eyes revealed distant Tartar blood, while his curved, full mouth was all voluptuary, framed by a trimmed, dark goatee. An arresting face that spoke of a life fully lived. She would have looked twice at him under any circumstances, but it was his hair that truly made her gape.

He'd shaved most of his head to dark stubble, but down the center of his head he'd let his hair grow longer, and it stood up in a dramatic crest, the tip colored crimson. Dimly, she remembered reading about the American Indians called Mohawks, who wore their hair in just such a fashion. Never before had she seen it on a non-Indian.

By rights, the style ought to look outlandish, or even ludicrous. Yet on Denisov, it was precisely right—dangerous, unexpected, and surprisingly alluring. Rings of graduated sizes ran along the edge of one ear, and a dagger-shaped pendant hung from the lobe of his other ear.

Though Denisov sat in a corner booth, his size was evident. His arms stretched out along the back of the booth, and he sprawled in a seemingly casual pose, his long legs sticking out from beneath the table. A small child could fit inside each of his tall, buckled boots. He wore what must have been his Russian Imperial Aerial Navy long coat, but he'd torn off the sleeves, and the once-somber gray wool now sported a motley assortment of chains, medals, ribbons, and bits of clockwork. A deliberate show of defiance. His coat proclaimed: *I'm no longer under any government's control.*

If he wore a shirt beneath his coat, she couldn't tell. His arms were bare, save for a thick leather gauntlet adorned with more buckles on one wrist.

Despite her years of fieldwork in the world's faraway places, Daphne could confidently say Denisov was by far the most extraordinary-looking individual she'd ever seen. She barely noticed the two men sitting with him, all three of them laughing boisterously over something Denisov said.

His laugh stopped abruptly. He trained his quartz blue gaze right at her.

As if filled with ether, her heart immediately soared into her throat. She felt as though she'd been targeted by a predator. Nowhere to turn, nowhere to run.

I'm not here to run.

When he crooked his finger, motioning for her to come toward him, she fought her impulse to flee. Instead, she put one foot in front of the other, approaching his booth until she stood before him. Even with the table separating them, she didn't feel protected. One sweep of his thickly muscled arm could toss the heavy oak aside as if it were paper.

"Your search has ended, *zaika*." His voice was heavily accented, deep as a cavern. "Here I am."

She wondered how he knew to speak to her in English rather than Italian, but, glancing down at her painfully tidy traveling costume, she realized she may as well have worn a sash bearing the Union Jack.

"How do you know it's you I seek?" she returned.

With one broad finger, he tapped his ear. The pendant hanging from his lobe swung slightly with the movement. "These tell me everyone's secrets."

Of course. Man O' Wars had hearing and eyesight far superior to a normal man's. He'd heard her fumbling her way toward him.

"What are *your* secrets, *zaika*?" Without straightening from his sprawl, he looked her up and down in bold perusal.

Heat flooded her cheeks and spread throughout her body. One would think, having lived in Italy for as long as she had, she'd be no stranger to a man's impudent stare. Something about the way Denisov stared at her, though, sent a new, hot awareness through her.

"I have no secrets," she lied.

A corner of his mouth turned up. "Everyone does. The fun is trying to discover what they are."

"I wonder at your definition of fun," she said, raising an eyebrow.

"No need to simply wonder." His smile turned blatantly carnal. "You can find out for yourself."

Good God. Blushing virgin, she most certainly wasn't. So why did she feel like one in his presence, and with every word from his mouth? And why did she get the feeling that most women took him up on his offer?

She straightened. "Mikhail Mikhailovich Denisov?"

"*Captain* Mikhail Mikhailovich Denisov," he answered. "I may have been drummed out of the tsar's navy, but I still captain my ship."

"Precisely why I sought you out." Records on rogue Man O' Wars were scarce, since most governments didn't like to make such knowledge public. But Denisov had been one of the Russian Imperial Aerial Navy's finest. Even in Britain, his desertion had been trumpeted in the newspapers. One thing all articles had left out was the reason *why* he'd gone rogue. Rogue Man O' Wars were notorious for keeping silent about their rationales for turning their backs on their countries, as if there was some kind of tacit agreement between them. Which only added to their aura of danger and mystery.

Since Denisov had broken from the Russian Navy, he'd become infamous as a mercenary willing to do almost anything for the right price. Which is exactly why she needed him. He was her only hope.

"Not for fun."

"Not for fun," she said. Finding him had not been easy, taking valuable time following leads through criminal networks—a world she knew very little about, but had needed to learn to navigate quickly. Fear and urgency had been her constant companions then, just as they were now. Her heart fluttered in her throat, and her palms were damp.

He affected a sigh, then kicked a chair toward her. "As you like. But if you change your mind . . ." His grin was all scoundrel. "All the stories you've heard about Man O' Wars are true."

As she took her seat, she could only speculate about the content of those stories. She didn't know if she was relieved or disappointed that she hadn't heard them.

One thing she now knew for certain: Denisov was not wearing a shirt beneath his coat, only a buckled waistcoat. The deep V-neck of the waistcoat revealed precisely delineated pectoral muscles, sprinkled with dark hair. As Denisov shifted slightly, light from the flickering gas lamp gleamed on a metallic surface on his chest. His telumium implants.

"Go ahead and look." His wry voice punctured her thoughts. Pulling aside the edge of his waistcoat, he revealed more of the implants.

She was a scholar, so she felt no compunction about studying them. Somehow, the metal had been grafted to his skin, covering his left pectoral. It looked as though it continued up onto his shoulder, as well. The telumium had been shaped so that it appeared part of his body, taking on the form of his muscles. Having done some research on Man O' Wars, she knew that there were telumium filaments leading from the implants to his heart, which created the process by which he powered an airship. Yet she was an anthropologist, not an engineer, and the whys and wherefores of the process remained arcane.

"Does it hurt?" she asked.

He frowned, as though the question caught him by surprise, and tugged his waistcoat back into place. "Not anymore."

She flattened her disappointment that she couldn't study his implants further. All that truly mattered was that Denisov had an airship, not how he could power it.

"Mister Denisov—"

"*Captain* Denisov."

"Captain," she began again. "Are you familiar with the current situation in the Arabian Peninsula?"

"As familiar as I need to be." He took a deep drink from his cup, and she tried not to watch the tendons in his neck as he swallowed. "Telumium was discovered there a few months ago."

"A very rich source," she confirmed. "Which means that the war has spread as nations vie for the telumium deposit. The allied English and Italians want it, and the Hapsburg-Russian alliance wants it. The entire region has destabilized as a result. Any remnants of the fragile peace between local tribes has been utterly shattered."

One of the men sitting with Denisov snorted derisively. "So?"

She glared at him. "*So*—my parents are archaeologists in the Arabian Peninsula. They were working on a dig when the telumium was discovered and everything went to hell." Turning her gaze to Denisov, she said, "My parents have been kidnapped. A warlord by the name of Haroun ibn Jalal al-Rahim has imprisoned them."

Denisov whistled lowly. "Heard of al-Rahim. A ruthless bastard, that one."

A cold spike of fear jammed into her chest, but she forced herself to ignore it. Nothing could be gained by panicking. The only way she could see this through was to remain calm and in control at all times.

"He took my parents and the local people working with them on the dig," she continued, "despite the fact that they were intruding on no one's territory."

"How'd you find out about this?"

"Al-Rahim sent a package to me in Florence." She swallowed hard, remembering the terror that chilled her as she'd unwrapped the paper and read the accompanying letter. "It contained my mother's wedding band and my father's prized knife. My mother gave it to him as an anniversary gift. They'd never willingly part with either of those things. So I knew al-Rahim's claims were true. I went straight to the British Embassy in Rome, asking for help."

"And they were no help at all," Denisov said.

Her hands curled into fists with remembered anger. "*The political situation is too tenuous.* That's what they told me. *It could cause further imbalance in the region.*"

"Meaning," Denisov said with a smirk, "they were looking after their own arses."

"The bloody telumium, too." She didn't care if her language was becoming coarse. The more she thought about how the British government, *her* government and the government of her parents, put its own financial and political interests ahead of the well-being of its citizens, the more infuriated she became.

Telumium was extremely rare, and an essential component in the creation of Man O' Wars. Having Man O' Wars meant a nation could have airships, which expanded their political and economic reach. Europe had been torn apart as countries allied with and vied against one another in the ongoing search for telumium. To Daphne, it seemed a ridiculous cycle. Going to war in order to give a country the resources to perpetuate war.

She never cared for politics. Her only interest was anthropology, studying the cultures of the world before they vanished beneath the grinding wheels of modernity. Yet now she cared about politics. Deeply.

"There's nothing for it," she said, her words hardening. "I have to try to free my parents on my own."

As she spoke, Denisov straightened, and his wry expression grew more serious. Though he was sitting, she still felt herself intimidated by his size. Motorized bicycle races could be held on his shoulders.

She pressed on. "The only way for me to reach my parents is via airship. *Your* airship."

The glint in his eyes vanished. "No."

"But—"

"The answer is no." Abruptly, he stood.

Oh, Lord, he was so . . . big. She had to tip her head back to look up at him, looming like an omen. An ether pistol was strapped to his thigh. She thought of the revolver in her handbag, and how tiny it seemed in comparison. Did ordinary bullets affect Man O' Wars? She wished she'd researched that topic more thoroughly before coming here tonight.

The men sitting beside Denisov scrambled out of the way as he stalked from the table. Leaving Daphne alone.

Was that it? One word from the Man O' War and her mission was over before it had truly begun?

She jumped to her feet and hurried after him. Given that he cleared a path through the tavern—people scuttling out of his way—she followed in his wake. Before he could reach the door, she jumped in front of him. Thank goodness he stopped walking, or else he would have rolled right over her like a tetrol-powered plow. Thank goodness, too, that she was desperate, or else the glower he gave her might have sent her scurrying for cover behind the bar.

"Captain Denisov, please—"

"Smuggling contraband Chinese automatons into the Kingdom of Brazil," he growled. "*Liberating* treasure from lead-lined vaults on behalf of wealthy clients. Those are the sorts of jobs I take on. Not some miniscule errand."

"There is nothing *miniscule* about saving my parents' lives," she shot back.

He crossed his arms over his chest, the substantial muscles of his biceps knotting. "Profit motivates me, *zaika*. Nothing else."

"You'd be compensated for your efforts."

"Not enough to make it worth my while. Since I've gone rogue, I stay well away from political pandemonium like the one in Arabia."

"As a rogue, doesn't that mean you aren't affiliated with any government? You have freedom to go where others cannot."

"The Russian Imperial Aerial Navy considers me a traitor against the tsar," he countered. "A thief, too, for stealing the *Bielyi Voron*. Any Russian Man O' War who finds and captures me is assured glory. They'll certainly be in Arabia, which means I won't be going there."

He set one massive hand on her shoulder. Though she wore a thick twill jacket, a cotton blouse, and chemise, his touch burned right through all her garments, as if he placed his hand upon her bare skin. Her heartbeat stuttered.

His brows lowered, as though this simple touch affected him just as strongly. With his hand still on her shoulder, he guided her out of his path, like a lion nudging aside a cub. He took his hand away, yet she noticed how he rubbed his fingers together afterward—either remembering or erasing the feel of her.

"Find someone else to help you," he said.

She blurted, "Come with me back to my *pensione*."

That teasing smile was back in place. "Changed your mind about the fun, *zaika*? Man O' Wars have a great deal of stamina."

"Just . . . come with me." She turned and hurried outside before her cheeks went up in flames. The salty night air did little to calm her or cool her face, but she took several deep breaths, steadying herself. A moment passed as she stood alone in the street. Then she heard Denisov's heavy steps on the pavement behind her. She didn't know whether to be relieved or terrified.

She walked toward her *pensione*, passing sailors and peddlers and men in front of tatty velvet curtains, hawking the latest in mechanized pleasure. She ignored the catcalls and exhortations thrown her way, her mind focused only on Denisov as he followed her. A quick glance over her shoulder revealed him moving through the gaslight and shadows, trailing after her with deliberate intent. He kept a distance between them, as though purposefully preserving the illusion that she led the chase. If he had wanted to, he could have caught up with her in a few strides. But the space between them only heightened the sense that he toyed with her.

The *pensione* was a tottering three-story building, paint and plaster chipping from its façade. There were finer places to stay in Palermo along the more genteel stretch of waterfront, grand hotels with jeweled mechanical peacocks strutting through their vast gardens, but she hadn't the funds for them. Briefly, she wondered if she ought to have taken a room there, to better indicate to Denisov that she had more than enough money. Too late now.

She took her key from the smirking *signora* at the desk. The woman's smirk faltered when she caught sight of Denisov striding through the doorway. Daphne felt the heat of him as he stood behind her. The *signora* glanced back and forth between Daphne and the Man O' War, and new respect gleamed in her eyes.

Daphne ignored the rattling, steam-powered elevator—it would be impossible to squeeze both herself and Denisov into that narrow metal box—and climbed the three flights of stairs to her room. As she unlocked her door, she caught the unmistakable sounds of a couple enjoying themselves in the room across the hall.

Denisov's chuckle rippled over her as she fumbled with her key. The door finally swung open. She stepped inside and switched on the gaslights.

He shut the door behind them. They were alone together.

Turning to face him, her heart beat faster than it had from the three-story climb. Her room was far from lavish, just big enough to contain a rickety table, a lamp, a dresser with a mirror hanging over it, and a bed. Denisov filled the chamber, not merely with his size, but his presence. With his hair, his coat, his very essence, he seemed a creature from the depths of dreams.

"I'm glad you changed your mind, *lapochka*." His smile was unalloyed wickedness as he stepped closer. He ran one finger along the side of her neck, sending electrical sparks through her. "I admit, you're not my usual sort, but then, I doubt I'm your typical choice."

"That's not . . . why I brought you here." A curious reluctance tore at her as she pulled away. She hurried around the side of the bed, then knelt on the dusty floor. Reaching beneath the bed, she felt for a handle. Her fingers closed around it, and she tugged. Hard.

She dragged the strongbox out from beneath the bed. Muscles straining with the effort, she hefted the metal box and set it down upon the coverlet. The container itself wasn't particularly large—the size of the tea caddy her mother used to take on digs so that she could enjoy her favorite beverage even in the field. But what this strongbox contained was far more valuable than Darjeeling tea.

Denisov watched her, his expression only mildly interested.

She entered a combination into the strongbox's keypad, her fingers flying over the enameled numeric buttons. There was a hiss as the brass locking system unbolted. She lifted the lid.

"*Blyat*," Denisov cursed.

A row of four gold ingots lay like gleaming soldiers within the strongbox. A modest fortune.

"This is half the payment," Daphne said. "You'll receive the other half after I'm taken to Arabia and my parents are freed."

He picked up one of the gold bars. Tested its weight in his hand, even giving the ingot a little toss into the air before catching it. Still, he wasn't satisfied, not until he scraped the gold bar across the surface of the mirror. It left no scratch upon the glass.

Turning back to her, he asked, "Where did you get this gold?"

"Does it matter?"

He thought about it for a moment. "No."

"As I said, all that is yours, if you'll agree to fly me to Arabia. To the city of Medinat al-Kadib, specifically. That's where I'm supposed to meet al-Rahim's emissary."

Setting the ingot down beside the others, he said in a deceptively light voice, "A big chance you've taken, *zaika*—"

"Daphne Carlisle," she cut in. "Of the *Accademia delle Arti e della Cultura* in Florence."

"Ah, a *professorsha*." He planted his hands on his hips. "Learned lady, what's to stop me from just taking this gold now?"

She eyed him, from the tip of his outrageous hair to the toes of his boots. "Nothing. Save the promise of more, if you fulfill your end of the bargain."

"Clever, Miss Carlisle, to use my greed against me." Yet he smiled as he said this.

"So," she pressed, "will you do it?"

She didn't know what she'd do if he said no. Tracking him down had been a Herculean effort, and if, by some miracle, she was able to find another rogue Man O' War willing to take on the task, it would likely be too late. She doubted al-Rahim would keep her parents alive indefinitely.

He glanced down at the strongbox, then up at the ceiling. Her heartbeat, her breath—everything stopped as she waited for him to make his decision.

Finally, he exhaled.

"My ship is anchored off of Capo Zafferano," he said. "We leave at nine o'clock tomorrow morning."

"I'll be there." Relief and trepidation fought for dominance inside her chest. "I wouldn't be averse to departing tonight."

"But my crew would. We've been on the move for weeks, and I promised them leave."

Considerate, despite the fact that it meant his crew were drinking and whoring all over Palermo. Doubtless the captain was intent on doing the same when she approached him in the tavern. Well, the night was hardly over. *So long as he's at his ship tomorrow morning, I don't care what he does between now and then.*

He moved to take the strongbox. She quickly shut the lid, the brass bolts inside sliding back into place. He flicked a glance toward her, one full of amused forbearance. Right. Doubtless he could smash the strongbox into fragments, regardless of its state-of-the-art security system.

Still, she said, "I'll bring it with me tomorrow. To ensure that you wait for me."

"Most women aren't worth waiting for."

"Neither are most men," she answered. "But, we're both rather exceptional."

He laughed, the sound as rich and deep as a summer night. Then he strode to the door and opened it. Daphne was relieved to note that the couple across the hall had concluded their endeavors.

Pausing at the doorway, Denisov said, "This is going to be a very interesting job, *professorsha*."

"I don't want it to be interesting, Captain Denisov. I only want it to be successful. My parents' lives depend on it."

At the mention of her parents, the Man O' War snorted, then turned and paced down the hall. He rattled the floorboards with each step. As soon as his footfalls faded, she hurried over and shut the door. Locked it, for good measure. Leaning against the door, she let out a long, shaking breath.

I've just made a deal with the telumium-enhanced Devil.

Chapter Two

MIKHAIL STOOD UPON the rocky shoreline, his face to the sun. Aquamarine water lapped at the beach, and a dog trotted along the edge of the sea, pausing to nose at bits of debris that had washed ashore. Pretty little villas dotted the hills overlooking the bay. The air was warm and mild. A perfect day for lying in the sunshine and drinking grappa, with a few lush, golden-skinned Sicilian women to keep him company.

Instead, he was about to fly off into risky skies for one freckled, narrow-hipped Englishwoman.

"She's late," muttered Levkov, standing beside him.

"Your timepiece is fast," Mikhail said. "Or broken." He glanced up at the sky. "It will be nine o'clock in ten minutes."

Levkov ran a kerchief over the shining dome of his bald head. "The time doesn't matter. What matters is that this job is a mistake."

"Good thing we're old friends, Piotr Romanovich," Mikhail murmured, "or else I'd throw you into the sea for contradicting your captain."

Levkov grumbled something under his breath that Mikhail decided to consider an apology.

"Besides," Mikhail continued, "it's not a mistake when the woman in question will pay us a tsar's ransom in gold." Perhaps it wasn't a tsar's ransom. More like a tsarevitch's ransom, but it was still more than Mikhail's crew had been paid in a long while. Smuggling those contraband tetrol processors into Oceania hadn't been as profitable as Mikhail had wanted, because the client turned out to have bigger promises than pockets.

"All the gold in the sodding world won't matter if we've got the navy up our bungholes."

"Then we'll just have to keep our bungholes clean." His acute hearing caught the sounds of a distant wagon approaching. "She'll be here in five minutes."

Sure enough, five minutes later, a smoke-spewing wagon appeared at the top of the road running past the beach. A boy sat at the wheel, and another young man sat beside him.

Mikhail frowned. He could've sworn that Miss Daphne Carlisle was nearing, as if a strange, other sense had told him that she was nearby. The same sense that had made him aware of her the moment she'd entered the tavern last night. Apparently, that perception had deserted him this morning. But as the wagon bounced nearer, he saw that the young man in the vehicle was Daphne Carlisle. She'd traded her stiff traveling clothes for a short leather jacket and pair of trousers tucked into tall, laced boots. The wagon came to a stop a few yards away, and Miss Carlisle jumped down, revealing just how snug her trousers were, and what an unexpectedly pretty round arse she had.

"Fuck your sister," Levkov muttered as she struggled to get her trunk down from the back of the wagon. The boy at the wheel offered no assistance. "The English-woman didn't look like that last night."

"I do like surprises," Mikhail said.

"No, you don't."

"I like *this* surprise." He strode to the wagon and plucked the trunk from the bed of the vehicle, then hoisted it onto his shoulder.

Miss Carlisle's moss green eyes widened, and he realized that she didn't have much experience with Man O' Wars, to find his strength so surprising. It had taken him nearly a year to get used to it himself.

Taking the opportunity to see her by daylight, he noted the sharp point of her chin, the fullness of her bottom lip, rose-colored in the morning sun, and the scattering of freckles across her cheeks and nose that were suggestive instead of girlish.

"I didn't know captains also offered luggage service," she said. Last night, she'd worn her light brown hair in a tight bun, but today she'd braided it, and the plait hung down between her shoulder blades. *What might it look like if the braid was undone? Would her hair be curly or straight? Coarse or soft?*

He suspected it would be soft, like satin against his fingers.

"We don't," he said. "But I don't want to watch you fight your baggage for half the day."

Saying nothing, she climbed into the bed of the wagon to retrieve her strongbox. It afforded him another fine opportunity to look at her figure. Her curves weren't generous, but they were definitely there, and she moved with an unexpected energy. But then, he had seen her neatly trip the drunkard accosting her at the tavern, so she possessed some skill. Perhaps she didn't spend all of her time in dusty university libraries.

Hefting the strongbox, she caught him staring. He only smiled at her glare.

Awkward beneath the weight of the metal box, she struggled to alight from the wagon.

"Happy to alleviate your burden," he said.

"Of that, I've no doubt." She grunted with effort as she clambered down. The moment her feet touched the ground, the wagon trundled away, coughing black smoke into the pure Mediterranean sky.

Levkov lumbered toward them.

"This ugly bastard is Levkov, my first mate," Mikhail said to her. "You need anything during the voyage, you go to him."

She eyed Levkov, who returned the look balefully. "I'm sure I'll be self-sufficient." She glanced around the bay. "You said your airship was anchored here."

He started walking down the rocky beach. "It's inland, near Ficuzza. Less visible."

"So, you weren't telling me the truth." She hurried after him as fast as she could, which wasn't fast at all, given that she carried a strongbox containing four bars of gold. Levkov followed, muttering.

"Wanted to make sure you weren't laying a trap for me."

"I'd never . . . do . . . such a thing." Her words were breathless with strain.

"Sure you don't want me to carry that for you?"

She threw him a look that answered his question. Then, "How are we supposed to get to your ship? Ficuzza is miles from here, and the wagon's gone."

"The journey hasn't even begun and you're already questioning me." He made a *tsk*ing sound, then nodded toward a jolly boat beached on the rocks. "There's our transportation."

"Ficuzza is inland."

"So it is." He set her trunk down in the jolly boat.

"This is a boat."

"Right again." Both he and Levkov climbed in and sat down on the planks that formed the seats, Mikhail by the tiller. "Get in."

He saw the moment she realized that the jolly boat was, in fact, hovering several inches off the ground. Her gaze moved to the brass-cased ether tank mounted on the aft of the vessel and the small turbine affixed to the stern.

"I've seen ether-borne patrol gliders," she said, climbing in with effort then setting the strongbox at her feet, "but never a boat like this."

"Strap yourself in." He fastened a harness across his lap. "I like to go fast."

"That comes as no surprise." She did as he instructed, then pulled a pair of goggles from her jacket's inside pocket and set them in place on her face.

"You were confident I'd agree to take you to Medinat al-Kadib." He tugged on the goggles that hung around his neck, and Levkov did the same.

Though the goggles partially hid her face, he could see the sharp determination in her gaze. "My only option is success."

Resolve—he had to credit her with that. As slight as she was, she had a will as hard as forged steel.

"Buckled in?" he asked. When she nodded, he said, "Good. Hang on."

He flipped a few switches, and the jolly boat rose up into the sky. Her gasp of surprise was caught upon the wind, but he heard it, just as he heard her murmurs of wonderment as he steered the boat high above the blue waters of the bay, and then inland. They flew over the white and green rocky hills, the little villages that at that height looked like illustrations from a child's picture book, the narrow ribbons of road.

For years, he'd known the sky. He knew what the world looked like from so high up. The first time he'd flown, he'd thought himself in the middle of his best boyhood dream. The intervening years had dulled that sense of wonder.

Yet seeing the naked awe on Miss Carlisle's face stirred something awake within him. The cobwebs of routine shook off. He saw the passing landscape with her eyes, and how flight was, in its way, miraculous. Only twenty

years earlier, theories of taking to the skies were just
that—theories. No one believed it possible. And now . . .
Now he was like that boy in the ancient story. Icarus. No,
Icarus had been a fool and had flown too high. His reckless stupidity had cost him his life. But his father, Daeda-
lus, he was the one who knew just how far up he could go
without being burned.

Lessons learned, by all of them.

For now, he could enjoy what it was to fly, and watch
the amazement of pretty Daphne Carlisle as the wind
tugged loose strands of her hair and the hillside towns
sped beneath them.

They crested a rugged hill, and she gave another gasp.
There, half a mile above the ground, was his airship.
Bielyi Voron. His stolen prize.

Like other airships, she had a wooden hull, with two
large turbines mounted in the stern. Russian airships had
their ether tanks in the aft, unlike their British and Italian foes. All naval insignias had long ago been scraped
or torn off the *Bielyi Voron*, though Mikhail left the scars
there as a badge of . . . honor. Or defiance. Both.

He'd kept the figurehead of the white raven that gave
the ship her name, but gouged out the imperial eagle on
its chest. That, he'd done himself, a blade in each hand
digging at the painted wood. At the time, he'd wished
he'd been burying the blades in one particular man's
chest, but the eagle had sufficed.

The entire top deck was open, save for the pilot house
at the middle of the ship, and crewmen hurried back
and forth as they went about their duties. Some of them

moved slower than others—a consequence of one wild night in Palermo.

Mikhail hadn't had a wild night. After leaving Daphne Carlisle's shabby *pensione*, he'd been restless, too restless to find another tavern or the arms of a willing woman, and he'd spent the hours before dawn pacing up and down the esplanade in Palermo, watching the ships enter and leave the harbor. Now he inwardly grimaced. A fine rogue Man O' War he made, brooding when he should have been carousing. As soon as this mission was over, he'd remedy that.

Bringing the jolly boat closer, he let his gaze stray from his airship to Miss Carlisle. She studied the ship, craning her neck to better see its different parts, completely absorbed with scrutinizing the *Bielyi Voron*. An academic, through and through. Although she didn't quite move like an academic.

Perhaps he could get more out of this job than her gold.

As the jolly boat approached, doors opened in the keel. He steered the boat up into the waiting cargo bay. The loading doors shut beneath it. Herrera, his quartermaster, came forward as soon as Mikhail brought the jolly boat down. Levkov immediately jumped out and stomped away.

Like the rest of the crew, Herrera had been told about their next job and Daphne Carlisle's presence on the ship. He simply nodded at her as she gaped at the interior of the cargo bay.

"Have Polzin and O'Keefe take Miss Carlisle's trunk to her cabin." Mikhail unbuckled his harness and leapt out of the jolly boat, then pulled his goggles down so they hung around his neck.

"What about that, Captain?" Herrera eyed the strongbox at Daphne Carlisle's feet.

"Take it to the strong room."

"I didn't agree to that," she said. Tugging off her goggles, she glared at Herrera and then Mikhail.

"It was yours until I took you aboard." He leaned over the edge of the boat and unfastened the harness around her lap. The backs of his hands brushed against her thighs. She tensed beneath him. "Now you're on the ship, and the gold is mine."

She ignored his offered assistance out of the jolly boat, climbing down on her own. "If you take the gold now, what's to keep you from pitching me overboard? We're, what, fifteen hundred feet above the ground? A bit difficult to survive that kind of trip over the side."

"Twenty-six hundred feet up," he said, "and nothing's stopping me."

"Except your honor."

He laughed at that.

She was less amused. "It stays in my cabin. At the very least, until we reach Medinat al-Kadib."

A token gesture. They both knew he could take it whenever he so desired. But he'd indulge her. Because it amused him.

"Carry it there yourself," he said.

After shooting him a look, she grabbed the handles of the strongbox and, with a groan, hefted it up. "Where is . . . my . . . cabin?"

He waved a hand at the quartermaster. "Herrera will take you there."

"I will?" Herrera asked. At Mikhail's stony stare, the quartermaster said, "I will."

"Wonderful," she said through gritted teeth, straining beneath the weight of the strongbox.

His hands itched. He fought his impulse to take the box from her—not for the gold, but to alleviate her burden. The results of a lifetime of instruction from his father in good manners, and the discipline drummed into him by the navy. But he wasn't his father's son anymore, nor was he a naval officer. He'd made himself into something, someone different.

No remorse. No looking back.

"Welcome to the *Bielyi Voron*, Miss Carlisle." With an ironic smile, he clicked his heels together and bowed. He strode toward the steps leading up to the next deck, then threw over his shoulder, "Don't get into trouble. I make enough of it on my own."

DAPHNE WATCHED HIS retreating back, torn between admiring the wide span of his shoulders and wanting to throw a gold ingot at his head. She did neither.

Turning to Herrera—who stared at her with wary curiosity—she said, "I'll go . . . to my cabin . . . now." Carrying a box full of gold made speaking in full sentences rather difficult.

The man shrugged and ambled away, taking the same set of steps that Denisov had used. It took her a good deal longer to climb them, huffing and panting the entire way, the muscles of her arms shouting with the effort. But she wouldn't relent. The only other option was to simply hand over the strongbox to Denisov, and that she couldn't do.

Herrera waited for her on the next deck. She followed him as he made his way through the airship, traveling down passageways and up stairs. Though the effort of carrying the strongbox taxed her, she couldn't help but stare in fascination at the ship. It was one thing to read about these modern wonders, quite another to finally see them, to be *inside* one.

Metal plates were mounted to the bulkheads. Batteries, if her research was correct. They actually drew their power from Denisov, a process made possible by his telumium implants. Copper tubes also traced along the bulkheads, conveying ether from the batteries to storage tanks like those she saw positioned at the rear of the airship. Presumably, the batteries generated enough ether to fill additional tanks, such as the one that had been on the small boat. Weapons, too, would take some of the surplus ether.

Almost all the crew that she passed wore ether pistols. She'd never been around so many firearms in her life, especially those given extra power from the potent gas.

Nor had she seen a ship's crew of such diversity. Mostly, they were men, but a small number of women were part of their ranks. They spoke a babel of languages. Primarily Russian, but she also heard Spanish, English, German, Chinese, and several others she couldn't place. Their clothing was equally collaged: pieces from naval uniforms, regular European civilian garments, Asian tunics, feathers and adornments from Central America. Goggles around their necks were standard. All the men wore their hair closely cropped, while the women kept theirs tucked beneath brightly printed kerchiefs. With their faces so exposed, an assortment of scars were revealed, evidence that they'd been in a fair number of fights and possibly battles.

What sort of people became mercenaries on an airship? What choices did they make in their lives? What sort of ethos did they possess, if any?

Though Daphne wanted to find these things out about the crew, if she were to be honest with herself, it was the captain of this airship that fascinated her the most.

A treatise suddenly popped into her mind: *The Habits and Customs of Airship Mercenaries, with Particular Examination of the Captain of Said Mercenaries,* by Doctor Daphne Sheridan Carlisle, PhD, AAC.

She burned to document everything she saw. Or perhaps it was her muscles that burned from hefting this bloody strongbox.

The crew seemed unsettled by her appearance on the ship. They simply stopped and watched her as she passed. Some were curious, others hostile. Despite the unease sitting like an oily snake in her belly, she tipped up her chin and met each man's gaze. In most cultures, when an outsider stepped into a closed society, the first engagements set the tone for the outsider's interactions and their position within the society. She couldn't show these mercenaries that she was intimidated. Especially not by the captain.

Herrera stopped in front of one door and opened it. With a halfhearted gesture, he waved her inside.

She stood in the doorway, peering in. Light seeped into the cabin from the small porthole, illuminating a narrow cot shoved against the bulkhead. An upended crate served as a table, one old-fashioned oil lamp sitting atop it. Coils of chain and half-assembled mechanical equipment covered most of the floor. The cabin smelled of tetrol fuel, metal, and a small amount of smoked paprika.

There was no dresser. A lumpy pillow and coarse wool blanket were thrown onto the cot.

Clearly, the *Bielyi Voron* was not outfitted as a passenger ship, nor did Denisov think she necessitated any special treatment. She supposed she ought to consider herself lucky that she had a cabin at all. Though it was more of a storage compartment than a berth.

She stepped inside and set the strongbox down. Resisting the need to massage her aching arms, she said, "I don't see a water closet or anywhere to bathe."

Herrera jerked a thumb toward the corridor. "Down the passageway."

Delightful. She could just picture herself in her nightgown and robe, walking past hard-bitten mercenaries so she could relieve herself or wash her face. Although, she did have a knife conveniently stashed in her boot. Best to make that her constant companion from now on.

The blade would probably bounce right off of Denisov.

Two crewmen appeared at the door, bearing her trunk

between them. They eyed the limited floor space. It took her several moments of shoving more junk against the bulkheads and even under her cot to make enough room, but finally the men deposited her luggage in the cabin. Did one give a gratuity to mercenaries?

Apparently not, for as soon as her trunk was set down, the crewmen disappeared.

"Got things to do," Herrera muttered, then he, too, vanished.

Daphne shut her cabin door. Rattling the handle, she discovered that it didn't actually lock.

This just gets better and better.

But she couldn't complain about the lack of comforts. At that very moment, her parents were the prisoners of a vicious warlord. A little lack of privacy and the smell of tetrol were nothing in comparison.

The floor began to vibrate. The turbines must be coming to life in preparation for departure. It felt not unlike being on a steamship, though there was a different sense of buoyancy. There was no water beneath the ship. Only air.

Her stomach leapt at the thought. But all her research had revealed no recorded airship crashes—unless they were shot out of the sky. Given Denisov's status as a rogue Man O' War, she couldn't discount that possibility. They were headed straight into a war zone, after all.

She shook her head, banishing the fear. Strength. She needed strength.

Besides, how many civilians get the opportunity to fly?

Picking her way through the jumble on the floor, she peered through the porthole. Small as the window was, and set high in the hull, she couldn't see much through it. Standing up on her tiptoes didn't help.

Curiosity gnawed at her.

Leaving her cabin, she made her way through the corridors and searched for the stairs that would lead her to the top deck. She tried to make herself inconspicuous, yet not appear meek—not an easy feat. While she had no idea of the layout of the ship, she attempted to move as though she knew exactly where she was going. Asking directions from the crew was out of the question.

She wound up in the magazine twice and a mess hall three times before she at last found herself climbing a set of stairs, and winding up on deck.

Sky. All around her. It felt endless, as though the airship was suspended in an azure sphere.

When she managed to tear her gaze from the sky, she watched the crew going back and forth across the deck, shouting at one another in their strange patois. Though they weren't part of a formal navy, they went about their duties with a confidence that bespoke years of experience. Some must have been seafaring men and women, for Man O' Wars and airships had come into existence only within the past decade.

Many of them sent her inquisitive looks, but they were too involved in preparing the ship for flight to give her much notice. She danced out of the way as a crewman hurried past her, and muttered an apology when she found herself in another man's path. The crew made adjustments to instrument panels set along the railings, pulled levers, turned dials.

Damn, why didn't I bring my writing tablet up here with me? There was so much to see, so much to document. She could watch the activity all day and never grow weary of it.

The nerves across the back of her neck and along her arms tightened. She had a sense of heat and energy like a dynamo. Without turning around, she knew exactly what—or rather, *who*—caused the sensation.

Yet she did turn around, and everything surrounding her dimmed. The sky, the ship . . . faded. She only saw him.

Denisov stood in front of the pilot house, directing his crew as they made the ship ready. His unconventional hair and long, embellished coat only served to emphasize his natural authority rather than undermine it, as she might have thought. As he pointed at some piece of equipment, his waistcoat gapped slightly, revealing an edge of his telumium implants. The metal glittered in the sunlight.

A corona of heat shimmered around him—though that had to be her imagination. Yet her body warmed as it recalled the tremendous warmth he gave off, how it had seemed to fill her room at the *pensione* long after he'd gone.

It's only a side effect of the implant. A scientific process, nothing more.

But it made her feel hot and breathless just the same.

Their gazes met across the length of the deck. And there went her pulse again.

As he'd done at the tavern, he motioned her toward him with a crook of his finger.

Daphne bristled. She was a tenured professor at a respected institute of higher learning. She was not summoned like a lackey. Certainly not in such an arrogant fashion.

But this was Denisov's ship. Overt defiance against the leader of a society—especially when one had no hope or even desire to supplant them from their position—led to conflict, if not outright ostracism. Or worse. Better to let her pride sting and play by Denisov's rules.

She walked to him with a deliberately measured pace.

"You're getting in the crew's way," he said without preamble. "Stay by me or go to your cabin."

"I can't see anything from that tiny aperture of a porthole."

"Then stay here." He pointed to the space beside him.

She moved to stand next to him, catching the scent of heated metal. For several moments, she was silent, observing him as he continued to direct the crew. He spoke to his men primarily in Russian, and the sound of that language on his tongue was an intoxicant.

They're only words.

The turbines' speed increased, the planks beneath her feet almost alive as they vibrated.

He moved to take the wheel from a crewman, and she had no choice but to follow him.

"Am I to stand next to you every time I'm above deck?" she asked.

"Only when we're preparing to leave." He didn't look at her as he spoke. "If you were next to me the whole voyage, it would be too . . ."

"Annoying," she filled in.

"Distracting."

After calling a command over his shoulder, he pulled a lever beside him. The ship began to move. A gradual slide forward, and then it picked up speed. The gentle breeze against her face grew in strength, from a soft breath into a scouring wind. She slid her goggles into place, as Denisov and the rest of the crew had also done.

From her position beside the captain, she could see edges of the landscape passing, the serrated tips of rocky peaks and the green fringe of trees.

Flight.

This was far different from being in a train, or even when she had been riding in the ether-borne boat. This was . . .

"Miraculous," she murmured.

She hadn't realized she'd spoken aloud until Denisov said with a wry smile, "Not a miracle. Science."

"That doesn't make it any less astonishing. There are some cultures that consider flight to be a god's power."

He shrugged. "You get used to it."

Closing her eyes, she concentrated on the feeling of wind upon her face. Fear for her parents continued to scrape at her heart, but she could only face each moment as it was presented to her. "I won't."

When she opened her eyes again, she found him watching her and not the sky. He wasn't wearing his habitual half smile. Instead, he seemed . . . intent. Slightly puzzled, but determined to solve the riddle.

And she was the riddle.

Oh, but he couldn't learn everything. That would be a disaster.

"I should unpack," she said abruptly. There was nothing for her to unpack into, but she needed a reason to get away from him. If she stayed beside him any longer, she might reveal things she shouldn't. Dangerous things.

Before he could speak, she hurried away, putting the vast sky and the intensity of his gaze behind her.

Chapter Three

"SHE'S DISTURBING THE CREW."

At Levkov's complaint, Mikhail looked up from studying the charts spread across the table in his stateroom. The skies over the Mediterranean swarmed with airships from every nation, especially Russia. His own nature, combined with the telumium implants, made him want to head *toward* a fight, not *away* from one—even years after turning rogue—but intelligence had to override instinct. His goals now were based solely on profit, not glory.

He'd have to be careful, very careful, getting his ship safely to Medinat al-Kadib.

He also knew without asking which "she" Levkov referred to. Not Bonita Marlowe, the ship's surgeon, not Rupa Patel, the carpenter's assistant, or any of the other dozen females on board the *Bielyi Voron*.

No, Levkov spoke of the only women on board Mikhail

couldn't stop thinking about, no matter how many maps he studied or evasive strategies he planned. How she watched the skies with fascination, how she moved with unexpected suppleness. How fear glinted in her eyes but she fought past that fear, and how he couldn't help admiring that, damn it.

"She's just a wisp of an Englishwoman." He used an aeroplotter to finish charting his course before turning to Levkov. "Every single member of this crew has been in blood-soaked battle. How could Daphne Carlisle disturb anyone?" He put this question more to himself than to his first mate.

"Go and see," Levkov said. "Right now, she's topside."

Mikhail wanted to bark that he was busy, he had a damn ship to run—but if his crew was troubled by her, then they'd not perform their duties properly. Another voice whispered at the back of his mind: *You just want to look at her again.*

Maybe he did. And maybe seeing that she was just an ordinary woman with no especially seductive charms would help him get the machinery of his brain back in working order.

Stalking from his cabin, he headed above deck, with Levkov on his heels. As Mikhail walked, he felt the subtle pull of the batteries lining the bulkheads, a silver-edged awareness as his *aurora vires* was transformed into the energy powering the ship. Seldom did he notice the feeling. It had become an ingrained, automatic part of him, like breathing or flight. Yet he sensed it now, and it was a measure of how her presence on his airship threw him off balance.

He emerged on the top deck and set his goggles into place. Man O' War he might be, with sharper vision and greater strength than a normal man, but the wind from the airship's velocity still pulled tears from his eyes.

Late afternoon sun spilled sideways across the deck. They'd made good progress today, already nearing Crete. Within a day and a half, the ship would reach Medinat al-Kadib, and then he could receive the second half of his payment. Bid farewell to Daphne Carlisle, and then go back to his usual business.

He saw her immediately. She sat upon a crate, a writing tablet across her lap. Struggling with the pages flapping wildly in the breeze, her hand sped across the paper as she wrote. Every now and then, she'd glance up and study the crew moving around her. Then she'd return to her notebook. The process repeated itself many times.

His crew tried to give her a wide berth. They'd take the most circuitous route to avoid her as they went about their duties. A crewman crossed all the way to the other side of the ship, although the valve he needed to adjust was mere steps away if he'd walked right past her. A damned inefficient way to run a ship. He wasn't in the navy anymore, but even rogue airships needed to function properly.

He and Levkov approached, but she didn't look up from her writing.

"You see what I mean," Levkov complained in Russian. "Sits there like a judging owl."

"Pretty owl, though," Mikhail answered in the same language. "Got some surprisingly lush plumage on her, even if she is a pain in my arse."

"Owls have talons, too," Daphne Carlisle said in Russian.

He gave a soft snort. Of course the *professorsha* knew his native tongue. Likely she knew dozens of languages. He'd have to remain vigilant around her.

He waved Levkov off, and the first mate seemed glad to put distance between himself and the Englishwoman.

She glanced up with an annoyed frown when Mikhail's shadow darkened the pages of her notebook, making it difficult to write. Straightening her shoulders, she tipped her head back to try to look him in the eye.

"You're bothering my crew," he said.

"I'm being perfectly unobtrusive," she countered.

"This is not being unobtrusive." He gestured toward the crew, who continued to edge around the deck like deer avoiding a wolf. A daft notion. She was only one slim-boned English academic. He knew for a fact that more than half his crew had bounties on their heads. He could make a good fortune by turning them in, but if he did, there'd be no one to help run his ship.

"This is precisely the same technique I use when making field notes." She stood, but took several steps back to keep distance between them. "At first, the subjects are wary of my presence. In time, they grow acclimated to me, and return to their usual patterns of behavior."

"My crew aren't *subjects*."

"But they're fascinating." She flipped through the pages of her writing tablet. "There's enough material on this airship to write a three-volume study. The power dy-

SKIES OF STEEL 43

namics. The societal structure. It's an entirely new culture that hasn't been investigated."

"With good reason." He plucked the notebook from her arms. "We don't want to be investigated."

He opened the writing tablet. Though she'd been on the ship for only a few hours, already she'd filled dozens of pages with her large but neat handwriting. He spoke English better than he read it, so figuring out exactly what she'd been documenting was a process that would take far too long. But he could identify the sketches of certain members of the crew. Diagrams also adorned the pages, but they were masses of lines, circles, and symbols as obscure as another language.

She snatched the notebook back and stuffed it into a satchel by her feet. "By my last count, there were at least two dozen rogue Man O' Wars. That certainly qualifies as a group large enough to warrant inquiry. Think of the benefit of such an analysis. It could shape national policy. For the better."

Her eyes shone behind the lenses of her goggles, and excitement chimed through her voice. A genuine smile formed at the corners of her mouth. With the low-hanging golden light tracing the curve of her cheek and the slim line of her neck, his annoyance sifted away, grain by grain.

"We've the English and Italians on one side," she continued, "the Hapsburgs and Russians on the other, plus all the other unallied nations like Brazil and China—every one of them vying for telumium and tetrol. It's as if the whole world is at war. But the rogue Man O' Wars make an already complex situation even more complicated with their own agendas. If governments had a better understanding of how rogue ships functioned, what their goals might be—"

Anger returned on a hot tide. "Then rogue ships like mine are fucked."

She didn't blink at his language.

"What you've got there," he said, nudging her satchel with the toe of his boot, "is a damned map to destroying rogues like me. Once governments know how we function, what our weaknesses might be, they'll take us down like that." He snapped his fingers an inch from her nose, and she recoiled. "Secrecy is what keeps us safe. As long as you're on my ship, there'll be no studies. No dissertations, or whatever the hell you call them."

Yet she held her ground. "It could be for my own edification. I'd make the findings available only to scholars and universities—"

"So you're forging a little knife instead of a scimitar." He shook his head. "The notebook stays in the bag."

Her mouth opened, as if she planned on some retort, but then she seemed to think better of it. Instead, she grabbed her satchel, slung it over her shoulder, and stepped around him. Her stride was long-legged as she headed to the foredeck. She stopped there, resting her arms on the railing, her legs braced wide on the deck.

The smart thing to do was go back to his stateroom and continue going over the charts. Or attend to the scores of duties that occupied him at every hour of every day. Definitely, that would be the intelligent thing to do.

His boots headed to the foredeck without thought. Maybe she had some kind of magnet sewn into her chemise that pulled him toward her.

He stood beside her at the rail. Together, they watched the Mediterranean glide below, the seafaring boats dancing across the sea and the white and green islands speckling the water.

"The boats will be coming in after a day fishing," she said without looking at him.

"They set out in the morning," he added. "Follow the tides and the currents."

She pulled a spyglass from her satchel and trained it on the boats below. "Good to see they're using nets to catch their fish."

"Instead of dynamite. Bad for the fish, bad for the coral."

Folding up her spyglass, she sent him a quick, surprised glance. "I didn't know rogue Man O' Wars noticed such things as the fishing practices near Crete."

His brow rose. "Think I'm too busy counting my plunder or plotting criminal schemes?" Resting his hands on the rail, he stared down at the water, but felt the few inches that separated his hand from the point of her elbow. "I was at sea in the Russian Navy for over a decade before I became a Man O' War."

"Doesn't mean you paid attention to anything beyond warfare. Or that you would care about preserving the health of the sea."

He shrugged, unsure where she was heading.

"You notice things," she said. "An observer, like me."

At this, he snorted. "A mercenary."

"Perhaps not always . . ." She sounded hopeful.

He had to set her straight. "Always." Fixing her gaze with his, he said flatly, "It's your gold that has me flying to Arabia. That's my only motivation."

She straightened. "And my only motivation is freeing my parents."

He tapped a finger against the satchel slung over her shoulder. "Not writing the first important study of rogue airships?"

Her gaze dropped, but her expression was taut. "I have to do something to occupy my mind during the journey. Thinking about my parents being held captive . . ." She clenched her hands, the knuckles whitening. "Tribal leaders in that area pride themselves on their hospitality, even to their hostages. Al-Rahim *must* treat my parents with respect. But with the world gone so chaotic, I don't know if there's anything that can be relied upon. Including a warlord's sense of honor."

Whether her parents were well treated—or even alive—shouldn't matter to him. She was only a woman offering him gold in exchange for passage to Medinat al-Kadib. Yet the pain in her voice seemed to puncture the metal covering his heart.

"Your parents are fine," he found himself saying. "Things may have gone to hell in Arabia, but tribal custom won't change just because some *ferengi* are fighting over telumium."

She took a breath. Her gaze became resolute. "You're right. Despite the changes in the region, al-Rahim won't risk his reputation just for my mother and father. He won't abuse or mistreat them. Especially not with the promise of a ransom."

Unease slid coldly down his neck. He shouldn't like seeing how she searched for—and found—courage and comfort from his words. No one relied on him for anything beyond his services as a mercenary. He'd proven a disappointment to far too many. Including himself.

Better to focus on his most accomplished, reliable skill: greed.

"Tell me about this ransom."

Her lips tightened. She wouldn't meet his eyes. "That's between al-Rahim and myself."

He couldn't blame her for being cagey. At least she didn't simply blurt her secrets like some soft-brained innocent. One could be intelligent without being shrewd. Clearly, Daphne Carlisle was both.

Respectable, that.

"As you like." He turned away. Dozens of things commanded his attention, and yet he stood here on the foredeck with her, as if this was a damned pleasure flight. They were speeding closer and closer to dangerous skies. Talking with her had made him forget that.

Before he took more than two steps, her voice stopped him. "Captain Denisov?"

He didn't face her. "What?"

"I'd read that you were a decorated member of the Russian Navy."

He'd once thought about throwing all his medals over the side of his ship, had pictured it many times: a ribboned and glittering tumble, and all those decorations lying at the bottom of the Black Sea. Had he done it, they'd be rusted or eaten away by now, lodged permanently in the belly of some fish. But something had compelled him to keep them, still pinned to their silk sash.

She continued, "Yet I couldn't find any records as to why you went rogue."

"Mother Russia doesn't send out telegrams announcing her failures," he said over his shoulder.

"So, you won't tell me, either," she answered.

"Nothing and no one on this ship goes into any essay or study."

"It's not for a study."

Her footsteps were light as she approached him from behind. Still, he wouldn't turn to look at her so she could see his face. He'd never made a good card player. A fact they'd teased him about in the naval academy.

"I'm just . . ." She hesitated. "Interested in you. In who *you* are."

Something hard and edged lodged itself in his throat. He couldn't remember the last time anyone had an interest in him beyond what he could do for them, as a sailor, a Man O' War, or a mercenary. Untrue. He did remember someone who had once been as close as a brother. Yet it wasn't brotherhood that man had finally offered. Only betrayal.

"Just a machine," he answered. "A machine that runs solely on profit."

He left her before either of them could say any more.

DAPHNE SAT ON the cot in her cabin, a tray balanced across her knees. A bowl of stew, a wedge of fine-crumbed bread, and a mug of what she assumed was beer comprised her dinner. As she dipped her spoon into the stew, she caught the scents of cinnamon, pepper, and lamb. A taste revealed the dish to be quite good—rich and warming, vaguely sensual.

It oughtn't come as a surprise that the food aboard the *Bielyi Voron* would be appetizing. It wasn't a naval ship any longer, and without the impetus of enforced order, the best way to keep a crew loyal was to treat them well. Empty or poorly fed bellies bred sedition.

More notes she couldn't put down in her notebook. Denisov had made himself clear on that. Risking his displeasure was dangerous. They had miles to go before reaching Medinat al-Kadib, so she had to stay as inconspicuous as possible. Avoiding him seemed the best policy.

They appeared to be in agreement on that point. Thus, she took her supper alone in her cabin rather than join the crew or even take a meal at the captain's table. Though, did mercenary airship captains maintain such regimented protocol? There weren't exactly senior officers aboard the ship, and though there was a hierarchy, distinctions such as rank didn't seem to matter as much as in the navy. For all she knew, Denisov ate with the rest of the crew. Or he dined alone in his stateroom.

As Daphne took a sip of her beer—it had the distinct malty flavor of a Belgian Trappist ale—she pictured him in his cabin. She hadn't actually seen it, but she could well imagine what it looked like. He'd have charts and maps, the furniture bolted to the floor so it wouldn't slide around. *Would he have books? What sort of books? Curios from years of traveling or prizes taken from piracy?*

She forced herself to concentrate on eating her meal, but her thoughts kept returning to Denisov. Every time they spoke, small fragments of his history and who he truly was emerged, sparking her interest—beyond the academic.

He likely did eat alone. For all the rough camaraderie he shared with his crew, there was something very . . . isolated about him. He was the only Man O' War on the airship, a fact that automatically made him different from everyone else. Yet, more than that, in his terse words, he revealed a greater separation. Almost a sense of loss.

A *failure*, he'd called himself. A failure to Russia. His words had been bitter, sharp. Revealing a wound that hadn't fully healed. What had happened? What had driven him to turn rogue and live as a perennial outcast, always hunted, always solitary.

Oh, for God's sake. He's a smuggler, a soldier of fortune. Not an exiled prince with a tragic history.

That had always been her weakness: ascribing nobler motivations to those who didn't merit them. Her anthropological work was a deliberate antidote. Seeing people for who they really were, all the good and all the bad. No one was a paragon. And, with a few exceptions, no one was a true villain, either.

And when they practice deliberate deception? What are they then?

She pushed the thought from her head, and concentrated on finishing her supper. Despite the quality of the food, it was a grim affair. A single gas lamp shed jaundiced light over the jumble of debris littering her tiny cabin, and turned the miniscule porthole into a yellow mirror reflecting the cramped little chamber.

With the last of her meal consumed, restlessness surged through her. She couldn't spend the whole of the evening trapped in here. She'd grown up at dig sites, and as an adult she was more often doing fieldwork than sitting in her office at the Accademia. Even in Florence, she had a habit of taking long rambles in the evening, crossing over the Ponte alle Grazie and heading up into the hills surrounding the city.

The *Bielyi Voron* wasn't a sizeable ship, but it was certainly big enough that she could avoid Denisov. Besides, the man was massive. He couldn't sneak up on her. The planks beneath his feet shook with each step, as though he were some massive god from the beginning of time, building mountains and scooping out oceans with his bare hands.

Grabbing her tray, she walked it back to the galley. It took several tries for her to find it, but at last she did, and a wary-eyed boy took the tray from her. He couldn't have been more than fourteen. The impulse to ask him about his history felt like an itch beneath her skin, so she quickly left the galley.

Bracing wind met her as she reached the top deck.

Full night had fallen, and with it, the temperature likewise dropped. The idea of going back down to her cabin to retrieve a coat didn't appeal, not when she could fill her lungs with the cool, fresh, evening air, and take her fill of the jeweled night sky. Flying during the daytime was wondrous, but being airborne at night was a waking dream. One she was determined to savor.

She walked further onto the deck, passing a few members of the crew but not, thankfully, Denisov. She wanted to enjoy these moments, and his presence deeply unsettled her. For so many reasons. Now, she could relish the unique experience of flying at night. Its lulling peace.

A burst of fire a mile away on the starboard side tore through the stillness. And then another. The airship rocked slightly from the concussive blasts. *What were they?*

Crewmen suddenly swarmed the deck. Yet none of them spoke. Eerie, how there were so many of them but they kept silent. Many of them were extinguishing the lamps and dimming the illumination devices in the panels lining the hull. Plunging the ship into utter darkness.

But the explosions on the starboard side continued. The fire flared, and half a moment later, she heard and felt the jolt. The flares of light dazzled her eyes. She couldn't make out what was causing the detonations.

"British and Russian airships," said a deep voice behind her. "Another territorial pissing match."

She whirled to face Denisov. In all the controlled

chaos, she hadn't heard or felt his approach. He came to stand beside her and together they stared out into the darkness.

Naturally, he could see what she could not. But in a moment, her vision adjusted, and she could just make out two British airships facing off against three Russian vessels. They unloaded their ether cannons on one another, lurid blossoms of fire bursting in the night sky. Ether-enhanced Gatling guns made rough, choppy sounds. The noise of wood shattering apart also tore through the air.

Something on one of the British ships caught fire. Crewmen seemed to work fast to put out the blaze, but it was clear the airship had suffered a bad blow.

Men were out there, dying. She couldn't see them, or hear them, but no crew could take that much bombardment without suffering loss of life.

Daphne's heart pounded in time with the ether cannon. Her mouth dried.

"I've never observed actual warfare before," she croaked. Oh, there had been some local tribal leaders' disputes that had resulted in spilled blood, but nothing on this industrialized scale.

Though she couldn't make out Denisov's expression, his words were flat. "It's just a skirmish. Hopefully, it's enough."

"Enough for what?" she asked, appalled.

"To get away unseen."

Thus the reason why all the lights aboard the *Bielyi Voron* were extinguished. With the British and Russians engaged in combat against each other, the rogue ship would appear to be nothing more than a patch of darkness in a cloudless sky, and not worth noting.

Not so cloudless. The formerly clear sky was rapidly dotting with gray, billowing clouds.

Which, to a sharp-eyed observer aboard one of the other airships, would throw the *Bielyi Voron* into perfect silhouette.

Denisov seemed to know this. When Levkov appeared, the captain ordered, "Get us out of here. Fast. But don't fire up the turbines too much, or they might spot us."

"Aye, Captain." Gone was Levkov's typical surliness as he hurried to obey Denisov's command.

The turbines whirred faster, and the wind picked up as the airship hastened to put distance between itself and the ongoing battle.

She felt the tension in her chest ease. They could steal away, with no one the wiser. Though she was a British citizen, somehow she doubted that would matter if a British airship got a rogue Man O' War's vessel in its sights. And Denisov had made clear that the Russians would hunt him down and kill him if given the chance.

But they wouldn't get that chance. Not tonight. The *Bielyi Voron* was disappearing into the night, and everything would be fine.

"*Blyat,*" Denisov cursed.

"What is it?"

"We've been spotted." He pointed into the darkness. "One of the Russian ships pulled away from the battle. They're coming after us."

Squinting, she just made out the large, dark form of the enemy airship. It looked a good deal bigger than the *Bielyi Voron*, which could slow them down. But it had larger turbines and ether tanks, too.

"We can outrun them," she said, hoping to convince herself. Then realized she spoke to no one, as Denisov was already striding across the deck toward the pilot house. Instinctively knowing that the safest place to be was with him, Daphne hurried after him.

"We *can* outrun them, can't we?" she pressed.

"That's the *Zelyonyi Oryol*." The way he said the ship's name made it clear that outrunning it was impossible. In the pilot house, he consulted with a dark-skinned man, speaking to him in a strange combination of a West African dialect and Russian. Daphne could make out every fourth word, words like *storm* and *protonic charge,* but even that didn't quite make sense. The African man hastened away to obey whatever order he'd been given.

"If we had anyplace to hide," Denisov said to her, "we might have a chance, but we're in the middle of the damned sea. There's nowhere to take cover."

With a sinking feeling, she realized he was right. A vast stretch of water offered no concealment.

Just as the understanding hit her, the ship rocked violently. The Russian ship was firing on them. Not expecting the jolt, she staggered and toppled toward the floor.

In a blur of movement, iron-hard arms scooped her up and set her on her feet. She pressed her palms against Denisov's forearms, the heat of him racing up through her limbs and mingling with the icy fear coursing through her veins.

But she felt herself steadied, and a moment later, stepped away.

"Go below," he commanded.

"Please, no." She didn't like the frightened tone of her voice, but, by God, she had good reason to be afraid. A massive Russian airship was determined to shoot them out of the sky, and if one could permit oneself a moment of fear, it would be now. "Huddling alone in that tiny cabin, wondering what was happening but not knowing . . . that's worse than facing the danger head-on."

He was silent. Her eyes had adjusted somewhat, and she could make out the hard, sharp contours of his face, the glint of his eyes. She thought that he'd sneer at her, and shove her below decks, but after a moment, he said in a strangely gentle voice, "All right. But stay close."

"I'm certainly not planning to caper around the deck," she answered.

A low, surprised chuckle rumbled up from his chest. "Save the capering for later. When we shake off our pursuer."

"I didn't think we could. They're faster, and we've no place to hide."

"All true. But," he added, and she could have sworn that he winked, "I didn't survive this long as a wanted man without having a few outrageous schemes."

Chapter Four

SHE FOLLOWED HIM as he strode to where the helmsman stood at the wheel. Despite the urgency of the situation, the crewman steering the ship betrayed no outward sign of fear, guiding the vessel with the same unflappable calm as if taking a pleasant afternoon flight. But the *zing* of ether rifles' fire and shuddering caused by the enemy's cannon made their flight anything but pleasant.

She struggled to keep herself as outwardly calm as any of the *Bielyi Voron*'s crew, even though her insides quaked.

"Steer us into those clouds ahead," Denisov commanded to the helmsman.

"Aye, sir."

"We can hide ourselves in them," she deduced.

Yet Denisov shook his head. "Any Man O' War could see through a cloud of that density. It's hardly cover."

"Then why—" But she silenced herself. Now wasn't

the time to question Denisov or his intentions. *He* was the air combat veteran, not she.

The ship plunged into the bank of clouds. Cold vapor surrounded them immediately, smelling faintly of sulfur and saline. It formed an eerie shroud, and she could barely make out the prow of the ship and forms of the crew through the mist. Yet she wasn't as cold as she ought to be. Because of Denisov. She stood close enough to him to feel the heat radiating from his body. Despite the cold, and the peril pursuing them, he seemed to grow even warmer as the hazard increased. As if the threat and the need to fight fed the heat within him—a furnace fueled by danger.

She glanced over at him. Yes—his eyes seemed to gleam with a new light, and she could almost sense his eagerness for combat as much as the heat spreading out from him.

But he wouldn't lead them into a fight, would he? Not with the odds against them so great?

The African man returned, holding a brass-hinged box in his hands. With him was another crewman, who carried what appeared to be an iron mortar. "I have them here, Captain."

"And not a minute to spare, Akua." Denisov took the box from the other man and headed toward the rear of the ship. Daphne, Akua, and the other crewman trailed after him as he climbed a set of steps to the poop deck. She fought for balance, gripping the rails on the steps, as the helmsman kept up evasive maneuvers, the ship veering from side to side like a deliberate drunkard. The clouds were thick on all sides, and the sound of enemy gunfire continued to tear the air apart.

Her only constant was Denisov, and she followed the massive breadth of his shoulders and the dark shadow of his long coat flaring out behind him as he moved with purpose.

Crewmen attending the aft-mounted ether tanks gave him respectful distance as he paced to the railing of the poop deck. He removed a contraption of intricate brass from the wooden box.

"Set the mortar up there," he directed Akua and the crewman with the weapon. "I want it at forty-five degrees."

The weapon was positioned near the railing, but what held Daphne's attention was the device that Denisov handled. It was spherical, consisting of various rings of brass, with a crank at one end. The captain pressed a latch and the sphere split apart. He took a handful of brilliant blue gems from a compartment within the wooden box, placed them inside the brass sphere, then latched the device shut.

Holding the metal orb in one hand, he started to turn the crank on the sphere's end. Rings within the orb began to spin. Faster and faster they turned as Denisov wound the device. Blue light sparkled to life within the apparatus, first in thin filaments, then with greater strength, until tendrils of electricity spread outward and covered the device. For that's what Denisov appeared to be doing: creating electricity. She would have thought generating that kind of charge would cause him pain. But as the light spilled outward and illuminated his face, he showed no sign of discomfort.

In truth, he looked like an elemental creature, all lurid light and hard angles, the rings in his ears glinting and his eyes ablaze. She didn't know whether to be frightened or enthralled.

"I think it's charged enough, Captain," Akua shouted above the din of gunfire.

Daphne glanced aft. She could just make out the form of the pursuing Russian airship. As Denisov had said, the clouds seemed to provide no impediment to the enemy's chase. But what, exactly, was Denisov doing that could give the *Bielyi Voron* any advantage?

"Shield yourselves," he directed. "Especially you," he added with a commanding look at Daphne.

She and the others did as they were bid. She stepped back from the mortar and lifted her arms to protect her face. Yet she couldn't resist peering through a small gap between her arms to see what he was doing.

"Prepare ether tanks for venting," he shouted above the din. Crewmen yelled back their readiness.

He dropped the crackling metallic sphere into the mortar. It immediately shot out with a low *thunk*.

Lowering her arms, Daphne watched the sphere arc into the clouds. Sizzling bolts of blue energy shot from the device. The artificial lightning threaded through the cloud, spreading like a jagged web with a snapping, crackling sound. It seemed to excite the energy within the clouds, and within moments, pale yellow filaments of electricity sparked to life.

At the same time, the brass orb split open and shot the azure-colored gems into the clouds. The clouds darkened into bruises.

She could feel it, smell it—the sulfuric tang of a gathering storm, moments away from bursting into full fury. The blue gems had to be some kind of storm seed, something she'd heard rumors about, but never actually seen. Now she'd not only seen them, but within moments, she'd be in the middle of their creation. A storm that would outpace anything from the Bible.

"Brace yourselves," Denisov said.

Though she didn't know what to expect, she held tight to the railing, bracing her feet wide.

He turned to the men at the ether tanks. "Vent them!"

The crewmen threw several levers. And the world fell from the sky.

The airship dropped rapidly, careening downward sharply. Her stomach did the same. A moment's blind terror. They were crashing! They'd plunge into the sea and sink to the bottom before anyone who survived the fall could have a chance to swim to the surface.

But the ship's free fall lasted only a moment. The next second, the vessel shot forward with incredible speed. It was as if dozens of turbines suddenly roared to life. The speed felt like a punch in the stomach. She couldn't catch her breath.

Unprepared for the velocity, she half stumbled and half crumpled against the railing. Only her arm looped around the wooden balustrade kept her from tumbling completely to the deck. Or, worse, overboard. Her feet dug at the planks and her arm shook from effort. She was about to tumble right over the rail.

"*Blyat*."

The huge, hot edifice of Denisov suddenly covered her, anchoring her down. His body formed a protective wall around her, his hands gripped the railing, effectively caging her. A typhoon couldn't dislodge her, not with him holding her steady.

His front pressed to her back, close as interlocking puzzle pieces. His skin carried the scent of leather and hot metal. He felt hard all over, solid as tempered steel, not an inch of give anywhere on his body. His breath was warm as it fanned across her neck and cheek. If she turned her head just a little, their lips would touch. Thinking of this, another kind of heat spread low in her belly.

"Told you to brace yourself," he growled.

"I did," she shot back, forcibly ignoring her awareness of him, and the almost intimate nature of their position. "Had no idea we'd be flung forward as if shot out of a cannon."

"Not a cannon, but when we vent the ether, it gives us an extra boost. We lose some height, but it's worth it for the speed."

She peered through the poop deck railing. The storm raged behind them, massive and dark as judgment, its peals of thunder and bolts of lightning seeming to crack the very sky apart. The device and storm seeds had created that—part of the marvel of modern science.

At least it was behind them, the venting of ether having pushed them ahead of the tempest.

"The other airship can do the same, though," she noted. "Vent their ether to catch up with us."

"They're stuck in the middle of the storm. Too dangerous to try the maneuver in the midst of that."

"So," she said, hopeful, "we've lost them."

He was more guarded, saying flatly, "Not going to breathe easy until I see nothing but night sky around us."

And *she* could not breathe easy until he no longer anchored her body with his own. Not when she felt the rise and fall of his chest, or the unyielding strength of his form. It sparked an awareness she did not want, one she could not afford.

"I can stand on my own now." Her voice was brusque, spinsterish.

After that initial, breathless burst of speed, the ship incrementally slowed. The black mirror of the sea below gained sharper definition as the *Bielyi Voron* decelerated.

"As you like." Despite his disinterested tone, he straightened gradually, as if making certain that she truly had stable footing. He kept his hands on the railing, however, even when she stood fully upright.

They both stared at the tempest. Though they had put distance between the ship and the storm, it continued to rage, shaking the sky with thunder and flashing with lightning. Yet she couldn't see the Russian ship. It had to be trapped within the storm.

She turned around, and found herself effectively pinned by Denisov against the railing. The span of a moth's wing separated them. Her awareness of him climbed higher. They'd skirted the battle between the

British and Russian airships, and evaded their pursuer. So why did her heart beat faster *now*?

He's metal and flesh. A handful of technological components grafted onto the body of an ordinary man. Nothing else.

Yet he seemed far more than that.

"Have you used that evasive technique before?" she asked, striving to sound calm.

His grin was audacious. "First time."

She felt her mouth drop open. "Was it dangerous?"

"Akua," Denisov said over his shoulder, "was what I did just now dangerous?"

"Ridiculously so, Captain," came the answer. "We had less than a five percent chance of surviving." Yet Akua didn't sound upset at all. He sounded . . . pleased. As if his captain's reckless behavior was something to celebrate.

A skewed value system these mercenaries have. Definitely something she would have liked to document more. Instead, she said aloud, "That's a ninety-five percent chance that we could've been killed."

"And if the *Zelyonyi Oryol* had gotten close enough, the odds were one hundred percent that we'd be blasted from the sky. I'm not much of a mathematician, but a five percent survival rate is better than none at all. We're alive now. We've lost our pursuers. That's all that matters."

Indeed, Denisov fairly glowed with arrogant pride as he stared down at her.

Dear God . . . they'd come so close to death. But his actions, audacious as they'd been, had prevented that.

A scoundrel of the first order. Wild, impulsive. Acquisitive and perfectly willing to go to outrageous lengths to save his own skin.

Yet he wasn't entirely self-serving. Had she fallen overboard when the ship had raced forward, the gold would be his, and he'd save himself a trip all the way to the dangerous Arabian Peninsula.

But he'd kept her safe. And she didn't know why.

She ducked under his arm. "I need a drink."

"There are two things you're guaranteed to find on a rogue Man O' War airship." He offered her a roguish smile. "Outlaws. And an abundance of alcohol."

ONLY WHEN MIKHAIL was certain that they'd lost the *Zelyonyi Oryol* and everything on his ship was relatively undamaged did he finally agree to leave the top deck. For security, he didn't permit any of the lights throughout the ship to be lit. The crew knew how to move in darkness from years of practice. As for himself, seeing in the dark simply came with the improvements he'd gained with his implants. Something that had taken some getting used to—opening his eyes in the middle of the night and being able to see as clearly as if it were high noon.

A very useful skill when navigating the night skies, a pitch-black treasure house, or a woman's bedroom in the smoky, seductive hours before dawn.

"Come with me," he said to Miss Carlisle. It was a measure of how shaken she'd been by what they'd just endured that she gave him no argument, no quick retort.

Instead, feeling her way carefully, she followed him. They walked down the companionway. Once they were below decks, however, the darkness was thick as secrets, and the night vision she acquired topside seemed to fail her in the black corridors. She shuffled along, and he heard the slide of her hand along the bulkheads lining the passageways.

She started when he took her hand in his.

"Easy," he muttered. "Just some guidance."

"Yes," she said. Then, with more strength, "Yes, that's fine."

Hand in hand, they continued down the passageway. Hers seemed tiny and cool in comparison to his, but it surprised him to feel small calluses on her palms and lightly edging her fingers. More surprising were the embers of awareness traveling from her hand to his, and up through his body. He'd been intrigued by her as a woman since the first moment he'd seen her, yet this went beyond his usual fast, simple want of a female's bodily pleasures. In their shared touch, as he led her through the passageway, he had knowledge of her—the unexpected resilience in her hand, how that same fortitude moved through her, and the surprising amount of desire it stirred within him.

All from holding a woman's hand. By God, had it been so long for him that this tiny touch affected him so strongly? He could barely remember the Portuguese courtesan he'd visited weeks ago, all the artful skills she'd employed as distant and uninvolving as if that night had happened to someone else.

Miss Carlisle's breathing, which had calmed somewhat, grew shallow again. Tension in her hand, as if she was torn between gripping him harder, or pulling away.

The same warring impulses he felt.

He stopped in front of one particular door, glancing back at her. Her eyes were opened wide.

"We're here." He pushed open the door and led her inside. To her eyes, the room would be filled with ashy light and silhouettes of furniture, but she wouldn't be able to guess where exactly he'd taken her.

When he released her hand, her fingers briefly curled, like she wanted to keep hold of him. Then they straightened, letting him go.

He moved through the chamber, closing heavy shutters. All the windows and portholes were covered, as well, throwing the chamber into a darkness as thick as it had been in the passageway.

Wryly, she asked, "Have you taken me to the brig?"

"This'd be a damn plush brig. Cover your eyes." With all the windows and portholes secured, he lit a quartz lamp, keeping it at its lowest setting. Dim green light glowed.

Slowly, she took her hand away from her eyes, blinking in the light. She turned in a slow circle. He watched her gaze flick around the room, alighting here and there. Bookcase. Chest. Desk. Bed—built to his specifications.

"This is your stateroom." She looked again at the bed. It certainly could hold two people comfortably, even if one was his size.

He didn't consider himself a particularly imaginative man, but he had no trouble conjuring images of her splayed out there, white sheets rumpled around her slim curves.

Difficult to read the look on her face as she glanced from the bed to him.

"If you haven't brought me here for a drink," she said, "I'm leaving."

He strode to a low cabinet and unlatched it. Cold air wafted out. He grabbed a bottle and two small glasses, and held them up. "This is more than a drink. It's the essence of Russia."

"Vodka."

He set the glasses down on the table, and filled them to their rims. "My country may have turned its back on me, but I can't change my Russian blood."

Before he could even offer her one of the glasses, she took it, and swallowed its contents in one gulp. Closing her eyes, she exhaled a low, fiery breath, and gave a delicate shudder. Then held out her glass.

He considered, then discarded, the idea of warning her about the vodka's potency. He had no plans to take advantage of an inebriated woman, but she was an adult, and if she wanted to get drunk, he wouldn't play disapproving nursemaid. So he filled her glass again.

At least this time she didn't immediately bolt down the vodka. She studied her drink.

"Every culture has its fermented beverages," she said, swirling the vodka around in her glass. "One of the first things any civilization does is find a way to create a drinkable intoxicant. Egyptians and the Babylonians had beer. The Chinese fermented rice and honey. But many of the earliest uses of alcohol were spiritual. A way of gaining a higher consciousness, connecting with the gods."

He tossed back his vodka, letting the cold burn all the way down to his belly.

When she finished her second glass of the spirit, he said, "You're not searching for God right now."

"But I prayed to Him only a few minutes ago." She set her glass down and began to move restlessly through his stateroom. Observant as she was, he had no doubt she took in every detail, from the naval-issue desk to the rows of bladed weapons mounted on the bulkhead, taken from armories and ships from around the globe. His belongings were scattered through the cabin: pairs of boots, empty bottles, a half-assembled clockwork dirigible he never got around to completing. She saw all of this.

Picked him apart.

He saw what she did. A scattered man. Who moved restlessly from one diversion to the other, without any real sense of purpose.

He'd had purpose once. And threw it away. Because of a moment of temptation offered to him by someone he'd thought a friend, an ally. No, more than a friend and ally—a brother. Who should he hate more—the one who tempted him, or himself, for giving in? It seemed he had enough hatred for both.

"You handled yourself well enough," he said. "Didn't scream or faint."

"But I *did* almost fall overboard."

Despite her dismissal, he'd spoken honestly. For someone who'd never been in the middle of an airship battle, she'd kept her wits. Fear hadn't paralyzed her. A surprise. But then, she'd also walked into one of Palermo's most dangerous taverns to find him. And she was heading right into the teeth of peril in order to help her parents. Not precisely a sheltered academic, this Daphne Carlisle. Not precisely anything he could easily define.

And that interested him.

"Still getting your air legs," he said.

She smiled at that, a little curl of a smile. "*Air legs*. It's a new world up here. With its own customs and language."

"So long as you only record it up here." He tapped his temple.

Folding her arms across her chest, she leaned against the table. "You seem awfully concerned about that."

"Secrecy is a rogue Man O' War's best weapon."

"Here I thought a Man O' War was himself a weapon and needed nothing else. Or," she added, tilting her head and studying him, "your insistence on secrecy hides something else. Such as the reason why you went rogue. Why there are no photographs of family members or loved ones in your stateroom. Unless you keep them hidden somewhere. In a locked drawer, perhaps."

He poured himself another drink and swallowed it down. Maybe this was why he seldom interacted with women of exceptional intelligence.

Like a needle she was, Daphne Carlisle, digging and jabbing, searching out the splinters beneath his skin, but leaving him raw and bleeding in the process.

He was a Man O' War. Metal and flesh. Science at

its most advanced. It took far more than one intriguing woman's questions to wound him.

Easy enough to show her how little she or her speculation could affect him.

From the bookshelf, he plucked out one volume. *A Statistical Inquiry Into the Irrigated Horticultural Practices of the Eastern Iberian Peninsula*. He handed her the book.

She read the title, frowning slightly. Then opened it, and her frown cleared.

The inside of the book had been hollowed out.

She pulled the small photograph from the compartment within the book. Walked it over to the quartz lamp and stared at the image in her hand.

He didn't need to see it. Every one of the people in the photograph, all of their faces, the way they posed formally in front of the photography studio's provided backdrop of a forest scene—all of it had been branded into the soft flesh of his brain, his eyes, his heart.

"You have a large family," she murmured.

"*Had*," he corrected. Four brothers, three sisters. For a time, his grandmother lived with them, but she wasn't in the photograph. His parents were, however. His father sat on a velvet-covered chair, impressive in his full beard and fierce eyebrows. Surrounding him were his children and wife, like planets around the sun, Mikhail amongst them, skinny and smug in his naval cadet uniform. He hadn't become a man yet, let alone a Man O' War. "*Had* a large family."

Her wide eyes met his. "They're dead? All of them?"

"I'm the one who died."

Photographs were strange things, turning living people into wax mannequins, or stopped automatons. One could never guess by looking at the picture that his mother loved practical jokes, or that his youngest brother Yuri drove them all mad by insisting on singing rather than speaking. Or that his sister Irina had to be bodily dragged from her study to eat. Even then, she'd take a book with her to the supper table. She'd looked up, though, when Mikhail had brought home a friend from the naval academy. Had Mikhail known what the result of that would be, he'd have locked Irina in the study. He'd also have plunged the carving knife into his friend's chest. But no one had known what betrayal lay ahead, least of all Mikhail.

One would never know from the photograph, either, that his father had bragged to the neighbors for months when Mikhail had been selected to become a Man O' War. A proud day that had been, when Mikhail had come home with the news.

Not just a Gimmel or a Bet, his father had kept repeating to whoever would listen. *An Aleph. The highest aurora vires ranking there is.*

None of them knew what lay ahead. If they had known, there would have been far less boasting, and more worry.

"See," he said, forcing his voice into a tone of lightness. "Nothing to hide. You wondered if I had any pictures of my family. There they are. As ordinary as bread."

"You don't look much like your father."

"I take after my mother's side. Some Tartar blood in there."

She glanced up at him. "I can see that. Here, in your

cheekbones, and here, in the shape of your eyes." As she said this, she lightly skimmed her fingertip across the features in question.

Silver heat spread through him. He wanted to lean into her touch—he wanted to shy away from it. Instead, he held himself still, as if unaffected.

"How old were you when this was taken?" she asked, looking back at the picture.

"Seventeen, eighteen. After that, I wasn't home long enough for us to get everyone to the photographer's studio."

Why did he continue to talk of this? When every word spoken felt like spikes of ice driven into his chest. But no; he kept speaking, as if to prove to not just her but himself that he was every bit as impervious as he claimed.

"You're the first Man O' War I've ever met," she murmured, "yet it seems odd to think that you have a father and mother, and a whole passel of siblings."

"Only part of me was made in a surgical theater." He nodded down at the implants. "I've got parents, just like anyone else."

She studied him for a moment, her gaze as uncomfortably precise as always. "It's been a long time since you've seen them, hasn't it?"

He snatched the photo from her. Tucking the picture back into its hiding place within the book, he growled, "You don't know a damned thing."

"My research revealed that you went rogue two years ago. Unless you've made secret trips back to Russia, or arranged meetings with them in relatively safe places, it's reasonable to assume you haven't seen them."

"The learned *professorsha* is right again." He stalked over to the vodka and drank directly from the bottle. It was getting too warm—the only way to truly drink it was cold as winter—but he didn't care for nuance. He only wanted a dulling of this unexpected pain. But the trouble with being a Man O' War was that it now took far more alcohol to achieve any kind of intoxication. A good, solid drunk required a case of vodka, not one paltry bottle.

In three long swallows, the bottle was empty, yet he couldn't feel it. "All my telegrams go unanswered."

"Maybe," she said gently, "they never received them."

She was the one who'd needed steadying after the airship battle, yet here she was, attempting to comfort *him*.

"Oh, they have," he answered. "Got some secret information channels that confirmed it. My parents are still in Tsaritsyn, same house they've been in my whole life. And the telegrams were delivered. But I never got a reply. Not to any of them."

"They could be protecting you," she offered. "In case the telegrams might be traced."

The sound he made was more of a rasp than a laugh. "Assigning my family such caution is admirable, *professorsha*, but unnecessary. I know the reason for their silence." He stared at her, feeling the twist of his mouth and hard knot in his belly. "They're ashamed. Of me. And they have every reason to be. I didn't just betray my country, I betrayed my family."

He waited for the disgust or disapproval in her gaze.

She'd had a bit to drink, so it might take her a moment to fully understand what he'd just revealed. But when she did understand, she'd turn away from him. As she should.

But he didn't realize until that moment how much her condemnation would wound him. This woman who, moments earlier, had defended him despite knowing he was nothing but a mercenary. She insisted that there could be something good within him. But there wasn't. Now she knew it. So he—who as a Man O' War could endure injury far greater than a normal man, and trained himself to feel as little as possible—braced himself for pain.

Chapter Five

OF ALL THE things she'd witnessed this evening—the battle between Russian and British airships, the pursuit by a Russian ship, the technologically induced storm—seeing the wariness and raw hurt in Denisov's eyes shook Daphne the most.

He played his part well. The braggadocio, the raffishness. The continued assertion that his only concern was profit. A ruthless mercenary. He claimed to be heartless, but no one without a heart could speak so painfully about the loss of his family.

Was she grasping at straws? Hoping to find some seed of honor and integrity in him, buried beneath telumium armor? Yet she knew that in everyone, including herself, there were moral ambiguities that made a person neither wholly good nor wholly bad. That there was always the possibility of error and forgiveness.

She returned the hollowed-out book to its place on the

SKIES OF STEEL 77

shelf, then crossed the stateroom to where he stood. His chary gaze never left her.

"You cut your hair after you went rogue," she guessed.

He looked briefly surprised at the abrupt change of topic. Had he been expecting a reaction from her at his revelation? It was as if . . . he feared her response. But that made no sense. To him, she was nothing, a paid assignment. Or so she'd thought. Since they'd gone into the privacy of his stateroom, it seemed as though layers of identity and persona had fallen away. Leaving them more exposed, more real.

He ran his broad hand over the crest of his hair. "Not standard issue for the Russian Imperial Aerial Navy."

"Reminds me of the Mohawk Indians. The Pawnee, too."

"Ukrainian Cossacks wear a *khokhol*. Similar, but not the same." The face he made clearly evinced that he wasn't patterning himself after those Cossacks.

"I wasn't aware that Russian Man O' Wars crossed paths with American Indians."

He shook his head. "Saw a handful of them once, in Paris. An Indian delegation trying to get French aid. They were on the city street, out of place, but damned proud. Wanted that for myself. That defiance. They wouldn't change how they looked to make anyone more comfortable."

His gaze fixed on the quartz lamp. "The rules for how they wanted us to look in the navy were strict." He snorted. "Uniformity. The tsar's *naval representatives*. We were not ourselves but Russia. Our hair could only be so long, combed in just such a way."

"Going rogue, you gave the navy the tonsorial equivalent of this." She made a rude hand gesture.

His laugh was low, but genuine. "Just so." Yet it faded all too soon. "Their lands were being taken away, the Indians. The American government made promises. Worthless promises."

"Did the ones you saw get the help they sought?"

"No idea. Doubt it, though," he added with a shrug. "The Americans might not have telumium, but they do have soya fields."

"Which means they have tetrol fuel."

"France won't risk breaking its trade alliance with the United States for the Indians' sake."

Her mouth tightened. "A common story," she muttered bitterly. "Progress and politics mercilessly move onward. And the price? Whole civilizations and cultures are being destroyed. Wiped clean from the slate of history."

"That makes you angry."

"Not angry—sad." She paused. "No, I'm angry, too. That any one culture decides it's more valuable than another, or that any human being considers itself superior to someone else. Think of everything that's being lost because of it!" She paced. "Vehicles that choke the air with smoke, and flying machines engineered strictly for war and destruction. How's any of that made the world a better place?"

Too late she realized how utterly insensitive her words must sound to him, the man who powered the flying machine.

She whirled to face him. "Oh, God, I didn't mean—"

"You meant it." He walked slowly toward her, the quartz light carving him into severe angles.

"I suppose I did." She lifted her chin to meet his gaze. "I *do* mean it. Sometimes I feel that technology ennobles humanity, and other times . . . most times, I feel it strips away the best part of us." She looked away, then back to him. "I imagine that must lower your opinion of me."

"Here I believed you didn't care what I thought of you." Humor tinged his voice. "If it helps you at all, I think you're right."

She gaped at him. "You do?"

"*Partially* right. Won't say what part, though. Can't make it easy on you." Reaching out, he playfully tugged on the end of her braid.

Just a quick, casual movement, that little tug, yet it made her heart beat a bit faster. It spoke of a growing intimacy, one she feared. And wanted.

"Have faith, Captain Denisov, that I am never at ease around you." Indeed, the more they spoke, talking of family, of beliefs, the more uncomfortable she became. Her awareness of him as a man only increased, as did a nascent, gleaming attraction. His outsized masculine appeal couldn't be denied, and there was something dreadfully alluring about a scoundrel that called to a usually well-behaved academic such as she. Made her wonder what kind of wildness within herself she could discover—with his expert assistance.

Worse, she was coming to know more of the man behind the telumium. She rather liked him.

This wasn't supposed to happen. It *shouldn't* happen. Yet, like so much of life, things had a way of slipping out of one's control, no matter how hard one struggled to keep hold.

"A shame," he murmured. "I'd like you to be relaxed around me."

A half smile teased his lips, and she wanted to trace her fingers along their intriguing curves. It had to be the two glasses of vodka she'd imbibed that made her want to do something so outrageous. No—she'd always had a strong tolerance for spirits. Her wits were as sharp as ever. This desire came from intoxication, but not from alcohol.

Somehow, the distance between them diminished, but whether it was because he drew nearer to her, or because she'd stepped closer to him, she couldn't tell. Whatever pulled them together, it seemed its own force, incapable of being reasoned with or neatly compartmentalized.

Danger from outside enemies had passed, for now. They were here, together, in his stateroom. The glow of the quartz lamp made the space seem small, intimate. Possibility and recklessness thickened the air.

Heat surrounded her, and the scent of hot metal. "Letting my guard down around you wouldn't be wise," she said, breathless.

"Most pleasure isn't wise, yet we crave it." His gaze went heavy-lidded. Each word he spoke strummed through her in low, sonorous ripples.

"We do."

She couldn't stop herself. She lifted her hands and ran

them up his chest, over the silk and wool of his waistcoat, feeling the fabric, the buckles, and the solid form of his torso beneath. He hissed in a breath as her hands traveled higher, to his exposed flesh above the vee of his waistcoat. He was impossibly firm under her palms. Yet through the telumium, she felt his heart beating furiously—as hers did.

A growl sounded deep in his chest. His expression tightened. He brought his own hands up, cupping one around the back of her neck, the other curving at her waist. Her eyes drifted shut from the feel of their bare skin touching. He was so warm, she felt as though she melted.

His head lowered. At the same time, she rose up on her toes. Bringing their bodies flush against each other. She thought she'd never felt anything as hard and unyielding as his body. Then their mouths met, and everything became satiny and sleek.

You shouldn't be doing this, her mind shouted.

I know and I don't care, her body shouted back.

His kiss was . . . overwhelming. Not in terms of physical force—his lips against hers were surprisingly tender. At first. But she sank into the kiss, and together they became resolute, determined to taste and know each other. Their boldness increased from breath to breath. His mouth was intent on seducing hers. He was audacious, then sensuous, then gentle, and back again. This was a man who knew the power of a kiss, who treated it not as a precursor to other pleasures, but as the pleasure itself.

It resonated everywhere in her. Her mouth was merely the conduit. She felt his kiss in her breasts, between her legs, all the places she might expect would respond to a devastating kiss. But also in the arches of her feet. In the crook of her elbows. Behind her eyelids. Not one part of her went unaffected.

His hands stayed precisely where they were, one covering her neck, the other at her waist. His fingers tightened, but only slightly. He was holding himself back, and for some reason, that touched her. That he could be so protective. A Man O' War's strength was legendary, but he wouldn't use it on her. He wouldn't hurt her.

Still, he pressed her closer, kissing her with growing hunger. Her own built to a towering height. She needed this, needed *him*. Needed to forget everything but the pure heat of desire.

Impossible. She couldn't allow herself that indulgence. Not now. Not with this man. Not with the secret weight on her conscience.

She made a pained sound, and ended the kiss. It was surprisingly easy to break from his hold, and she realized again how careful he'd been with her. *Damn it.*

"I hurt you," he said, voice rough with self-recrimination. His hands dropped to his sides, and he scowled fiercely.

"Not a single bruise. It was . . . I've never had a kiss like that." She backed toward the door. "I must get back to my cabin."

"Stay." His words were rumbled seduction. "It's good between us. That kiss was just the beginning."

A belated drunkenness seemed to hit her. Her legs

were unstable, and when she shook her head, she did so wildly. "Have to go." She stumbled for the door.

When he appeared beside her, she started. But it was herself she feared, not him.

"Take this." He thrust the quartz lamp into her hand. "Don't want you out there losing your bearings in the dark."

She barely managed a thanks before opening the door and lurching into the passageway. With a sense of dream-like unreality, she navigated her way back to her cabin. Once inside, she sank down onto her cot.

He'd warned her about going astray, but it was too late.

I'm already lost.

MIKHAIL WASN'T SURPRISED that Daphne Carlisle kept herself scarce for the rest of the night and most of the following day. Much as she'd enjoyed the kiss—and participated eagerly—something about it had upset her. Maybe she considered the idea of going to bed with a mercenary distasteful, when she herself seemed to possess such high scruples.

But, damn, she didn't kiss him like a high-minded woman.

He now stood on the forecastle, watching the approaching Egyptian coastline. The ship cruised at half a mile up.

But he barely saw the shore. His thoughts and body remembered the taste of her, the feel of her. The glittering flame she became when finally allowing herself to burn brightly. His hands tingled, recalling the feel of her slim but soft curves, and his cock stirred with memories of her hips pressed tight to his.

More than the desire between them, there was a pull stronger than just physical need. She didn't know the facts of what he'd done to go rogue, though he'd made it clear he deserved censure. No condemnation in her gaze, however. Whatever she thought of him, she spoke to him as though he wasn't a technologically enhanced soldier of fortune, and she wasn't a stiff-backed academic. As if they were simply a woman and a man. Equals.

It had been a long time since he'd enjoyed a woman's company so much, even out of bed. But if he got her into bed . . . They'd set the skies to burning, the air thick with smoke from the fire they created between them.

He gritted his teeth. Later. He'd consider those delicious possibilities later. Right now, the ship was about to make landfall, a critical juncture at this point in the voyage.

"Fetch Miss Carlisle," he said to a crewman. "And have her bring her strongbox."

The crewman hurried off to obey the order. She appeared a few minutes later, carrying not only the strongbox, but a sharp sense of caution. In the bright light of the eastern Mediterranean sun, she looked more severe, shadows of fatigue ringing her eyes. She hadn't slept well. Because of him?

"We cannot be at Medinat al-Kadib yet," she said without preamble.

"Half day from here."

"Then there's no need for me to bring this"—she hefted the strongbox—"to you."

"There's every need." He nodded toward the coastline, and its fringe of palm trees. "We're nearly in the Shepherdess's territory. She's the eyes of this part of the sea. Knows about everyone coming in and going out."

Miss Carlisle frowned. "Does she have her own airship?"

"That'd be impossible, since there are no female Man O' Wars, and she doesn't have a rogue one in her employ." He pointed at a small shape half a mile distant from the ship. "There, and there. Autonomously controlled observation dirigibles."

"No one pilots them?"

"Not a soul. All day and night, they follow prescribed patrol patterns."

"They can't run continuously."

"Every now and then they land to be rewound. Then, it's back on patrol. The Shepherdess has them all over the coast. Their lenses send visual data to the ground, and she collects it all on specially engineered cinemagraph screens."

Her eyes widened. "I had no idea such a thing was possible."

He grinned. "Clever thinkers they have out in this part of the world."

"Arabic inventors are more advanced than the ones in Europe, but this goes beyond anything I've ever seen. Self-propelled surveillance dirigibles." She squinted at one of the small craft.

Her caution had been forgotten in the discovery of the Shepherdess's mechanical spies, and it troubled him how her soft smile of wonderment echoed in warm pulses in his chest.

But he had to be pragmatic, especially at this critical juncture of the voyage.

"Astonishing, yes," he said. "Regular old human spies are on the ground, too. Know why she's called the Shepherdess?"

"I haven't the smallest idea."

"She's not a shepherdess of a flock, not even of people. Information is what she herds. Anyone clamoring to get into the Arabian Peninsula has to pay the Shepherdess. They pay for intelligence about who else might be lurking around the area. And they pay to keep her quiet about their own presence."

Miss Carlisle nodded. "Baksheesh. A common and venerable practice in these parts." She raised a brow. "But if the Shepherdess is paid to be silent about our presence here, what's to say she won't stay mute on the possibility of other threats in the area? The airspace could be thick with enemies who've also paid her. She could be playing everyone for fools, and collect as much baksheesh as she likes."

He had to appreciate how quickly her mind moved to devious schemes. "Pay her enough, we get the most reliable information. That's why I had you bring up this." He rapped a knuckle against the strongbox. "Nothing ensures security and intelligence like a bar of gold."

She took a step back, cradling the strongbox against

her chest. Her arms shook with the effort of holding the heavy container, but she didn't loosen her hold. "Use your own gold."

"That *is* my gold," he pointed out. Kiss or no kiss, he was in the business of protecting himself and his crew, and earning profit. "Here or in Medinat al-Kadib, it's mine. And it's what I'm going to use to pay the Shepherdess."

"There has to be something else on this ship that can serve the same purpose."

"Nothing as valuable as what you've got there." He made an impatient gesture. "Hand it over."

She scowled, but clearly saw that there was no winning this argument. Crouching, she set the strongbox down onto the planks and entered the combination. It unlocked with a hiss. She lifted the lid, shielding the contents from his sight.

All the color drained from her face, turning her white as ash, with her freckles standing out like scars. Her breathing stopped. For a moment, Mikhail actually thought she might be sick, or faint.

"Oh, God," she croaked. "Too soon."

His first thought was that she'd been struck by air madness, a rare ailment that briefly robbed airgoing travelers of their senses. But they hadn't been flying for more than a few days, not long enough for her to succumb to that sickness.

Concerned, he stepped closer. And saw the interior of the strongbox.

The ingots of gold were gone. In their place were bars of clay.

"The hell?" he growled. Picking up one of the bars, he saw it was exactly the same shape as an ingot of gold. Its heft wasn't the same, though. With one hand, he snapped the bar in half. Dried clay sifted away on the wind. Particles caught in her hair and dusted her clothing. The rest disappeared, blown out to sea.

He'd given express orders to his crew not to go into Daphne Carlisle's cabin, nor disturb any of her belongings. Including the strongbox. He didn't doubt that for someone like Akua, breaking the code for the combination lock was as easy as cracking a walnut. But Akua prided himself on not just his mental skill, but his scrupulous integrity. The chief engineer would never break into Miss Carlisle's strongbox, steal the gold, and replace it with bars of clay.

The answer was as obvious as the freckles on her chalky face. She'd fooled Mikhail.

"How'd you do it?"

She tore her horrified gaze from the strongbox to him. Slowly, she rose. He watched her silently debate her different options. Lie to him? Jump overboard and hope she survived the fall?

Finally, she said, "An alchemical process I'd learned in Morocco." Her voice was surprisingly steady for a woman caught in the middle of a massive lie.

Anger like acid poured through him. "Didn't think I'd notice the difference between clay and gold?"

"The transformation was supposed to last longer. The saline air might've affected its stability. The alchemist who showed me the process didn't say anything about it."

"Should've been more thorough in your education." He picked up the strongbox and flung it overboard.

She winced, but he couldn't find the means to care. This little Englishwoman with her notebooks and moss green eyes and sweet, hot kisses—she'd played him for a fool, deceiving him ever since the beginning. Duping *him*, the mercenary.

It wasn't the first time he'd been led astray by someone he thought he could trust, and the burn of it singed through his veins.

"Set the ship down," she said after a moment. "Or we can use the jolly boat."

"Now you're giving orders on my ship? What the hell for?" he demanded.

"All you need to do is drop me off as soon as we make land. I can go the rest of the way on my own."

From where the ship was now, it was a journey of nearly eight hundred miles to Medinat al-Kadib. A journey she planned on making by herself. With the Shepherdess aware of her every movement.

"Not a damned chance," he snarled, taking a step closer. "Tell me what you plan on using to pay for your parents' release. Better not be more of that false gold."

She hesitated. "There's a diamond mine—"

He snorted in disbelief.

"There truly is," she retorted. "An ancient mine I found with my parents several years ago. We didn't tell anyone about it because we were afraid it would draw unscrupulous treasure hunters into the area."

"So you were going to lead al-Rahim to the mine in exchange for your parents."

She swallowed, and nodded.

He swung away to pace the length of the forecastle. They were a half mile in the air, and just making land now. The waves lapped at the sandy coast in a froth of blue and white. Palm trees waved gently like dancers. But he barely saw the beauty of the scene. His mind churned. Anger continued to pump poison into his chest. He couldn't decide with whom he was most angry—her, for deceiving him, or himself, for being misled. *Again.*

But he'd survived this long because he was a devious bastard. That hadn't changed.

He shouted down the length of the ship, "I want Petrovsky!" Mikhail could have used the shipboard auditory device to call for his master-at-arms, but it felt a hell of a lot more satisfying to yell.

Petrovsky appeared a minute later. His broad chest and thick arms usually intimidated the crew into maintaining order, as his duties demanded. Seeing him, Miss Carlisle's brief display of bravado withered a little. She looked back and forth between Petrovsky and Mikhail.

"Keep an eye on Miss Carlisle," Mikhail ordered. "Take her to her cabin and post a guard outside. I don't want her trying to sneak off the ship while I'm gone. And confiscate the knife in her boot."

Petrovsky reached for her, but she jerked away from his grasp. "Physically accosting me isn't necessary," she said tartly. "I'll go to my cabin peaceably. And unarmed." She handed over her knife.

After taking the blade from her, the master-at-arms looked to Mikhail for guidance. He gave Petrovsky a small nod. Unlikely that Miss Carlisle would attempt an escape, or a fight with any of his crew. Unexpectedly fierce as she might be, his crew were all trained in combat. They could easily overpower her.

Hell—did she know what kind of a risk she'd been taking? Paying a rogue Man O' War with false gold? The danger she'd taken upon herself made his blood cold . . . until he realized he was furious with her, and he wasn't supposed to care if anything happened to her.

"Let's go, miss," Petrovsky said. He motioned for her to walk ahead of him.

She took a step, then stopped.

"You said that I was to be guarded while you were off the ship," she said. "Where are you going?"

His lip curled into a sneer. "Not in any position to ask me questions. But it doesn't matter." He planted his hands on his hips. "The Shepherdess and I are going to have a little chat. Baksheesh she wants. Baksheesh she gets. Damn lucky I keep a cache of jewels for times just like this."

Miss Carlisle stared at him. "We're continuing on to Medinat al-Kadib?"

"We are." His smile was merely a baring of his teeth. "Now you can sit in your cabin and think of all the ways you'll have to repay me."

DAPHNE WAS NEVER comfortable with keeping still, and was even less enamored of being confined in small places.

But with a large crewman outside her cabin door, she had no choice but to pace as best she could in the narrow berth and stew over Denisov's words.

What did he plan? For her and for the rest of the voyage? How was she supposed to repay him? Her resources were extremely limited, and they had to be reserved for freeing her parents. Beyond that, she had nothing to offer him.

A woman always has one means of payment.

It was a sad truth, but an old one. Women frequently paid with their bodies. It was often their most valued commodity. Could she do it? Be forced to sleep with him? The attraction between them couldn't be refuted—if he even still desired her after her deception—but going willingly to someone's bed and being coerced into doing so were vastly different things.

But if it meant saving her parents' lives . . .

God, she'd never been in this kind of a quandary before; it was far more complex than anything she'd ever faced. Made worse by the fact that, much as she tried, she couldn't get her brain to function logically. The violent, blistering-hot simoom wind was trapped in her mind, and a suffocating khamsin whirled in her heart. She couldn't document and analyze what she felt, what she thought. Always so much easier to pick apart someone else's culture than scrutinize herself.

What she did know: Denisov had been enraged at her deception. With good cause.

She stopped her frantic pacing and tried to look through the porthole. As usual, she could barely see anything, just a sliver of sky. How long had Denisov been gone? She'd been too preoccupied to check her pocket watch, and now she'd no idea if it had been ten minutes or two hours. And she didn't know what would happen when he finally did return to the ship. This fretting and worrying was driving her closer and closer to madness.

She had to remain as collected as possible. No matter what happened with Denisov, she still had to consider what to do about her mother and father. They were relying on her. Whatever it took, she'd find a way to get them free. She had to think of solutions, possibilities.

With that in mind, she grabbed her notebook. Thoughts came more easily to her if she wrote them down. Yet no sooner did she reach for her pencil than the sound of heavy footfalls resounded in the passageway. Only one person on this ship walked with such weight and single-minded purpose.

She managed to compose herself just as the door to her cabin banged open, revealing Denisov.

Though she'd seen him many times, his appearance continued to rob her of breath. He was so large, so dangerous with his untamed air. She'd thought him menacing the first time she'd ever seen him—had it only been a few days ago?—but they had started to build a strange, fragile connection during the voyage, especially after they'd kissed.

That connection was gone now. His expression was hard as granite, and his eyes blasted her with cold as he stared at her.

He stepped into her cabin and kicked the door shut

behind him. It rattled all the way into her bones as she faced him.

"The Shepherdess is paid," he said without preamble. "We're in the clear. Now, you're going to take me to that diamond mine."

"Give up my only leverage?" She shook her head. "No one goes near the mine until I get my parents back." Her own audacity stunned her, but she had to play the game intelligently.

He, too, looked momentarily surprised that she would dare contradict him. "Could force you to tell me where it is. The navy taught me all kinds of techniques for obtaining information. And I've since learned some things that would make the Russian Admiralty choke on their tea."

She could believe that. "It doesn't matter what you do to me. The only person who gets the location of the mine is al-Rahim."

Though he didn't move, she had the sense that he seemed to grow even larger, filling the cramped space of her cabin with his presence. Her heart slammed in her chest, a drum beating the march to the gallows.

Finally, he said, "This is how it'll work: I'll take you to get your parents back. You tell al-Rahim where the mine is. He gets the diamonds from the mine. Then I'm taking the diamonds from al-Rahim."

"Those are quite a few steps until you receive any sort of financial recompense," she answered. "Why not simply cut your losses and put me down here? Let me deal with al-Rahim on my own."

He folded his arms across his chest, muscles bunching impressively, and the miniscule cabin shrank even more. "I've flown across the whole damned Mediterranean, skirted a battle between airships, outrun a Russian ship eager for my blood. My crew and I have to get something out of this. A mine full of diamonds should settle the bill."

She supposed she ought to be grateful that he'd take her the rest of the way. Crossing the Arabian Peninsula on her own could be done, but the trek would be much longer and far more dangerous.

"All right," she said after a moment.

"Delighted that you approve of my plan. Until we reach Medinat al-Kadib, you're confined to your quarters." He turned on his heel and took a step toward the door.

"Is that . . . all?"

Her voice stopped him, and he turned back to face her. "Ah, I see. The *professorsha* thinks I'm going to demand another kind of payment from her." His gaze raked her, and he smirked. "I don't force a woman into my bed. When she comes, she comes willingly. And she always wants to stay." His smirk faded, replaced by cold scorn. "You've lost any chance of ever becoming my lover."

He left her then. She didn't know if she was relieved that he wasn't coercing her into his bed, or if she was disappointed that she'd cost them whatever chance they might have had to become something more to each other.

Chapter Six

DAPHNE HAD LEARNED patience early in life. One couldn't grow up in innumerable archaeological dig sites without developing some sense of equanimity. Digs were most assuredly not hotbeds of excitement—involving long, tedious hours of carefully sifting through dust, meticulously brushing away said dust from minute fragments, and painstakingly documenting every step of the process. And this could go on for weeks, months.

She'd always received stern rebukes from her parents if she ever whined, or if she kicked up dust as she ran around the site. So she'd forced herself to become calm, the very soul of self-restraint. One of her parents' long-term workers was from Gujarat, and had helped immensely by teaching Daphne meditative techniques to make those interminable, sunbaked hours tolerable.

Then again, as soon as she was old enough to go to university, she hadn't studied archaeology, as her parents had hoped, but anthropology. Far more interesting, and active, living with people of different cultures and participating in routines of their daily lives.

Academic life could try anyone's patience, so she spent as little time at the Accademia as possible.

But now she had to draw on her early training, spending the whole of the day confined to her cabin as the airship traveled toward Medinat al-Kadib. She would've gone quite mad if she didn't invoke some of Chandra's techniques in quieting her mind for the duration of the journey. The sky outside the porthole shifted from the bright blue of morning to the deeper sapphire of approaching dusk. She made herself watch this slow transformation with infinite calm, emptying her thoughts of everything but the color of the sky.

Even so, by the time Denisov appeared at her door, she leapt to her feet, all sense of peace forgotten.

It wasn't merely the endless day spent trapped in her cabin. It was him. He had a way of doing that to her—shattering her calm, unsettling her profoundly.

"We've reached the periphery of the city," he said, voice flat.

"I could see the lights," she answered, and felt ridiculous for offering up such an inane observation.

"How are you going to let al-Rahim know you've arrived?"

She pulled a piece of crumpled paper from a pocket in her satchel. "I'm to find a telegraph office and send a wire to this address. Then an emissary is supposed to respond with the location of our meeting. That's what al-Rahim said in his letter to me. From there . . ."—she shrugged—"I'm to receive further instruction."

"Makes sense al-Rahim wouldn't come in person," Denisov murmured to himself. "He'd keep your parents in his custody until he was certain of payment." His gaze was glacial. "His caution's understandable."

Perhaps it was being too long imprisoned in her cabin, but she snapped, "I'm an *academic*, Captain. I can barely afford to eat. Did you really think I'd have bars of gold in my possession?"

"I've got the vision of a hawk, but your virtuous appearance fooled me, *professorsha*," he replied, "as much as those fake gold bars. But I'm a quick study, and won't be deceived again. Not by you."

She hurriedly grabbed her satchel, avoiding his eyes. "I'll need someone to ferry me down in the jolly boat."

"Come on, then." He jerked his head toward the passageway, and she tried to walk past him. He made no move to step aside or get out of her way, so she was forced to edge around him, feeling the heat radiating from his body and brushing up against the unyielding muscles of his chest and arms. A flare of a different heat moved through her, reminding her how only last night she'd been pressed close to him, his hands holding her with a rough tenderness.

She shoved such thoughts away. They'd serve her no purpose now.

Denisov led her through the ship, back down to the cargo hold. The jolly boat waited there, along with Levkov and the crewman named Herrera.

"You're to take the jolly boat back to the ship," Denisov said to Herrera. "Wait for me on the outskirts of the city. Should be back within a day, but if I'm going to be any longer, I'll send word."

"Aye, sir. Hear they've got clockwork scarabs that carry messages. Cheap, and reliable, too. You can use one of 'em."

"Why, Herrera," Denisov said with a wry smile. "Here I thought we kept you around for your pretty face."

"Ain't that your job, Captain?"

While Levkov rolled his eyes, Daphne frowned.

She stared at Denisov. "Wait—*you're* coming with me? I thought you'd just have a crewman drop me off."

"Protecting my investment," he answered. "Medinat al-Kadib isn't the Boboli Gardens. Who knows what kind of trouble you'd get yourself into down there."

"Your master-at-arms could accompany me."

Denisov snorted. "Petrovsky's strong, but a Man O' War is stronger than any man." He glanced down at the visible edge of his implants. "Only person I trust for this job is me."

"Are you my protection," she demanded, "or my warden?"

His mouth firmed. "Wardens are for people who can't be trusted. You figure out what I'm supposed to be." He nodded toward the jolly boat. "Get in and secure yourself."

She had to agree that having a Man O' War accompanying her in what was a notoriously dangerous city had its merits. Not all of Medinat al-Kadib was perilous—

most of its citizens made their living through honest means such as trade and manufacturing—but she had a feeling that al-Rahim's emissary wouldn't want to meet anywhere respectable.

So without further disagreement, she climbed into the jolly boat and fastened the safety harness around her lap. Herrera took up a position in the front of the boat.

Denisov slipped his arms through the straps of a pack. Levkov was placing brass cylinders the size of loaves of bread into it. A band of leather wrapped around the middle of each cylinder, and they were topped by plates of what appeared to be telumium.

"Spare batteries," Herrera explained.

"For the jolly boat?" she asked.

"For me," Denisov said, jumping lightly into the vessel. He positioned himself at the tiller. "If a Man O' War's away from his ship for more than a few days, the energy within him builds up. A lot."

"Too much," Herrera added. "Could trigger an uncontrollable rage. Battle madness."

"Getting damned mouthy, Herrera," Denisov growled. The crewman looked away, chastised.

"God," she said. "I had no idea." Being so utterly out of control . . . it sounded terrifying.

He shrugged. "You become a Man O' War, you take some risks."

"And the spare batteries in your pack draw off your energy when you're apart from your ship," she deduced.

"Gives me a week away rather than just a few days."

He made adjustments to the jolly boat's control panel, readying it for flight.

As indifferent as he sounded to the prospect, it distressed her. "In essence, you're tethered to your ship. It's part of you, and you're part of it. Does that . . . trouble you?"

"No." He scowled at her. "Think I'm going to overload on purpose and punish you for your deception?"

She swallowed hard. "I hadn't considered that."

"I'm not going to put myself through that just for you."

Well, that was a relief. "I just mean . . ." She struggled to find the right words. "It'd be like I had an airship-sized millstone around my neck. Shackled. I can't think you'd find that to be a pleasant feeling." She eyed his crest of hair, the rings in his ears, everything that proclaimed him to be a maverick. "Freedom's very valuable to you."

He started, as if she'd jabbed a knife between his ribs. "You don't know a damned thing about me." Busying himself with preparing the jolly boat, he muttered, "Long as I have these"—he glanced at the pack containing the batteries—"I can have as much life on land as I want. But the skies are a hell of a lot more free. Better to have wings than be trapped on the dull ground like a commonplace man."

"You most certainly aren't commonplace." She smiled.

He didn't return the smile. "Flattering me is a useless pastime."

"I wasn't trying to. Merely stating a truth."

The look he gave her showed just how much faith he

had in her definition of *truth*. She deserved his mistrust. Yet she couldn't dwell on it. At last, she'd reached Medinat al-Kadib, which meant she was one step closer to freeing her parents. As perilous as the past few days had been—on many levels—the real danger was about to begin.

Levkov pulled the lever opening the cargo doors, and the jolly boat plunged downward.

She clung to the sides of the vessel as it plummeted. A terrifying sensation. Yet oddly familiar. Ever since she'd received word that her parents had been kidnapped, her life had been in perpetual free fall. It would be a long, long time before she felt solid ground beneath her feet.

MIKHAIL HAD BEEN to Medinat al-Kadib only once, but it was a city that left an indelible impression, like a burn. Its outer walls ran right up against the coast of the Red Sea, thick fortifications built to repel the water pirates that had long plagued the city. Ether cannons atop the battlements stood poised to repel any seagoing threat, and steam-powered dhows patrolled the harbor, Gatling guns mounted on their prows.

Safer for him and Daphne Carlisle to approach from the landward side. Dusk fell rapidly as they neared the eastern gate. The walls enclosing the city had been built hundreds of years ago, but now the huge, elaborately carved wooden door at the gate had a complex me-chanical lock that could bolt into place at the first sign of trouble.

A stream of traffic led both into and out of the city.

SKIES OF STEEL 103

Shepherds and farmers poured out, having concluded their business for the day. Many drove steam wagons, no longer reliant on donkeys or horses to draw their vehicles. They seemed eager to leave the city, eyeing warily the men and women who deliberately came to Medinat al-Kadib at night in order to sample its sensual pleasures.

Mikhail wouldn't be enjoying those pleasures. Not tonight. Right now, his task was to escort Miss Carlisle to the nearest telegraph office, and then see what the rest of the night brought.

They joined the line of people making their way through the eastern gate. Fortunately, he didn't have to tell Miss Carlisle to stay close. She did so on her own. She had a strong sense of self-preservation—he'd had ample evidence of that already. He kept one eye on her, one on their surroundings. He had no doubt he could handle any trouble that came his way, but she was far more vulnerable in a place known for its wildness.

No one would hurt or harass her, not so long as he was around.

Protecting my investment.

But as they crossed through the gate and entered the winding, jeweled labyrinth of the city's streets, he thought back to how distressed she'd seemed at the idea that he and the *Bielyi Voron* were forever tied to each other. As if she actually cared about him.

Don't be a sentimental ass. She's a mercenary, like you are, except she disguises it behind a fancy vocabulary and a pair of wide green eyes.

He was grateful, at least, that she didn't gawk at their

surroundings like a guileless innocent—or a keen-eyed academic eagerly researching new subject matter. She kept her gaze level and dispassionate. Yet if ever there was a place that might deserve dumbfounded stares, it was Medinat al-Kadib. Mosaics covered almost every surface, glittering in the spherical gas lamps that hovered above the streets. Small rotor blades atop the lamps kept them aloft. Clockwork scarabs also filled the air, the city's messenger system, and the metallic whir of their wings droned beneath the constant beat of the *doumbek* drum and strum of the *oud*.

Some people walked down the twisting streets, a few rode donkeys, and there were others who drove steam-powered palanquins. Some of the vehicles were ornately gilded and shaped, their interior compartments curtained with bright silk. Yet other palanquins looked as though they'd been driven across the desert and back and encountered herds of angry camels along the way.

Steam power, not tetrol, was the fuel of choice here. The East hadn't made the necessary alliances to secure the American fuel and didn't have the land and climate to grow their own soya.

Men sat outside cafés, smoking hookahs that were periodically refilled by wheeled automatons. The mechanical servers also carried trays of tea and plates of honey-soaked pastries. There was laughter and song, and the continuous chatter of voices poured out from screened windows.

"The city's different from the last time I was here," Miss Carlisle said quietly. "It's become . . . downtrodden."

"Don't see a lot of suffering here," he answered, also pitching his voice low.

"Look closer." She subtly nodded toward the narrower lanes leading off the main thoroughfares. A woman and her three children wrapped in tattered blankets were crouched beside a brazier, their hollow gazes fixed on the flames. "There never used to be people living on the streets. I see hunger in many faces."

As she pointed this out, he did see signs that the once-prosperous city was in decline. More beggars, and buildings in need of repair. Of course she would notice these things, for she was the kind of woman uniquely attuned to the lives of others.

"A kind of desperation, too, in the merriment." The laughter seemed forced, the music strained.

She nodded. "The effects of the war. People here are caught between two major powers, and they're suffering for it." Her expression turned even more grim. "Just as my parents were caught up in the conflict, and now they could be killed."

What would he do to save the lives of his family? They'd rejected him, and yet, would he travel to the ends of the earth to keep them alive? Would he use any attack or trick to ensure their safety?

I would. I'd deceive anyone if it meant their survival.

The thought shook him, that he could possibly understand why Daphne Carlisle had deliberately misled him.

Whatever her motivations, he had to consider his own benefit and prosperity. Sympathy didn't pay his crew, or put gold and jewels in his coffers.

"Telegraph office is ahead on the right," he said gruffly.

They entered the office, where a woman sat behind a desk, idly leafing through a frayed book. Telegraphs must not be in high demand in Medinat al-Kadib, for the clerk jumped up in surprise when Mikhail and Miss Carlisle approached the counter. The clerk eyed him guardedly, but he was used to such a response.

"I need to send a telegram to this address," Miss Carlisle said in Arabic.

Fortunately, there were a few members of Mikhail's crew who hailed from this part of the world, so he knew the language passably well.

The clerk read the address. "But that's the telegraph office on the other side of the city. You'd be better off using the scarab couriers."

"Not a good practice," he said, "telling your customers to take their business elsewhere."

The clerk blushed and stammered. "Of course, *sayyid*." After Daphne Carlisle wrote out her message, the clerk hurried off to tap it into her telegraph machine.

"It makes sense that I'd send a telegram rather than a courier," Miss Carlisle said as the clerk worked. "The scarab would go directly to al-Rahim's emissary, making it easier to track his whereabouts."

"But if he has someone posted at the other telegraph office," Mikhail noted, "they'd get the message and take it to the emissary, without revealing where he'd be found."

She exhaled through her nose. "This subterfuge makes me uneasy." Catching his eye, she said pointedly, "*All* of this duplicity."

It wasn't an apology, and he didn't mistake it for one.

Silently, they waited for the clerk to finish sending the telegraph.

"It may take some time before we receive a response," the clerk explained when she was done. "Hours, or days."

But no sooner had she spoken than the telegraph receiver beeped to life. The clerk transcribed the message as it came through, and handed it to Miss Carlisle.

"We're to meet at the Café Ifrit in an hour."

"Oh, that is not a good place, *sayidati*," the clerk exclaimed. "Bad people go to the Café Ifrit. Dangerous men."

"She'll be safe," Mikhail said.

The clerk looked him up and down. "So she will, *insha'Allah*."

"Not God's will," Mikhail answered, "but mine."

FULL NIGHT HAD descended by the time Daphne and Denisov left the telegraph office. Between the hovering gas lamps and a few strands of garish electric lights, the streets held an unnatural brightness. Not all the streets, though, for the alleys and side paths were shadowed and punctuated by furtive movement—human or other animal.

The desperation in the merriment that Denisov had noted earlier had increased, too. Harsher notes in the laughter, more discordant tones in the music. As if the city itself realized that it balanced precariously over a chasm, with the British and Italian allies on one side, the

Hapsburgs and Russians on the other, both willing to shove the local populace to their doom if it would serve the greater cause.

She stayed close beside him as they navigated the streets. He'd thrown barbs at her at the telegraph office, barbs she deserved yet they still stung. For all her deception with him, she liked to consider herself an honest person.

She hadn't time to consider moral conundrums. Every step she took beside Denisov brought her that much closer to freeing her parents. Yet those steps were like treading on dynamite. Danger lay in all directions. Including the man striding next to her. But he'd said that he would protect his investment, and his investment was her.

Walking beside him was like strolling beside a massive shark, with all the smaller fishes giving him ample space. His size, his appearance, the air of power just on the verge of slipping its tether—no one wanted to cross Denisov. It wasn't merely that he was a Man O' War, but that he had a means of moving, lethal and direct, with a sinister grace, that both drew everyone's attention and caused them to shrink away.

She wondered why the men who looked at her would suddenly blanch and hurry off, until she saw the threatening glares Denisov sent their way. His crystalline eyes seemed to glow with warning. *One word, one touch, and I'll tear you into shreds.*

Ever since the Mechanical Transformation that had happened fifty years earlier, providing the leveling ground of technology, women had finally gained more equality.

They were no longer limited to roles as wives, seam-stresses, and shopgirls, but could take their place in the world as the equal of men. Men gradually—sometimes reluctantly—realized that the female gender possessed the same faculties, the same intelligence and fortitude as men. There were female politicians, scientists, ship captains. Professors, such as herself.

For all that egalitarianism, she was damned grateful to have a massive Man O' War providing protection as she wove her way through the streets of Medinat al-Kadib.

A commotion up ahead made her slow in her steps. Distinctly English music and voices poured out an open door, and European men in British uniforms loitered around the door, shouting rowdily at the passersby.

"That's a British officers' club," she murmured to Denisov. "Unofficial, of course. No one nation has claim over the city."

"British officers making asses of themselves," he muttered back.

The soldiers in question all had faces reddened with drink and belligerence as they spilled out into the street. Amusing themselves, they yelled epithets and slurs at the people walking by. One lieutenant shoved the shoulder of a local man, causing him to stumble back into the arms of other citizens.

Crowds gathered, both British and Arabian, facing each other in the street. More insults were hurled, and the knife edge of potential violence cut through the heavy air. It was clear by the jaded expressions on the locals' faces that this wasn't the first time they had been harassed by foreign soldiers, but they were certainly ready to meet aggression with aggression.

"This place'll be better off once Britain gets her hands on it," a major boasted, swaggering in front of the collected citizens. "Replace all this foreign nonsense with proper culture."

"*Proper culture?*" a young local retorted, stepping close. "When it was *our* culture that gave you infidels mathematics, chemistry, astronomy, medicine?"

"All improved by British minds," the major sneered.

"And if we hadn't given you *ferengi* coffee, you'd all still be drunk." The young man sniffed, then wrinkled his nose. "Never mind, you're still drunk."

Both sides of the crowd stirred restively, tension climbing higher.

"We need to leave," she whispered to Denisov. "*Now.*" In moments, the street would explode into a chaotic melee.

Instead, Denisov strode right into the middle of the gathered mob. The British major and the local man stepped back as Denisov placed himself between them. He towered over both men, and stared at them as if gazing at the antics of strutting roosters.

Though the British soldier turned chalky, he tried to cover it with bravado. "Siding with these dark-skinned idolaters?"

"We don't need any outsider's help," the local man declared.

"Taking sides is for those too weak to stand on their own," Denisov answered. He pulled aside the edge of his waistcoat, revealing his telumium implant. "Going to assume you know what this means."

Mutters of shock and amazement greeted this revelation. The words *Man O' War* were repeated over and over, in both English and Arabic.

The major paled even further. He gazed at Denisov's hair, his long gray naval coat now sleeveless and adorned with chains and gears, and it looked as though the pieces slowly began fitting together in the inebriated man's mind.

"A rogue," he gulped.

"So you haven't drunk your wits away completely," Denisov said, affable. "Damned freeing, being rogue. Allows me all kinds of moral flexibility. Let's say I take on every man here and lay them all out, broken and bleeding. I'll have no superiors to report to. No local officials I'll have to offer excuses." He spread his massive hands. "I can do whatever I like, whenever I like. To whomever I like. And I can't be stopped."

"There are many of us," the young local man said, "yet only one of you."

"Except for *her*," the British soldier added, leering at Daphne.

Just as she was about to assert loudly and angrily that she was a British citizen, and expected to be treated with respect by her own countrymen, Denisov's low growl stopped her reprimand.

"You so much as *look* at her, and you'll be chewing on your own testicles."

Immediately, every man present pretended that Daphne

had turned invisible, and their gazes studiously avoided her.

"It's true," Denisov continued, "that there's only one of me, and many more of you. Yet allow me to offer you a brief illustration." He strode to a metal railing that demarcated a café's terrace, then pulled the railing up with a quick tug. Gasps rose up from the crowd when, with just a simple movement, he twisted the railing into a thick beam, then bent it into an arc. He tossed the bowed metal onto the ground, where it landed with a loud clang.

No one spoke. Even Daphne didn't dare to breathe. She'd known, intellectually, that Man O' Wars were extraordinarily strong. This was her first true demonstration of that strength, and it left her astounded. All this time, he'd been carrying that strength within him. It was terrifying. Thrilling. In a very primal way, she reminded herself.

"It's my esteemed opinion," Denisov continued pleasantly, as if he hadn't just twisted thick metal with his bare hands, "that the whole lot of you should either get inside"—he directed this comment to the British officers—"or get the hell home," he said to the locals.

Almost at once, the street cleared. The British officers filed meekly back into their club, and the citizens dispersed, sifting away like so much sand. Calm descended, the kind of calm enforced by the possibility of violence. Daphne's pulse continued to race in the aftermath.

"We lost time," Denisov said, turning to her. "Let's go."

She quickened her steps to once again walk beside him. As they snaked through the streets, stunned and wary faces stared back at them from shops and behind screened windows. Word had already spread of Denisov's presence, and the threats he could easily make good on.

"Why?"

At her question, he glanced at her, frowning. "Why what?"

"Step in the middle of that scenario. There was no reason for you to get involved."

He offered a negligent shrug. "They were blocking the street. We would've lost time finding another route to the meeting point."

She placed a hand on his forearm. The contact of skin to skin blazed through her, but she wouldn't pull back and reveal just how much touching him affected her.

"Finding another way would've taken only a minute," she countered.

His gaze remained fastened to where her hand rested on his arm. Instead of disgust or antipathy in his expression, however, she saw desire. Fast, and quickly banked, but there all the same.

Finally, he exhaled, looking away. "Let's say a fight breaks out between the locals and the British officers. Men hurt or killed. Bad as it is in the city now, after that it'd get a hell of a lot worse. Life would get damned tough for the locals. The officers could keep food from getting into the city. They'd shut down businesses. Conduct raids. Rogue Man O' Wars, though, we don't have any political affiliations. I step in, and it can't be chalked up to any particular side." He watched as a barefoot girl led her young sister quickly down the street, until they disappeared into an alley. "Everyone comes out clean. What?" he demanded, when he caught Daphne gazing intently at him.

She said, "What you just did back there seems awfully inconsistent for a man who claims to only be concerned about profit. Is it possible? The mercenary actually cares about others, even if there's no profit in it?"

He scowled. "You don't know a damned thing about me."

"So you've noted," she conceded, "and I agree. But what I am learning is fascinating." Including the fact that he didn't like to be reminded of his sense of humanity or justice. He seemed determined to show himself in the very worst light.

Mikhail Mikhailovich Denisov had to be the most enthralling man she'd ever met, and she had encountered a good many people in her studies. He was more than a binary of good or bad, far more complex than he was willing to allow. And that captivated her, as much as she was drawn to him by their shared attraction.

"I don't want your intrigue," he said, pulling his arm away. "Just your diamonds." He moved on, and she had to follow.

The threat surrounding her had never been greater. She tried to put aside thoughts of Denisov's complicated nature and the even more complicated bond between them, yet whatever peril she faced, she faced with and from him.

Chapter Seven

SHADOW-SHROUDED, FULL OF professional thieves and killers for hire, places like the Café Ifrit existed all over the world—and Mikhail had been to most of them. Hell, he was on a first-name basis with half the scum who frequented those places. They knew him for the cold-blooded mercenary he was, and they also knew that only a fool would ever give him trouble. Being a Man O' War made him an aberration, but it also granted him deserved respect. He never feared for his safety when walking into yet another seedy watering hole.

Yet setting foot inside the Café Ifrit with Daphne Carlisle by his side, he was hamstrung in a way he hadn't ever felt. She had no telumium implants. She couldn't hear a blade being drawn from its scabbard halfway across a crowded room. She couldn't see a cold-eyed assassin hiding deep within the darkness. Miss Carlisle was simply a woman. For all her claimed experience out in the field, she wasn't battle-tested. Could she handle herself if things got rough? Could he protect her if she were in danger?

He'd met her in a place just like this one, and she'd handled herself fine. Hell, when she'd set foot in that tavern in Palermo, she'd done so with every intention of deceiving him. And he'd had no idea. In that grimy Sicilian watering hole, she'd seemed like just a prim scholar, but her starched appearance had hidden a very different woman—one who tricked an expert at deception. It was almost admirable, that skill, if he hadn't been on the receiving end of it.

No wide-eyed innocent, this Miss Carlisle. She'd find a way to survive.

Even so, the leer the British officer had given her still made fire surge through his veins. Mikhail had meant exactly what he'd said: anyone who tried to harm her would learn new definitions of pain.

That had been out in the street. Walking into the smoky café, with its many chipped, tiled columns and an abundance of sinister looks from its patrons—most of whom sported daggers up their sleeves or tucked into their robes—Mikhail knew he'd have a harder fight on his hands if anything happened in this place. But he'd emerge the winner. He always did. He'd just have to keep Miss Carlisle safe in the process.

She's an investment. That's all.

Tension showed in her eyes as she scanned the room. "The emissary said we're supposed to meet him in a back room."

"Of course he did," Mikhail muttered. He rested his hand on the ether pistol strapped to his thigh. A brief hesitation, and then he pressed something into her hand.

"My revolver," she exclaimed. "I didn't know you'd taken it from me."

His ship was crewed with thieves who could steal the Pope's miter while it was on his head. "Now you've got it back. Don't waver if you have to use it."

"Never have in the past." At his surprised expression, she continued, "Sometimes out in the field, bandits or raiders tried extortion. They wanted gold or jewels, or me." With a practiced movement, she checked the Webley's cylinder to ensure it was loaded, then snapped it back into place. She tucked the weapon into her jacket's inside pocket.

"And got neither for their trouble," he surmised.

"I couldn't send them on their way empty-handed. So I gave them limps, or pretty holes right in the middle of their shooting hands."

"Ought to rethink my opinion of academics," he murmured, reluctantly impressed.

She sent him a smile that spread light through his chest. "We're not all trapped behind desks or squabbling over tenure." But her smile quickly faded, replaced by the same tension that had followed her into the café. "Where the hell is this back room? We find it, then I get my parents back."

He doubted it would be that simple. Few things in life ever were.

Before they took another step, a man in a robe and

vest approached them, saying in Arabic, "This way, *say-idati*." He walked briskly ahead, his arm outstretched as he guided them around columns and tables, past a boy rattling a tambourine, until they reached a curtained chamber. The man pulled the curtain back and waved them inside.

Neither Mikhail nor Daphne Carlisle moved.

"Ah, Miss Carlisle. I am Abdul Shakur al-Zaman." A man with a neatly trimmed white beard rose up from the table at which he'd been sitting. His robe was richly dyed, and golden threads wove through the sash at his waist. A curve-handled blade was tucked into his sash. He bowed, not very deeply. "Very punctual. A British quality I so admire. Though I hear you nearly caused a brawl outside the *ferengis'* club."

It wasn't a surprise that whoever this man was, he had eyes all over the city. And it didn't shock Mikhail that the emissary spoke smooth, elegant English.

The shock, however, came from the two men who stood directly behind al-Zaman.

Two other rogue Man O' Wars. One, Mikhail had never seen in his life. But the other, he knew very well. He'd killed him in his dreams many times.

"The hell are you doing here, Olevski?" Mikhail demanded.

Olevski smirked. "Earning a living, just like you." His gaze flicked up to Mikhail's hair, and down his altered coat. "How you've changed, old friend."

"Treachery agrees with you," Mikhail answered. "As ugly as ever." Which wasn't entirely true. Olevski still had the square jaw and blond hair that had made him so favored in the navy. And by Mikhail's sister, Irina. But the bastard's face turned Mikhail's stomach.

The other rogue Man O' War had long black hair, worn tied back with a bandana. He looked bored by the exchange between Mikhail and Olevski. A true mercenary, that one.

Miss Carlisle's gaze shot back and forth between Mikhail and Olevski. "Whatever bad blood you two share," she said tightly, "it's going to have to wait." She turned her attention to al-Zaman. "I demand to see my parents."

Al-Zaman merely smiled. "Of course I would not bring them to a disreputable place such as this. My master wants them as safe and well cared for as possible."

"How courteous," she shot back. "But I need evidence that your master is, in fact, keeping them safe and cared for. That they aren't, in fact"—she swallowed hard—"dead."

The pain in her voice pierced through the red haze of anger engulfing Mikhail.

"It wounds me that you would doubt my master." Al-Zaman pressed a hand to his heart.

"Go cry on your mother's tits," Mikhail growled. "Give us proof."

Al-Zaman heaved a put-upon sigh, then nodded at the unknown Man O' War. The man muttered something in French, then placed a wood-and-brass box upon the table and opened it. A square of white silk was attached to the front inside edge of the lid, while the bottom of the fabric was affixed to the inside edge of the box itself. As the lid was positioned, the silk stretched taut.

Al-Zaman snapped a small brass crank into place on the side of the box. He began to turn it. Doing so, he activated a small lamp inside. Light illuminated the square of silk from behind. The emissary continued to turn the crank, and more delicate machinery within the box came alive.

Daphne Carlisle gasped as tiny figures in a tiny room appeared on the silk. They were, in fact, projected images, with the silk acting as a screen. Film scrolled past the lamp within.

"A miniature cinemagraph," she whispered. "I've never seen anything like it."

"We are an advanced culture," said al-Zaman. "You asked for proof, and so here it is."

She peered closer at the screen. "Those are my parents! Their assistants, too."

Though the images upon the screen were small, Mikhail identified the Carlisles immediately. They wore a mixture of European and Arabic clothing, and there could be no denying the fact that Daphne Carlisle had her mother's gentle beauty. In the footage, the middle-aged couple stood side by side, Mr. Carlisle's arm around his wife's shoulders, and they both stared at the camera, their expressions tense but not pained. Their assistants gathered around them, some standing, some crouching.

"That cinemagraph reel was taken only yesterday," al-Zaman explained. "As you see, they are kept in a very pleasant chamber within my master's abode. It has a courtyard and a fountain. See how sleek and well they look? My master does not starve nor beat them. He is a man of honor."

"Honorable enough to take two harmless English people and their workers hostage," Mikhail noted.

Al-Zaman merely shrugged.

"This footage could have been taken weeks ago," she snapped.

"A moment's patience." Al-Zaman held up a finger. "Ah, here it is."

A burly local man stepped in front of the camera and held up a newspaper. It took a moment for the lens to focus, but when it did, it narrowed in on writing printed in the upper corner of the newspaper. Mikhail could speak some Arabic, but he couldn't read it, so the words meant nothing to him.

"Yesterday's date." Miss Carlisle gave a small exhalation of relief, then narrowed her eyes. "Anything might've happened to them between yesterday and today."

"Herein you must trust my master," al-Zaman said.

"Fine," Mikhail rumbled, conscious of Olevski's continued smirk. "The Carlisles are alive. Now it's time for you to hand them and their assistants over."

"Oh, but that is not possible," al-Zaman answered, remorseful.

"Why the hell not?" Miss Carlisle demanded.

"This standing is indeed tiring, and we've much to discuss." Al-Zaman gestured to the table, where glasses of tea and a plate of sweetmeats were arrayed. "Shall we all sit and refresh ourselves first?"

"I don't need any sodding refreshment," she said, banging her hand on the table, causing the glasses to rattle. Mikhail liked how her language coarsened, the angrier she got. "I want my parents back."

"And you shall have them safe in your custody very soon," al-Zaman said. "But there is something that my master requires first."

"Ransom," Mikhail said.

Yet the emissary shook his head. "That is to be considered later. He has a very special task for you, *sayidati* Carlisle, and if you are successful in that task, then, and only then, will we discuss the terms of your parents' release."

Olevski chuckled, and Mikhail knew the bastard enjoyed watching al-Zaman make him dance.

Frost crept up the back of Mikhail's neck. Nothing good could come of this. He deliberately let the muscles of his body loosen, as if in preparation for a fight.

"What is this *special task*?" she said through gritted teeth.

"You spent much of your youth with your parents, did you not? Robbing from graves."

"Archaeology isn't grave robbing," she said tartly.

"Oh, you English and your love of semantics." Al-Zaman sounded almost cheerful. "Regardless of how you justify your work, it *is* theft. Thus, you are the perfect candidate for the task my master wishes completed."

"You want her to steal something," Mikhail said.

Miss Carlisle made a sound of outrage, but al-Zaman spoke over her protests. "There is a prized astrolabe, a marvel of engineering, and of surpassing age. It is currently in the

possession of Khalida bint Afra al-Nazari. Though Khalida
and her tribe keep to the desert, the astrolabe is kept in a
specially guarded vault here in the city. Here, I am gracious
enough to give you a map to the vault in question." He set
a folded square of paper on the table and slid it toward her.

Though Mikhail didn't know all the intricacies
of tribal politics in this part of the world, even he had
heard of Khalida. The woman was one of the fiercest and
most respected warlords in the whole of the Arabian
Peninsula. She was also al-Rahim's greatest rival, their
feud long-standing and marked by episodes of blood-
soaked violence.

Stealing the astrolabe would be a prime means for
al-Rahim to strike a symbolic blow against his most powerful enemy. Khalida might lose the confidence of her
followers, may even be deserted by her warriors, giving
al-Rahim the perfect opportunity to surpass her as the
region's dominant force.

Daphne Carlisle knew this, too, and her freckles darkened with her anger. "I'm not going to play a role in your
master's schemes for more unrest. Aren't the people of
Arabia suffering enough with the presence of the Europeans?"

"Perhaps my master could bring peace to his home-
land," al-Zaman offered.

Both Mikhail and Daphne Carlisle snorted in disbelief.

"Even if I were to agree," she said, "Khalida is a known
ally of Britain. If word were to get out that a British citizen robbed her, the consequences would be disastrous."

"Then you must be very clever," the emissary said, "and not reveal your nationality to anyone. Nor get caught." As she started to object, al-Zaman said with a voice like iron, "This is not open to negotiation. If you do not steal the astrolabe from Khalida, my master's hospitality will be at an end, and your parents will die."

Mikhail could only imagine how well guarded the vault holding the astrolabe had to be. Most likely it was an impenetrable fortress. Not only was Khalida's power legendary, so was her wealth. Without a doubt, she'd have spent a fortune to keep her most prized possession secure.

"You've got two Man O' Wars in your pocket," Mikhail said with contempt. "Have them do it for you."

"Ah, but it must be a Briton who purloins the astrolabe."

The task al-Rahim had set was preposterous for anyone who wasn't a Man O' War. The best thief couldn't breach the vault's security. Anger stirred embers in Mikhail's chest, that al-Rahim could be so sadistic as to torment Daphne Carlisle with hope that wasn't truly hope. Just a heartless exercise in cruelty.

Mikhail glanced down at her, anticipating her despair. If faced with the same unwinnable situation, most people would crumble.

Instead, her face was dark with anger. For an instant, Mikhail believed she'd actually launch herself across the table and curl her hands around al-Zaman's neck. She certainly seemed capable of violence at that moment. He readied himself to wrap his arms around her and hold her back.

Keeps on surprising me, my professorsha.

She drew in a few ragged breaths, fighting for calm. "When must this theft be accomplished?" she said through clenched teeth.

"The sooner it is done," al-Zaman said, "the sooner your mother and father will be returned to you."

"Tomorrow morning," she said without hesitation. "We'll meet here. You'll have your damned astrolabe."

Mikhail wasn't the only man in the room to be surprised. Al-Zaman raised his brows, and both Olevski and the French rogue Man O' War wore similar stunned expressions.

"In the morning, then," al-Zaman finally said. "If you do not appear by noon, I'll assume that either you have run away or you have failed."

"I'll do neither." She grabbed the map, turned on her heel, and left the chamber.

For a moment, Mikhail didn't move. His gaze locked with Olevski's. All Mikhail wanted to do was kick the table aside and unleash years of rage and hatred on the bastard. His telumium implants goaded him, too. They demanded and fed his aggression, scorching his veins, his muscles, with fury that had to be released. He didn't care about the other Man O' War. Al-Zaman meant nothing. Finally, Mikhail had a chance to face the son of a bitch who'd led him into ruin, who'd betrayed him and his family so bitterly. A moment he'd been craving for years.

But Daphne Carlisle was out there, headed toward what would surely be her death.

He made the choice without thinking. He threw

Olevski one final glare before stalking from the room and through the café.

She was already in the street by the time he caught up with her. Rather than looking afraid, she seemed determined, drawn forward by unshakable resolve.

"You can't really mean to do it," he said. "It's a madman's errand."

She barely glanced at him as she strode onward, occasionally glancing down to consult the map. "I've got no choice in the matter."

"There's always a choice." He'd made more than a few wrong choices in his life, however.

"Not in this, there isn't." She turned a corner, away from the more populated avenues, and he kept pace. They negotiated narrow, snaking lanes and alleyways where the hovering gas lamps were fewer in number, the shadows abundant. He was almost too large to navigate through the alleys, turning sideways so he could fit. Her steps didn't hesitate, resolutely moving ahead.

Goddamn it, he didn't want to respect her courage. He didn't want to appreciate how she was rising to meet an insurmountable challenge. But ever since he laid eyes on her in that tavern in Palermo, she'd shown nothing but courage in the face of danger.

And deception, too. Don't forget that.

"What happened between you and that other Russian Man O' War?" she asked abruptly.

Merely the thought of Olevski relit the fuse of Mikhail's anger. "The *professorsha* is a dancer, too. Spins and turns around the topic."

She glanced up at him. "Whereas you simply stomp on anything you don't want to discuss."

"History," he finally answered. "Nothing more than that."

"Yet you would've ripped his throat out if given the opportunity."

"I might, still." He didn't know if killing Olevski would grant him any sense of peace, resolution, or even exoneration. It certainly wouldn't give him his family back. But he didn't much care. Spilling that bastard's blood would be enough.

The narrow lane abruptly ended, leading them into a plaza. They quickly stepped back into the shadows to get a better look at the plaza's lone structure: Khalida's vault.

The two-story structure was adorned sparsely, only a few mosaics decorating the walls. There were no windows on the ground floor, but the second story appeared to be surrounded by an enclosed catwalk. Here and there along the outer wall of the catwalk were windows covered with metal lattices. Crenellations ran along the very top of the building, offering a good vantage for anyone trying to defend the vault against attack. A large, heavy door was the only entrance, guarded by a burly man with both a gun and a scimitar tucked into his sash. For now, the guard hadn't noticed them. He looked, actually, bored as hell.

Despite these protective measures, the vault itself seemed less defended than Mikhail would've expected. A prized item lay inside, something that bestowed its owner with tremendous symbolic power. Why was the guard outside so bored? Why weren't there more sentries, more defenses, more weapons?

He understood why: there was no need. All of the vault's true fortifications were inside. Only a fool would attempt to get himself inside.

"I'll go," he said. "I'll get the astrolabe."

OF ALL THE things she expected Denisov to say to her—including trying to dissuade her—what he just said ranked at the very bottom of the list.

"You said yourself it's a madman's errand."

"Haven't been sane for a long time now," he answered. As she started to object, he spoke over her. "More guards will be inside. Other security apparatuses, too. Tough warlord like Khalida won't be satisfied with a simple locked safe or a few booby traps. Whatever she's got in there is going to be big, and dangerous."

"And outwitted," she added.

"I can take more physical punishment than you can. I'm stronger and faster. Trained in combat and evasion. You're . . ." He took her measure, and she felt the thoroughness of his perusal. As if he was seeing into every part of her. "Brave and clever you might be, but that's not enough."

She flushed at his words, that he would think of her as anything good, let alone brave and clever.

"My parents' lives depend on this," she said.

His eyes flashed. "I'm not going to fail."

"I never said that you would." She struggled to find the right words. "I can't simply hand over the fate of my mother and father to someone else. Can't sit back idly hoping it works out. I need . . . I need to be a part of this. To know I did my damnedest to help. That I never took the easy way out." Frustration curled her hands into fists. "Hell. I'm not making much sense."

"Makes perfect sense," he said with surprising thoughtfulness. "Still, it's safer if I go it alone."

She glanced toward the door of the vault. It was massive, nearly fifteen feet high, and the man guarding it seemed almost as big.

"If you were to try to breach the vault," she said, "what would be your plan?"

Denisov also gazed at the guarded door. "He's a big bastard, but I could take him down easily. Then force my way inside."

"But look. There are patrolling guards, too." As she spoke, another large, well-armed man walked past the guard standing outside the door. The two men exchanged nods, and the patrolling guard moved on. "The moment they see any trouble, they'll come running. And there's the strong possibility that once the guards see something's happening outside, they'll activate a higher level of security inside. Which will make the task of getting to the astrolabe even more difficult."

Denisov must have seen the logic of her reasoning, because he cursed under his breath. "I can find another way in besides the front door."

They moved through the shadows ringing the building. "There doesn't appear to be any other entrance or exit. Wait, no, I see something. It's on the side wall."

She pointed to a spout ten feet up the wall. It would serve to drain off any rainwater from the catwalk. The spout appeared to be about a foot and a half in diameter, with a stone lip on its bottom edge to help direct water away from the building.

"Climb in through the rainspout," he murmured, approving. "That'd work."

"You'll never be able to fit into it." She glanced back and forth between the spout and Denisov's incredibly broad shoulders. "Unless Man O' Wars have collapsible skeletons."

He scowled. "Not part of the design plan." He nodded toward a grated window on the catwalk. "I'll get in that way. Easy enough for me to run up the wall or jump to the height of the window's sill, then pull it open."

Though she marveled at the idea that he could so easily scale the height, his plan held flaws. "Doubtless the grate covering the window is locked from the inside. Even if you could pull the grate off, it'd make so much noise that you'll alert the guards."

He crossed his arms over his chest, clearly becoming exasperated. "All right, *professorsha*. Since you seem so learned when it comes to breaking into highly secured vaults, tell me what *you'd* do."

She gave him a small smile. "It's not what *I* would do, or what *you* would do, it's what *we* will do."

CREDIT WAS DUE. He listened to her plan, and didn't once snort or scoff or dismiss her. Though it didn't look as though the scheme entirely pleased him, either.

"Wish there was another way to do this that didn't involve you," he muttered. "It's going to be dangerous."

"I may be an academic, Captain," she said, "but I assure you, I have a strong sense of self-preservation."

His rueful smile did alarming things to her pulse. He didn't trust her, had no reason to, and claimed to be involved for purely mercenary reasons. Yet he sought to protect her. Here was a man who was far more complex than he even knew.

At the least, they seemed to be in agreement about her plan.

They waited until a patrolling guard passed by and turned the corner. At the same time, the guard in front of the door became distracted by the sound of music and women's laughter spiraling out from an adjoining street. He turned toward the source of the noise, tapping his foot in time with the beat of the *doumbek*.

This was the moment they needed. Daphne and Mikhail hurried around the side of the vault, keeping low and to the shadows. They stood at the base of the wall, just below the rainspout. At her nod, he quickly picked her up. She felt like a dandelion puff in his hands, he lifted her so easily.

She stretched up, trying to reach the lip of the spout. Her fingers just skimmed it—not enough for a decent purchase. She strained higher. Finally, she had enough height to grip the lip and stare into it. The wall it traversed was nearly two feet thick. Not too far a distance for her to crawl through. But being this close, she realized that the passage would be a tight squeeze to wriggle through, even in her jacket, boots, and trousers. For the first time in her life, she was grateful she didn't have elaborate feminine curves or wear fussy gowns and dresses.

No time for hesitation. She took a breath and then pulled herself up and into the spout. Though she'd explored the passageways of narrow tombs, she had been a child at the time. Now, she squirmed her way through the rainspout, one arm forward, one arm trailing, as if she were swimming. Breath wasn't easy to come by. It was as if she was willingly being swallowed by a boa constrictor.

Finally, she got her hand out of the spout, using the tiled floor for leverage. She pulled her head through the opening. A quick check in both directions revealed that no guards were around. With very unladylike grunts, she managed to writhe the rest of her body through the spout. It took her a moment to regain the ability to breathe, but once she had, she took stock of the situation.

She was inside the catwalk running around the perimeter of the vault. But the vault wasn't built like a European structure, all solid walls and enclosed spaces. For one thing, European vaults wouldn't have an interior courtyard. From her vantage on the catwalk, she peered through the columns. A guard smoking a pipe stood in the enclosure below. Further investigation had to wait. She needed to open the grated window for Denisov, and she must act quickly.

Daphne swore under her breath when she saw the mechanized lock on the window. Curse it, she was an anthropologist, not an engineer. Arabic numerals were marked on enameled buttons, indicating that there was a code that needed to be entered. No doubt if she entered the wrong code sequence, an alarm would go off, finding her trapped inside the vault and Denisov stuck outside.

What numbers might be important to Khalida? Warlords were notorious for their arrogance, so it had to be a number that held significance. She didn't know Khalida's birthday, or the date that the warlord took over as the leader of her tribe. It had to be an important number. But what?

Words flashed into her mind, words from the sacred text of Islam.

And He it is Who has made the stars for you that you might follow the right way thereby in the darkness of the land and the sea; truly We have made plain the communications for a people who know.

A fitting description for the astrolabe.

Fingers working quickly, she keyed in the number six, and then ninety-seven, for that passage in the Qur'an was from Surah 6, Ayah 97.

Breath lodged in her throat, she waited.

The lock gave a single, soft chime, then opened.

Resisting the impulse to yelp in triumph, Daphne carefully unlatched the grate and pushed it open. She peered down, and there was Denisov, looking as dangerous and alluring as ever.

He winked at her—a weapon, that wink—then, taking only a few steps back, ran twelve feet up the wall and grabbed hold of the window sill. Despite his size, he did it quickly, effortlessly, as if flying. She couldn't help but lose her breath at this display of acrobatic grace. With the same fluid movement, he pulled himself up and inside, landing noiselessly.

She closed the window, making sure to cover their tracks.

"Damned clever of you," he said, "deciphering a lock like this."

Her face heated from his praise, but thankfully he didn't notice, his interest trained on the lock in question. "I've seen these types of devices before," he noted. "They're attuned to sound. Gunfire, specifically. If a gun goes off, the locks respond, become double-enforced."

"Then we can't let anyone fire a gun," she whispered in response. "But," she added, striving for optimism, "we've done it. We're inside."

She and Denisov peered down into the central courtyard. Here, too, only one guard stood, but she caught the movement of a few others patrolling beneath the arcade formed by the catwalk.

His mouth curled. "That was the easy part."

Chapter Eight

INSIDE THE VAULT at last, and it would only get more difficult from here. Damn Denisov for pointing that out. Yet he was right, and from this point forward, she needed all her wits, all her vigilance.

She did have a particular skill: observing. So she took careful note of the courtyard. It held a few potted palms, and the columns surrounding it were painted with traditional patterns. One object in particular caught Daphne's attention.

"What is that?" she whispered to Denisov, pointing to the item in question.

"A ladder of some kind. Looks like it can be extended."

"Why would there be a guard for a ladder?" For the man stood close to it as it lay upon the tiled floor. The ladder was on wheels, like a small wagon.

"Some part of the vault's security, I can only assume." He stared intently into the courtyard. "There are at least five guards down there, and I'm guessing at least one of them will patrol up here soon."

She understood. They couldn't puzzle out the uses for the ladder, when they had a much more important errand that required attention. Crouching so they couldn't be seen by any of the sentries below, they hurried along the catwalk. A set of stairs heading downward lay at the end.

It had to lead somewhere, and wherever they wound up, they could figure out their next move.

"Not much of interest there," he said, glancing toward the courtyard. "Best bet is the door at the bottom of the stairs."

"But the guard can see it—and us, if we try to use it."

"The guard's pipe is losing its glow."

Despite her best efforts, she couldn't see what he could. Only a Man O' War could make out such detail at this distance.

"He'll have to relight it," Denisov continued. "Away from the draft that's coming down the stairs."

Just as Denisov predicted, the guard turned his back to the stairs in order to relight his pipe.

The moment they'd waited for. They both hurried down the stairs.

It seemed strange that the door at the bottom was unlocked, but they stepped through the doorway. She shut the door quickly behind them to ensure the guard wouldn't be made aware of their presence.

As she turned back to face the chamber, she solved the mystery of the unlocked door.

"What the hell is this?" Denisov growled.

"Remember those security systems we talked about earlier? This must be one of them."

They stood at one end of a corridor. Its walls were at least twenty feet high, but there was no ceiling. Instead, the corridor was open to the air. It seemed a strange thing to have a hallway thus exposed, but looking up, Daphne saw that bladed fans were suspended on axles between the walls. The fans turned in the breeze. Their axles were attached to what she thought might be small electromagnetic generators bolted to the tops of the walls.

The open ceiling, fans, and generators weren't the only odd features of the corridor. Suspended six inches off the floor was a grid of braided wires. The grid itself was anchored to the walls of the hallway with metal bolts.

"Look there." Denisov indicated the wires that ran from the generators down to the grid. "They're supplying power to it." He turned to her. "Got anything leather in that satchel of yours?"

She rifled through her bag until she produced her compass, enclosed in a small leather case. After removing the compass, she handed the case to Denisov. He tossed it onto the metal grid.

Smoke. The acrid smell of burnt leather. She threw her arm up to protect herself from the sparks. The case finally fell to the ground, black and charred.

Dear God, the whole grid was electrified. And the fan-driven generators supplied the power. If anyone tried to cross the passageway, they'd be turned to a scorched husk.

"Perhaps we ought to find another route," she said.

"We're right where we're supposed to be." He nodded toward the door at the other end of the corridor. "You don't use a Gatling gun to defend a pile of dung. Whatever's behind that door, it's damned valuable."

"The astrolabe." She glanced toward a key-shaped slot in the wall directly behind them. "Here's how Khalida comes and goes without being broiled."

"Can't pick a lock like that," he said with the air of a man who possessed knowledge of such things. He scowled at the door at the other end of the corridor, and cursed. "It's too far to jump, and the only way I can fly is with an airship."

"So we turn off the generators." She stared at the conduit connecting the generators to the grid. "Divert their power, perhaps."

Silence fell as both she and Denisov mulled this over. Her mind churned through possibilities, yet none of them seemed right. How could they do this? It seemed an impossible task, but she couldn't give up. There *was* a solution . . . somewhere.

Her mind kept hitching on the notion of diverting the generators' power. What could be used for that purpose?

Standing close to Denisov, she felt his heat, the power he emanated. As though he gave off as much power as the grid.

He *did*. Because of his implants. Her gaze fell on the pack he wore. And suddenly, inspiration struck.

"Your batteries," she said. "We can use them to absorb the generators' power."

His expression hardened. "Want to see me rip this

place down with my bare hands? Or maybe you'd like to watch me literally tear the guards apart? Because that's what'll happen if I don't have the batteries drawing energy from me. Battle madness." His eyes grew dark. "I saw it once. In training. They kept a Man O' War from discharging his energy. Poor bastard. He punched holes in solid stone walls. Killed two officers."

He pinned her with his gaze. "Friend or foe, it won't matter if the madness gets me. Nobody would be safe. Including you."

The chill of his voice made her shiver. Having seen glimpses of Denisov's strength, she could only imagine the destruction he'd wreak if his control broke and he lost his mind. "Have you tested that on yourself?"

"Seeing it was enough."

"It would be. But," she pressed, "if we took just *one* battery, surely that won't compromise you overmuch."

"It means I have less time away from my ship. Five days instead of seven." He ran his hand over his chin, considering. "But I don't plan on spending a long holiday here." Quickly, he removed one of the batteries from his knapsack and handed it to her.

The brass cylinder was lighter than she expected. Another marvel of the modern era she didn't fully understand. But she didn't need to know how or why it worked, only that it did. The telumium plate atop the battery should siphon energy away from the grid. Gingerly, she moved to place the battery's contact onto the electrified grid.

He suddenly grabbed the battery from her hands.

"Electricity's going to be flying. I'll absorb the shock better than you."

She couldn't object to this, so she waited, heart pounding and breath scarce. He said he could handle the electrical current better than she could, but he wasn't immortal or impervious to harm.

Denisov edged close to the grid, battery in hand. Then, in a swift movement, propped the battery onto the grid. He took a step back.

"Let's see if it worked," she said.

He made a sound of surprise when she placed her hand on his abdomen. Even through the fabric of his waistcoat, the steel of his muscles twitched beneath her touch.

What's more electrifying? The metal grid, or him?

"Trying to get back in my favor?" he asked, sardonic.

"Trying to keep us alive." She tugged, then held up a silver buckle. Glancing down to see the loose thread on his waistcoat, he smirked.

She tossed the buckle onto the grid. It touched the wires, and a much smaller spark than the one before sizzled. The buckle then simply fell to the ground. The battery was working, drawing most of the electrical charge into itself.

Denisov's brows rose. Clearly, he hadn't been certain her strategy would work, and she couldn't help feeling a flare of gratification.

She inhaled deeply, steadying herself, then she and Denisov took the first step together, stepping into the open spaces in the grid. She winced when her shin contacted one of the wires, but all she felt was a mild buzzing sensation, nothing like the fatal shock she would have received without the battery's assistance.

They made their way quickly down the corridor. Once they reached the door at the other end, she finally allowed herself a full exhalation. They'd done it!

Her relief wasn't going to last long. "There's more danger on the other side of this door, isn't there?"

To his credit, he didn't try to feed her palliative lies. "Most likely. One way to find out."

She reached out, and opened the door.

SHE KEPT IMPRESSING him with her courage. Mikhail didn't want to admire her, not after her duplicity. Still, his respect for her reluctantly grew as Daphne Carlisle gamely pressed forward.

The door swung open, revealing a long, wide set of stairs leading downward. Gas lamps flickered on the stone walls, and the air held a distinct subterranean smell. Wherever these steps led, they'd take them deep beneath the city.

With Miss Carlisle following, he descended the stairs, cautious in case any of the steps were booby-trapped.

"Those tapestries are beautiful," she murmured behind him.

He glanced up. The tapestries hung at regular intervals from the walls, the upper corners of the weavings anchored into the stone. They were, in fact, quite striking, depicting the heavens—constellations and celestial bodies in gold upon deep indigo skies—the craftsmanship so fine that they had to have been woven by hand and not machine.

"Never seen anything like them," he said.

"They must be centuries old. Precious." Her brow furrowed. "What a waste to keep them hidden here, where no one can see them."

"Khalida can, whenever she wants." His mention of the warlord was enough to get them moving again. Yet they hadn't taken more than a few steps when he flung out an arm, keeping her from going any farther.

"Think I know what that extendable ladder is for," he said.

She gave a low gasp. A huge gap lay between the step on which they now stood and where the stairs resumed. Between the two solid steps was a sheer chasm that disappeared into darkness. Rough rocks lined the walls of the abyss, and a dank breeze swirled up from the void. An airship captain couldn't be afraid of heights, but with his acute vision he could see jagged stone spikes at the bottom of the chasm and had a distinct image of himself—or, worse, Miss Carlisle—impaled on them.

"You've got your airship to cross distances," she said. "Khalida has the ladder. Perhaps we could go back and try to take it from the guard."

"And bring everyone running like it's penny night at the brothel." He shook his head. "Need to find another way across." He studied the gap between the stairs. Forty feet separated them. "*Blyat*. This distance is too far for me to jump it. What's the use of being a damned Man O' War if I can't do things like this?"

"I imagine that breaking into an Arabian warlord's vault on behalf of her arch-nemesis wasn't part of the navy's intended use of Man O' Wars," she said drily. "Not very farsighted of those naval committees."

No, this little Englishwoman could never be considered timid or reserved .

He glanced up again at the tapestries, especially the two hanging beside the chasm, an idea percolating. "You may be exceedingly clever, *professorsha*," he said, "but my Man O' War strength's going to get us to the other side. Point of fact," he added, thoughtfully studying the woven wall hangings, "I've got some cleverness of my own."

"I never doubted it," she answered.

He searched for a sign of sarcasm or hint of mockery in her words, her face, and found none. Echoes of heat still played across his stomach where she'd touched him; her slim fingers had been nimble and deft as they'd plucked a button from his waistcoat. The taste of her still lingered, and the softness of her lips against his. Hell, it had been just a kiss, just the press of her hand against his abdomen. He'd had far more carnal encounters, but those sensations had faded quickly, while Daphne Carlisle's few touches continued to ring through him.

Misha, he snarled at himself, *don't be a sodding idiot. The woman meant to cheat you. She's a green-eyed liar. Get the astrolabe, get out. Get your diamonds and move on.*

"Are you a good jumper?" he asked her.

"My father told me I once leapt six feet straight into the air when I saw a millipede." She shuddered. "I hate things with lots of legs."

He crouched down. "At my signal, just imagine a dozen millipedes crawling up your ankles." Energy and strength coiled within him, readying, eager for release.

"What—?"

He didn't wait for the rest of her question. Using all the strength of his legs, he sprang up toward the wall. He stepped onto the wall and ran along it. The moment he got close enough to the tapestry, he grabbed hold. He gripped the fabric, clinging to it. The abyss yawned below him. He prayed that the tapestry's weaver had made the piece good and durable, strong enough to hold his bulk. So far, it held, but that could change in an instant.

Reaching out, he tore at the tapestry's farthest corner, ripping it away from its anchoring in the wall. He fought to hold on as the fabric swung like a pendulum with his weight.

Miss Carlisle muttered several curses in many different languages.

"Get ready to jump," he called to her.

"I can't leap that far," she protested, "no matter how many millipedes are crawling after me."

"I'll come to you." Using the tapestry like a rope, he gripped it with one hand. He braced his feet against the now-uncovered wall, balancing on his toes. Using the tapestry for support, he ran lightly along the wall, in one direction, then the other. Back and forth he went, gaining momentum, gaining distance with each pass.

He pushed against the wall with his feet, propelling himself closer to where Daphne Carlisle readied in a crouch on the steps. A foot closer, then another, then—

"Now!" He held out his hand, stretching toward her.

Only a moment's hesitation flickered across her face before she jumped. The vision of her, flying, braid whipping behind her, expression set and determined. Her hand reached for his. For the barest moment, he feared they wouldn't be able to get hold of each other. But then her palm found his, his fingers wrapped around her wrist, and he pulled. Carefully, though. He could dislocate her arm if he wasn't cautious.

She grabbed the tapestry, as he'd hoped. They hung like that for a few moments, both clinging to their improvised rope, pressed close against each other. He could sense all of her—lithe strength, tensed muscles, her rapid inhalations and exhalations. A woman who'd just trusted him to catch her, trusted him with her life.

"My God," she gulped. "I can't believe I just did that." Her eyes were perfect circles of shock.

"Like a St. Petersburg acrobat." But she was still pale. What she needed was some distraction. "This is fun. Reminds me of the rope swing that hung over the swimming hole near my family's summer cottage."

She seemed eager for the distraction. "We'd spend summers with my grandparents in Northumberland. It was dull as blazes, but we couldn't dig during the warmer months."

"Wager you got into lots of trouble during the summer."

A small smile tugged at her mouth. "My father got quite proficient at apologizing to the neighbors. *I'm so very sorry Daphne let your sheep out of their pen. My regrets for the hole in your roof; Daphne takes after her mother's side of the family.* Everyone was relieved when it was time to head back out into the field."

He found himself chuckling at the image of a young Daphne Carlisle wreaking havoc on a sleepy English village. Damned strange to be sharing childhood memories with her, revealing her to be a woman with a life, a history. Human, and flawed. Same as he himself was flawed.

She glanced down, and her face went pale.

"Don't do that," he commanded. "Keep your eyes on mine."

She dragged her wide gaze back up to his. "At least you have beautiful eyes. Palest aquamarine. I could stare into them for hours. Thought so from the moment I saw you."

He was hanging above an impossibly deep chasm, with jagged stone spikes below ensuring death to any who had the misfortune to fall on them, and there were guards and security systems throughout this vault, but he found himself actually blushing. Apparently, madness had set in. He said, "Danger seems to make you confess."

"Seems that it does." True to his direction, she continued to hold his gaze, allowing him to see that her green eyes held flecks of gold, like treasure in a forest.

God, not only was he mad, he was turning into that most dreaded of all creatures: a poet. Hazardous directions indeed. He was made for war, not sonnets.

He nodded toward the next tapestry beside them, fifteen feet away. "Ready to do it all over again?"

"I was looking forward to becoming a permanent part of Khalida's tapestry collection." She heaved a sigh, but her breath was shaky, revealing her fear. "But I guess that's not to be."

"It's simple as letting sheep out of a pen. Feet on the wall. Run back and forth. Build momentum. Then I reach the next tapestry."

She did as he directed, bracing her boots against the wall. At first, they bumped against each other, their feet and bodies out of alignment as they made several clumsy tries. Finally, they found a smooth and easy rhythm, moving naturally together.

Parts of him were machine, but the majority of him was a man. Establishing this kind of rhythm with her turned his mind, and other parts of him, to other activities that required their bodies to move together.

He needed to focus. Or else they'd both go tumbling tits over arse and wind up impaled.

There—he had enough momentum. "Hang on tight," he commanded her. "I'm going to leave you here while I go for the other one." Then he leapt, reaching out for the next tapestry.

But he was hasty. His hold of the fabric wasn't secure. It skidded through his fingers. He slid down along the edge of the tapestry. Clenching his teeth, he managed to grab a firmer hold just before he slipped off the hanging entirely.

A moment ticked by with infinite slowness as he dangled from the bottom corner. Hand over hand, he climbed up the tapestry. Until he was level with Miss Carlisle, who looked white as talc as she clung to the other tapestry.

Her voice shook as she said, "Don't frighten me like that."

"My apologies. Unforgivably rude of me to almost fall to my death."

She glared at him, which was far better than the fear she'd shown a moment earlier. "Let's just get on with it," she said, jaw tight.

Mikhail repeated the process, tearing the opposite corner of the tapestry from its anchor, then using the fabric as a rope as he gained momentum, running back and forth along the wall. She did the same, pushing herself nearer and nearer to him. Once again, at the high point of his approach, he reached for her, and she jumped. Their hands met and held.

It came as a shock, the relief and pleasure of touching her, even here in this blasted subterranean vault.

When she'd grabbed hold of the tapestry, and they were side by side, they ran together on the wall, building power. Until he felt they had enough, and with a burst of power, he let go of the tapestry and jumped for the bottom portion of the stairs.

He landed in a crouch, and forced all of his strength into his thighs so he wouldn't be thrown forward and roll down the stairs. A tumble like that could play hell with the batteries in his pack. Losing one battery wasn't too bad, but it'd be chancy if he damaged the rest. Once he was sure he'd gotten his footing, he stood and turned back to Daphne Carlisle.

She still clung to the tapestry, which continued to sway after he'd jumped.

"Same as before. Run along the wall," he directed her. "Then jump." When she dubiously eyed the distance between the tapestry and the stairs, he said, "I'll catch you."

Brave she might be, but she still needed to take a calming breath. He got a nice view—able to see the supple movement of her body, her lithe agility. She *did* remind him of the famous acrobats of St. Petersburg, women in gauzy costumes who flew and danced through the air like carefree butterflies. Except Miss Daphne Carlisle wore a leather jacket, snug trousers, and laced boots, more grimly determined than carefree.

She seemed to have decided she'd gotten enough momentum, and at the closest point of her run, let go of the tapestry. His heart stuttered as he beheld her in midair, entirely unsupported, momentarily fragile. He stretched his arms out to her.

And grabbed her. He felt the impact of her body against his, absorbed her energy into himself, and pulled her close, her arms around his shoulders, her legs around his hips. Impressions rocked through him—her taut muscles, the subtle tremors running through her, sinking into him.

They were like that for some time, his arms wrapped about her. Her breath puffed hotly against his neck. He pressed his mouth to the top of her head, feeling the silken threads of her hair against his lips, and against his chest her heart pounded.

An intimate embrace, the kind reserved for lovers. They appeared to become aware of that at the same time—she stiffened slightly in his embrace and dropped her legs from around his waist—yet neither seemed willing to let go. Not quite yet.

"Nicely done, *professorsha*," he whispered. "More impressive than defending a dissertation."

"You've never been before a dissertation committee." She pulled back, just enough to hold his gaze. "I don't think I would've trusted anyone else to catch me."

Her words pierced him. *Trust.* Something that seemed to ebb and flow between them. Why should she trust him? She'd deceived him, and his motivations were far from charitable. It was there, though, that thing binding them together.

"You're not a heavy burden," he said.

Her lips curved into a smile. Need burned through him to feel that curve against his own lips. But he knew that once he kissed her, no matter where they happened to be, stopping would be impossible. Reluctantly, he loosened his arms around her. She, too, let go, but the slide of her hands down his body was exquisite torture.

Once they'd both gained their feet, they continued on down the stairs. The steps ended in yet another door.

"The astrolabe better be behind this," he muttered, hand on the doorknob. "It's been a damned long night. Only cure for it is several gallons of vodka."

"Me, too." She glanced at the door. "Sadly, the bacchanalia has to wait."

He pushed the door open, and together they stepped inside a vast circular chamber lit by a ring of quartz lamps. The walls of the chamber were made of huge stone boulders. They must be far beneath the city.

"Look down," she whispered.

The floor was elaborately carved, covered in symbols

and curved lines in different configurations. It seemed to be in layers, too. A large circular plate was its base, and another plate chiseled into curves and arcs lay on top of that. A straight piece of stone crossed the whole floor, with a column in the middle. The entire design looked familiar. The large scale of it, though, made it a puzzle to place.

"My God," she said, wonder in her voice. "It's an astrolabe."

Blyat, he should have seen that sooner. All the parts of the device were there, carved into the floor. She walked over the mater and plate that made up the base of the astrolabe, with its straight and curved lines showing things such as horizon, tropics, direction, and latitude. It took her several strides to cross the rete atop the plate, with its star pointers and stereographic projection of the ecliptic. She studied the straight piece of stone that crossed these parts. It had to be the rule, which located positions on the plate or rete.

The astrolabe was beautiful . . . and massive.

There was no door on the opposite side of the room. This chamber was their final destination.

All the excitement and energy he'd gotten from swinging on the tapestries, the heat that had fired through him from holding Daphne Carlisle close—it all drained out of him. Ice flowed through his body. He was never cold. But now he fought the chill spreading through him as if he stood in his own tomb.

"That son of a bitch," he cursed. "Al-Zaman sent us on a fool's errand." He pointed angrily to the floor. "*This* is the astrolabe he wants us to steal."

Chapter Nine

TORN BETWEEN DESPAIR and hysterical laughter, Daphne stared down at the floor. The astrolabe carving had to be at least thirty feet in diameter. No denying its beauty or the skill of the artisan who'd made it: in every aspect, it faithfully reproduced the complex device's different components and markings, all in polished stone. But artistic merit didn't help solve the problem of how, exactly, she was supposed to remove it from the vault, or transport it to al-Zaman.

"There has to be some way of getting it out of here," she muttered.

For a moment, Denisov looked at her as if she were mad—which she supposed she was, to even consider hauling a massive stone astrolabe from this impenetrable place.

But then his gaze became thoughtful. "We'd have to dynamite it out of the floor. There's TNT on board the

Bielyi Voron, and no one knows how to set a charge better than Akua. Once it's blasted out, the ship could haul it up."

"That would necessitate us leaving the vault, getting to the ship, then returning here to set off what will likely be a massive explosion, and contending with the security systems and the guards." She ticked the obstacles off on her fingers. "And since this chamber must be far below the surface, we'd need to find a way to transport the astrolabe up to your ship. It just cannot be done."

"Man O' Wars thrive on impossible situations." His grin was audacious.

Her pulse leapt in response. "Much as I appreciate your resolve, Captain—"

"Mikhail," he said. "When you were leaping into my arms a few minutes ago, were you thinking, *Captain* or *Mikhail*?"

"I was thinking, *Please, God, don't let me fall*."

"Don't need to call me *God*—Mikhail will do. And I'll call you Daphne."

"Now I lay me down to sleep. I pray to Mikhail my soul to keep." The feel of his name on her lips had a strange resonance, like an old enchantment buried in her memory. She felt a subtle shift between them, an easing of mistrust. The sharing of first names wasn't something done lightly. And when he chuckled lowly at her words, she felt the knot of his suspicion loosen even further.

You need to tell him the truth, her conscience demanded. *All of the truth.*

If I tell him now, he'll desert me, and I need him more than ever.

Yet it felt like a blade she scored down her own heart, knowing that she continued to deceive him. What choice did she have?

"Admirable as your determination is, I'm certain that this"—she gestured to the carved floor—"can't be what we're seeking."

He frowned. "Don't see heaps of astrolabes piled in the corners."

She turned in a slow circle, studying the chamber. "Cleverness is valued in this culture as much as physical strength. Think of all the tales of quick-witted men and women who survive and triumph by outthinking a situation or adversary."

"Ali Baba or Scheherazade."

She nodded. "This has to be a puzzle or riddle. I'm certain of it. And listen."

They both fell silent. A soft ticking sound resounded through the chamber, like a massive clockwork device. "There *is* a mechanical component here. Meaning there's a riddle serving as a security system. The question is: what's the puzzle, and how do we solve it?"

For the first time, she noticed seven white marble spheres the size of cannonballs around the perimeter of the chamber. Examining them closer, she discovered that some had crescents carved into them, and some bore other ovoid or nearly circular shapes. A kind of tinting had been applied to the surface of the spheres, making them appear partially white and partly dark. Only one was smooth, polished marble.

"The moon," Mikhail said, coming up behind her. At

her curious glance, he explained, "These pieces of marble look like the phases of the moon." He pointed to them in turn. "Waxing crescent. First quarter. Waxing gibbous."

The more she looked at the spheres, the more she realized he was right. The marble orbs were representations of the moon's phases. Of course, a sailor and airship captain would know the night sky.

"What's the current phase of the moon?" she asked.

"Waning crescent," he answered without hesitation.

She turned back to the astrolabe hewn into the floor. Constellations dotted its surface. "And where is the moon right now?"

He closed his eyes, as if conjuring up the sky in his imagination. "In Virgo." His eyes flew open, and she and Mikhail stared at each other. Could this be the solution they needed?

"That ticking sound must be some device that keeps track of the sky and the moon." She couldn't keep the excitement from her voice.

Before she finished speaking, he'd picked up the marble orb representing the waning crescent moon. He held it in one hand, though she was certain it would take all of her strength to get it a few inches off the floor. He strode quickly to where the constellation of Virgo was depicted on the floor, then closed his eyes again. Though she couldn't read his thoughts, she knew he was recalling exactly where in the constellation the moon would be found at that moment.

This small action reminded her that he had a whole life, a history and knowledge, of which she had no real understanding. He'd been a sailor, an airship captain for the Russian Navy. There was so much to him she'd yet to know and explore.

He remained opaque, and she realized she wanted more. His thoughts, his feelings, the things he wished for in the depths of night.

False as you are, you've no right to want more from him.
But I do.

Opening his eyes again, he set the moon carving down in a specific part of Virgo.

For a moment, nothing happened. Disappointment hollowed her. She'd nearly convinced herself that they had solved the enigma, and were that much closer to freeing her parents.

Mikhail glanced toward her. She could have sworn that there was sympathy in his gaze. As though feeling her frustration and dismay. Of all the times to finally gain a measure of his compassion, she felt herself stretched too thin now, veering dangerously close to either sorrow or rage. His concern made her all the more vulnerable.

"Damn it," she growled. Yet she wouldn't let defeat claim her. "There has to be another way. Something we're overlooking—"

The entire chamber shook. She braced her legs wide against the force of the vibrations, looking around wildly for their source. Mikhail already had his ether pistol in hand as he glanced about the stone room, his gaze sharp and ready for any threat.

There was a heavy grinding sound that shook the chamber even more. One of the large rocks that formed the wall slid to one side, then stopped moving. Revealing a dark space. Gas lamps flared to life inside, one by one, showing the space to be a small room.

Cautiously, she approached, Mikhail right beside her. They stepped across the threshold to investigate. The room was perfectly round, its domed ceiling covered with blue and gold tile work, representing the night sky. But what held her attention was the thing right in the center of the room.

A carved alabaster column stood waist-high. A richly embroidered cushion sat atop the column. And sitting on the cushion, gleaming brilliantly in the gas lamps' glare, was the astrolabe.

SLOWLY, DAPHNE ADVANCED. Part of her wanted to rush toward the astrolabe and snatch it up like a greedy child, this object that had taken every ounce of strength and mental agility to attain. Another part of her urged caution, and was, in fact, dubious that at last she and Mikhail had finally reached their objective.

The astrolabe itself was beautiful, an intricate device of highly decorated and shaped brass, and it shined beneath the lamplight like the eye of a god. It held a slight patina from age and use—it was as ancient as al-Zaman had said, several centuries old at the least. The Accademia had one in its collection, but she'd never seen it, never handled the device. Her hands hovered over the astrolabe, as though reluctant to touch it.

"Go on," Mikhail urged. "It's what we're here for. No time for shyness."

Her laugh was strained, and she rubbed her damp palms on her trousers. Then, warily, reached out and picked up the astrolabe. It was the size of a dinner plate, with a ring at the top, which she used to lift it up. Though it wasn't heavy, it had a satisfying weight, as though dense with use and importance. She imagined the man who'd fashioned it hundreds of years earlier, employing all the subtle and advanced skill of his culture to create this gracefully complicated implement. Whole empires had been forged using a device such as this. Her mind fairly spun with all the implications.

"I have no idea how to use one of these," she admitted.

"I'll give you a lesson," he answered. "Later. Now, we need to get the hell out of here."

Very true. She gently tucked the astrolabe into her satchel, wishing she'd had the foresight to carry a scarf or something that might cushion it.

Once it had been safely stowed, they left the small room and quickly strode across the larger chamber, with its carved mechanical floor. Reaching the doorway at the other end, they were confronted once again by the flight of stairs and its yawning abyss.

"Oh, God," she muttered. "We have to do this again."

"But now we know how." He grinned, and she returned the cheeky smile. His audacity was contagious.

Mikhail had to jump farther to reach the tapestries, yet he moved with speed and strength. He moved fluidly, powerfully, leaping onto the torn tapestry and impelling it closer to her. She took a running jump and grasped his outstretched hand. Amazing how, in such a short amount of time, she'd come to know the feel of his hand clasping hers, and the surge of confidence it gave her.

They'd found their rhythm. It seemed instinctual now, as if they'd always known how to work and move together. She remembered Giovanni, a fellow professor at the Accademia. For all their shared interests, their similar backgrounds, she and Giovanni could never quite find a connection, a natural flow. Not like this, with Mikhail. As though they were two pieces of a machine that worked in deft harmony.

Yet one part of the machine was untrustworthy. He thought he knew the depths of her treachery, but he had no idea. Not truly.

He swung to the next tapestry, and she soon followed. In a matter of moments, they stood upon the other side of the chasm.

"Impossible tasks aren't so impossible, once you get used to them," she said, eyeing the deep abyss.

He looked offended. "No credit for your partner?"

"Gallons of credit." Which mollified him somewhat. Had he realized he'd called himself her partner?

They hurried up the rest of the stairs, through the doorway into the corridor with the electrified grid. He nudged the grid with his boot. "Battery's still drawing power, but it's nearly full. The shock won't be as dulled this time across." He looked at her with a frown of concern. "It's going to hurt. I'll carry you."

"I can handle a jolt or two." She started across before he could argue to try to stop her. It was a struggle to keep from swearing aloud at each shock. It had to be endured.

Finally, she reached the other end, and felt certain that whatever hair wasn't confined in her braid now stood straight up. Her bones seemed to jump within her body. But she'd made it across on her own.

He also made his way across, reaching the other end of the corridor. As he passed the battery, he grabbed it.

Mikhail seemed utterly unfazed by the shocks. Naturally. He handed her the battery. "No words once we're on the other side of the door," he said. "Any of the guards hear us and fire a weapon, it'll alert the other bastards."

"And trigger the locks on the windows and doors, too."

"Trapping us like whores in church."

Her brows lifted at the analogy. "We've got two options for getting out of here. The fastest way would be straight through the courtyard and out the front door. That entails sneaking past the guard standing sentry, and then finding a way through the door. Doubtless it's got an even more impenetrable lock than any of the windows on the catwalk."

"Up the stairs, then." He cracked open the door. They both peered out, and seeing the top of the stairs to be clear, started up them.

A patrolling guard suddenly appeared at the top of the stairs. The man's eyes widened. He opened his mouth to shout an alarm. Mikhail became a blur as he leapt up the stairs and tackled the guard. From her position at the bottom of the steps, she couldn't see everything, but caught glimpses of the guard's flailing limbs as Mikhail grappled with him. The sentry abruptly stilled, his limbs hanging loosely. But she observed that the man's chest still rose and fell. Mikhail must have knocked him unconscious. He appeared at the top of the stairs and motioned for her to follow.

Relieved that they'd have a relatively easy route out, Daphne was about to start up the steps, when a voice in Arabic rang out.

"Intruder!"

She swung about to see that the guard in the courtyard had caught sight of her. Barely had she moved when Mikhail jumped down from the catwalk, right into the courtyard. He flung himself at the guard, and they fell to the ground. As the guard went down, he managed to fire a single shot into a column.

Thunk! Thunk! Thunk! In waves, the locks on the door and windows all slid firmly into place. At the sound, her heart sank, too. There'd be no getting out of here.

Mikhail punched the guard in the face, and the man's eyes rolled back. Despite the fact that the guard was unconscious, the noise of other guards' boots both inside and outside the vault meant the problem was far from over.

A dozen sentries poured into the courtyard. Without hesitation, Mikhail launched himself at them.

She'd never seen him fight before, nor had she ever witnessed a Man O' War in the middle of combat, but the sight was mesmerizing. He was all action, strength, and purpose. No matter how many guards came at him, he met them all unwaveringly. She saw then how a Man O' War truly was a weapon, for as the guards attacked him with their clubs and knives, he parried every move. He used the sentries against themselves, dodging their blows with re-markable speed so that the guards wounded one another. Everything was chaos, and yet he was in complete control, playing several moves ahead. They were mere mortals, but he was a mythological warrior.

All of the guards focused their attention on Mikhail, but three more sentries came running, right at Daphne. Burdened with the battery, she couldn't draw her revolver to hold them back. Spotting the extendable ladder on the ground, she used all of her strength to kick it toward the advancing guards. The ladder swiveled on its wheels, right into the feet of the oncoming guards. Tripping, they toppled like ninepins.

Shouting came from outside the vault's walls. More guards. She and Mikhail would be trapped if they didn't get out, and now.

"Mikhail!" she shouted.

The guards surrounding him flew as he knocked them all back. He emerged from the melee, and she caught her first good view of him since the sentries had begun their attack. Instead of looking angry or beleaguered, he grinned broadly. As if he enjoyed this free-for-all. Which made a strange kind of sense. He was made for combat. All this skulking around must rankle the part of him that wanted nothing more than a stand-up fight. Still, it caught her by surprise, his battle-induced gratification.

"Head for the door," he called across the courtyard.

"Can you break it down?"

"Absolutely, if I had two other Man O' Wars with

me. Got another idea in this thick head of mine. Run, woman!"

They both sped toward the front door. A large metal bolt barred the way, with a thick lock set atop the bolt. It would take at least ten Man O' Wars to break through. Yet she and Mikhail were running straight toward it.

"Throw the battery," he commanded. "Right at the door."

She had no idea what he intended, but with the fallen guards all getting to their feet behind them, and the impenetrable door ahead of them, this wasn't the opportune moment to question him.

Mustering as much force as she could, she tossed the battery toward the door. Mikhail lunged in front of her. He drew his ether pistol and fired. With incredible accuracy, the bullet slammed into the battery. There was a spark, and then a massive explosion. Even protected by his solid bulk, she felt the force of it, fighting to stay on her feet.

He grabbed her hand and pulled her toward what was now a gaping, smoking hole where the vault's front door once stood.

The sound of gunshots punctured the air. Bullets from the guards' weapons sped through the air around her and Mikhail as they ran. She crouched low but kept on going. Dear Lord, she'd never been shot at before! There wasn't time to pull her own revolver and return fire. All she could do was run, her hand clasped in Mikhail's.

They crossed the threshold of the vault and hurried out into the street. Several dazed sentries lay on the ground, knocked down by the blast to the door.

A dozen more guards sprinted toward them. Mikhail dropped her hand and faced the guard closest to him. He grabbed the man's rifle and broke the weapon in two, then threw the pieces to the ground. The guard stared in shock at what had been his gun.

Close as she was standing to Mikhail, she could feel his body's eagerness for battle. He lurched toward the other advancing guards, then he suddenly changed direction. He grabbed her hand again and sprinted down an alley, towing her behind him. The guards shouted and gave chase, more bullets flying.

"You get us out of here," he growled to her. "I'll throw a little lead in their path."

She hurried ahead of him. He shot back at the pursuing sentries. A few men cried out and fell.

With such chaotic noise behind her, Daphne ran as fast as she could, weaving her way through the shadow-strewn maze of the city, hoping to lose their pursuers. She knew the city well enough, but all her mental maps scrambled in the heat of being hunted.

She turned down an alley and cursed. "Dead end," she snarled. She glanced around them. A balcony was some fifteen feet above them, and a rooftop another ten feet higher, but there were no other doors or ways out.

However, retracing their steps meant they'd come face-to-face with the guards. Mikhail, however, didn't appear troubled.

"Climb on my back," he said.

Immediately, she did as he directed, wrapping her arms around his shoulders. The pack he wore dug into her stomach, but she paid it no mind. "I'm not exactly light as thistledown."

He threw her a deadpan glance over his shoulder, letting her know exactly what he thought of her warning.

"Hold tight," he advised. Then she felt it as he crouched slightly—the astonishing sensation of his powerful body coiling, tensing, as if a steel bow were being drawn. And loosed.

It was indeed like being an arrow shot from a bow. For they flew up straight into the air. Her breath felt knocked from her lungs, her abdomen. She managed to glance down to see the faces of the guards staring up, their mouths all open in wonderment.

Flight stopped as Mikhail grabbed hold of the balcony's railing and pulled them both up. Yet he wasn't finished. He balanced on the edge of the railing and jumped to grip the edge of the roof. The guards seemed to come to their senses, for they began shooting. Their bullets punched holes in the walls, clouds of plaster flying.

Mikhail hauled himself and Daphne up onto the roof. Only when he took several steps back from the edge, did he say, "You can let go now."

And only then did she permit her death grip on his shoulders to loosen. She slid down to stand on the tiled roof, her legs like blancmange. From their vantage, she and Mikhail had a view of Medinat al-Kadib's skyline, the buildings crowded haphazardly together, jostling for position beneath the night sky.

The guards' shouts could still be heard below, followed by their footsteps.

"They're going to look for a way up," Mikhail said. "We need to keep moving."

She willed her legs back to stability. The danger hadn't passed, and she needed to hang on to her courage.

"Afraid of heights?" he asked.

"Not tonight," she answered.

A flash of admiration glinted in his eyes, and then he turned away. He leapt from rooftop to rooftop, agile as a jaguar. His long coat flew out behind him with each vault. She followed, grateful that the city's age meant the distance between buildings was minimal. Her own jumps weren't half as nimble as his, and more than once she had to scrabble for a handhold on a tiled roof, or steady herself to keep from tumbling into nothingness. Whenever she found herself struggling for balance, he was there with a steadying hand and even more steadying presence. But her confidence grew after each jump, as did her stability. Soon, she could vault the narrow space between structures without a stab of panic, and land with confidence.

As she and Mikhail danced across the city's rooftops, a strange kind of pleasure bloomed in her chest. Far above the streets, she felt herself and Mikhail separate from the world, two secret creatures who lived for flight and movement, drawing strength from the star-strewn sky above. Liberating. Exhilarating. And together, they had solved the riddle of the astrolabe. It had taken both of them to decipher the enigma.

Somehow, it was just right that she should share this

experience with him. A man who'd set himself apart from ordinary life.

Yet she *was* an ordinary human, and hadn't his telumium-enhanced endurance. Her legs ached with weariness, her breath coming in shallow gasps. This had been an extraordinary and long night.

"Need . . . a break . . ." she panted.

He immediately stopped, his gaze both sharp and concerned. Tilting his head, he listened intently. "We've lost them."

"They might still be patrolling the streets, looking for us." She glanced around, taking note of their surroundings. "There's a cupola on that rooftop. We could have a rest until it's time to meet al-Zaman."

"I don't need much sleep," he answered, then added with a frown, "but you look ready to collapse."

There was no use in pretending she was superhuman. "Wouldn't mind sitting down for a few minutes."

They headed toward the cupola. Mikhail plucked a few blankets from wash lines along the way. Normally, she didn't condone thievery, but tonight—indeed, this whole voyage—had already played havoc with her ethics, so she didn't object. She most certainly didn't complain when Mikhail leapt over the cupola's low wall and lay the blankets down upon the dusty floor.

Once she was inside the small structure, she finally allowed her legs to give out from under her, sinking to the blankets with a long exhale. She leaned against the wall and stretched her legs out, debating whether or not to unlace her boots. Better to keep them on, just in case she needed to run. At last, however, she could have a few moments' respite.

His back to her, Mikhail stood at the wall, hands braced on the stone. With the lights of the city all around, his stance wide and confident, he was an emperor surveying the lands that depended on his protection. Tonight he'd proven himself both physically capable and a strategist. But he wouldn't have risen in the navy, and wouldn't have been chosen to be a Man O' War candidate, if he was merely brawn.

Nor was he simply a mercenary, as he claimed. Again and again, this very night, he'd protected her.

Because he wants his diamonds.

No, it went beyond merely protecting what he thought was his investment. She'd seen it in his gaze, in the way he feared for her, encouraged her. At some point during the night, a boundary between them had been crossed.

Tell him. Tell him now. He needs to know.

"There's the waning crescent moon." He pointed to the sliver hanging in the sky. "In Virgo."

"Looks like a scimitar," she said.

He chuckled lowly, and despite her exhaustion, the sound of his laughter sparked her nerves to life. Brilliant little constellations of awareness.

Words formed within her, words she needed to tell him. Yet they couldn't move past her lips. The connection they had created tonight would be shattered, and she was selfish enough to want to cling to it a little longer.

From her satchel, she pulled out the astrolabe. It was dark in the cupola, so she couldn't make out much of its detail, but her fingers traced etched lines and ornate plates.

"A wondrous device," she murmured, "fashioned long before such things as tetrol and telumium."

To her surprise, he moved to sit beside her. To her even greater surprise, his legs pressed against hers, their arms touching, and the pace of her heartbeat quickened. The cupola was a small space, she reminded herself, so naturally he needed to sit close. His heat soaked into her, making her both languid and energized.

"All we had were dreams and wind-filled sails." A small, bittersweet smile curved his mouth. "That's what brought me to the sea. Dreams of faraway places. And dreams of glory," he added, a note of self-deprecation in his voice.

"And now?"

"I've got faraway places in abundance. But glory . . ." He shrugged his wide shoulders. "That dream slipped through my fingers."

They were silent for a long while, hearing the distant sounds of the city far below. Despite the lateness of the hour, the strained merriment continued in Medinat al-Kadib. As much as she enjoyed studying human societies and cultures, this night she found greater pleasure in looking at the sky, and the uncomplicated mysteries of distant stars.

She tucked the astrolabe back into her satchel. It had to be kept safe until she could hand it off to al-Zaman.

"An academic and a mercenary," she said softly. "Not the most likely of teams."

"A good one, though." Approval warmed his words. "We did a top-notch heist."

She didn't anticipate how much gratification she'd feel, both to be commended for her skills at theft, and to receive his praise. In only a few days, she'd become entirely altered, far more wicked, decidedly more bold.

I think I like it.

Exhaustion ebbed. Energy and potential moved through her like a golden tide, glimmering within. And with it, hunger for him surged just as brightly. She'd seen him at his most deadly tonight, and his most insightful. They'd worked together with an uncanny ability. As though they had a natural affinity for each other.

He broke the silence. "Get some rest. Dawn will be here in a few hours, and then we're convening with al-Zaman. I'll keep watch while you sleep."

Her secret was enclosed her heart as if by a cage of iron. She held the key, yet dreaded freeing what would surely destroy everything she and Mikhail had created together.

She bargained with herself. A little while longer with him like this. That's all she wanted. She would suffer later.

"It's a strange thing," she murmured, staring at the sharp, clean lines of his profile and the sensuous fullness of his bottom lip. "Tonight alone, I met the emissary of the warlord who's keeping my parents prisoner. I broke into one of the most secure buildings in the entire Arabian Peninsula. Crossed electrified grids. Swung across chasms, solved riddles, was chased by armed guards. Ran through the city and jumped across rooftops. One would think I'd be weary beyond imagining, and desperate for sleep."

Her heart pounding, she cupped the side of his face with her palm. The bristle of his close-cropped beard prickled against her skin, another reminder of his potent masculinity. She turned his face toward her.

"But I'm not sleepy," she whispered. "Not in the slightest." Their faces were close, and lambent light from the streets below gleamed in his sharply hot gaze. The guardedness in his eyes had fallen away. She saw desire there, and respect. Over the course of the night, they had each transformed, both within themselves, and to each other.

His hands came up to cradle her head. His face was a tight mask of need. "To hell with sleep."

"That's exactly what I was thinking." And then their lips came together, and she stopped thinking entirely.

Chapter Ten

FEVER BURNED IN Mikhail. It had started long ago, when he'd first kissed Daphne, setting him afire with the promise of what could be. He'd thought her dishonesty would have annihilated his desire for her, but that wasn't the case. They had worked perfectly together tonight. He'd seen her intelligence, her bravery. She'd trusted him, and his own mistrust had slowly peeled away.

Need for her burned brighter than ever. His blood was already aflame from the night's adventure, his control barely in check. And when he saw the hunger in her eyes, the same desire blazing through her, control snapped.

As they kissed, he took her mouth savagely, tasting her, drinking her deep. She met his kiss eagerly, her tongue stroking against his. The same boldness she'd shown in the vault was here, too, in the way they tangled like tigers, fighting for more, and more.

She rose up onto her knees and pushed at his coat. He readily shucked it. But that wasn't enough. Skin to skin— that's what they wanted. She tugged at the buckles of his waistcoat, and though he wanted to feel her hands on his bare flesh, he allowed himself the sweet torture of her fingers playing over him, the tease and frolic of her hands taunting him through the fabric.

He hissed in a breath when she dipped a finger between the buckles, stroking over the taut skin of his abdomen.

"Not a *professorsha*," he said, hoarse, "but a tantalizing minx."

Her smile was as ageless as Woman. "Always joy in the process of discovery."

"Enough of process," he rumbled. "Your hands on me. And mine on you."

Buckles scattered as he pulled his waistcoat open, then threw it aside. Finally, he was bared to the waist. He turned to her, so they knelt and faced each other.

She softly gasped, and her eyes widened as she held herself still. He willed himself patience. Few people ever saw a Man O' War. It had to come as a surprise to her, the way his body had been transformed and shaped by his implants.

"You're . . . incredible," she whispered.

His body was a weapon. Sometimes a lure to women. Until this moment, he'd cared only how it could serve him as a tool. But maybe it could be something more. Maybe . . . *he* could be something more.

Through her exploration, he changed. Her hands

traced over the ridges of his stomach, the dips of muscle on his hips. There was power in her touch, his need brought higher and higher by it, his blood loud in his ears. She slid her palms up over his chest. Damn that he couldn't feel her though the telumium implant that covered his right pectoral and continued up onto his shoulder. The admiration and amazement in her gaze was almost enough.

"Like armor," she murmured. "But it isn't rigid. And it gives off so much heat."

"Keeps its flexibility when implanted." He went to work on the buttons of her blouse. *Keep your damned hands steady, Misha.* But desire throbbed through him. Much as he wanted to tear the damn thing off of her, he had to keep himself under control. The implants pushed him to the very limits of his discipline.

As the buttons parted, revealing the column of her neck, his mouth followed the path, tasting her, biting and licking. Blessed saints, the sweet and smoky taste of her skin.

She moaned, tipping her head back.

Opening her blouse fully, he revealed a necklace covering the hollow of her throat. Three rocks were strung on the necklace, each the size of a walnut. An odd and unlovely ornament for a woman as pretty as she, and he reached to unfasten the clasp so he might get to the bare flesh of her throat.

Her hand stopped his, and her voice was tight. "Leave it on."

He wasn't about to argue, not when he was so close to

uncovering more of her skin, so, ignoring the necklace, he continued to work at the buttons of her blouse.

Finally, the garment parted open fully, and this was also thrown aside. Beneath her blouse, she wore only a chemise, her breasts tantalizing and ripe beneath the thin muslin. He'd once thought her prim and straitlaced. He'd known nothing. Here she was now, uncovered, soft, keen with desire. This was the real woman.

But he didn't want to waste time with more fabric. Impatient, he tugged her chemise up and away. Then she, too, was bare above the waist, save for the necklace. Erotic, seeing her naked but for this ornament.

His large hands fully covered her breasts. Such sweet handfuls. He stroked and caressed them, toying with the tight points of her nipples. She writhed against him, her hips pressed to his, and his aching cock couldn't decide if the sensation was torture or ecstasy.

Bending down, he took one of her nipples in his mouth. His tongue swirled around the bud, drawing more moans from deep in her throat. One of her hands gripped his shoulder, the other cupped the back of his head, urging him closer, demanding more.

He was only too happy to oblige. He took her nipple between his lips, lightly pinching. Ah, the sounds she made . . . Opening herself to him, not hiding from her desire for him. He shuddered with wanting her, this woman who'd proven herself again and again with her courage. Her fearlessness stoked his need, and he wanted inside of her, to know her in every way.

Somehow, he managed to get the front of her trousers

open, and worked his hand down within them, through the opening in her drawers. Until he found her pussy, slick and hot.

"So wet, my *professorsha*." His voice was nothing more than a rasp. "So wet for me."

He considered it a triumph that she was too lost in sensation to have an answer beyond a low, husky moan.

As he continued to lick and gently bite on her nipples, his fingers stroked her pussy, between her lips, rubbing tight circles around her clit. Her back arched, continuous sounds of pleasure spiraling up from the back of her throat.

"Need to know," she gasped, her hand going to the waistband of his trousers. "If you want me the way I want you."

"No doubt of that." He wasted no time undoing the buttons. Groaning, he freed his cock, and gripped it tightly in his hand. He couldn't remember ever being this hard, this desperate.

"This is what you want." He held it out, an offering and a tease—for them both.

"Yes." Her hand wrapped around the base of his cock, and they both gasped at the feel. Though her hand was too small to fully encircle him, he didn't care—all he cared about was the sensation of her fingers around him. He released his own grip, and let her stroke him, up and down, circling the swollen head. "Yes," she murmured again, or it could have been him who said it. All he knew was the marvel of her touch, bold and tender.

He continued to stroke her, too, caressing her folds,

finding all the places that made her whimper and keen with sensation. His lips covered hers, swallowing her sounds with lush, open-mouthed kisses. The more he touched her, the more open she became, her tongue stroking against his. And all the while, her hand continued to pump him, slow, then fast, then lightly, then firmly. She seemed born with an instinct to torment and pleasure him.

It was as if he'd been made not for war, but for this, for her. To feel the growing demands of her body. To sate those demands. All for her, and no other.

She stiffened, whole body tensing. *Yes*, he thought, savage, when sounds of ecstasy tore from her. Her climax was powerful as a hurricane, and just as leveling. The woman who'd moved self-consciously through the tavern in Palermo was gone. This woman cried out in pleasure, trusting him, free in herself.

But he needed, *demanded*, more. The last of her shudders subsided. He wasted no time in unlacing and removing her boots, before peeling off her trousers. Pliant with release, her eyes heavy-lidded, she watched him strip her—but she wasn't entirely passive. When the bottom cuff of her trousers caught on her heel, she helped tug it free. And then she was nude.

He caressed her everywhere, feeling the sleek softness of her limbs, all her rounded, sweet places that had fascinated him from the moment he saw her. The freckles dotting the bows of her collarbones. The curve of her waist. The trim lengths of her legs. She didn't shy away from his touch, but curled into it, purring and sensuous.

"This is how you're meant to be, *lapochka*," he rumbled. "Naked and pleasured. Not stuck away in some dusty library."

"Almost never in libraries," she said, her voice a honeyed rasp. "And it's not mutually exclusive—being a scholar and a wanton."

"I'll have both." Knowing these two aspects of her was exciting, that she could be rosy from orgasm, and also possess a mind as bright and clear as a diamond.

He moved so he leaned against the railing, legs stretched out in front of him. She straddled him. Reaching down, she adjusted his cock so it was at the perfect angle, the head just skimming her entrance. He held them like that for a moment, savoring. When she struggled against his grip, wanting to lower herself down onto him, his hold remained firm. Taunting them both with what could be, what would be.

She growled in complaint. "Now, Mikhail."

The sound of her commanding him snapped the very last filament of his control. He brought her down, hard, in one thick thrust. His eyes closed, and a groan tore from him. God, she was so slick, so tight. As hot as he ran, she burned him with her own heat.

She tensed all around him. He pried open his eyes, and his heart seized when he saw the faint flicker of pain in her face.

Damn him—he'd forgotten. He'd never been a little man, but the telumium implants had made him bigger. Everywhere. She was so small, so snug. He must be hurting her. And he'd gone plowing into her without any gentleness, like a rutting bull.

Though it almost killed him to do so, he started to lift her up. She gripped his wrists.

"No," she gasped. "Need . . . only a moment . . ."

"Don't want to hurt you."

"I'm not . . . I'm . . ." She took several deep breaths. "So full. It's . . ." In gradual waves, the pain left her face, replaced by rich pleasure, and she sank down onto him, taking him fully within her. "Ah. Yes . . . so good."

If he could form words, he would have agreed with her. But he had no vocabulary. No thought beyond the feel of her delicious sheath all around him and the look of ecstasy on her face. He surged up into her. Riding him, she gripped his shoulders. Their sounds of pleasure mingled together with each thrust.

She angled her hips, grinding hard against him. A tiny frown of concentration appeared between her brows as she hunted more sensation. Eager to give it to her, he twisted up to press tighter against her clit. He loved watching her grow frenzied, eagerly taking his every firm thrust, straining toward release. That he could take her beyond the limits of her control, the way she'd freed him from his.

Another climax hit her even harder than before. Her mouth opened soundlessly. Heat stained her cheeks, her chest. She was a tableau of pleasure. No artist could have captured a finer image of a woman in ecstasy.

His own release gathered. He couldn't hold back much longer.

He pulled out, then stood them both up, and turned her around. Placing her hands on the railing, he widened her legs. Over her shoulder, she cast him a look of such raw demand, he nearly came from that alone. The view was perfect: her shapely arse, the slickness of her waiting pussy, the curve of her back and lust in her eyes. And the whole of the city and night sky spread out before them.

"This," he rumbled. "How we're meant to be."

She gasped in response, "Yes."

He surged into her. Again. And again. Her hands gripped the railing, yet she pushed back into him, demanding as much as he could give her.

His thrusts increased in tempo. He was more than an ordinary man, and the speed of his strokes made her moan and pant. This was a vision he'd prize forever: the lights of the city all around, the crescent moon above, and her, frenzied with pleasure.

But he couldn't let it end too soon. He slowed his pace, almost pulling out entirely, then plunging into her, inch by inch. Teasing her with the crown of his cock. And then fucking her hard, her breasts bouncing with each thrust.

One of her hands released the railing to cover her mouth. Even behind her cupped hand, her screamed release reverberated through him.

Then it had him, too. His climax came from every part of him, tearing him open with devastating pleasure. His orgasm went on and on. He gritted his teeth to keep his own shout muffled, and felt the burn in his throat from the effort.

By the saints and stars, he'd never come like that before. His legs actually shook.

For a few moments, all he could do was bend over her,

pressing kisses to the juncture where her neck and shoulder met. His heart thundered in his chest. She turned her head to take his mouth with her own.

Finally, he slid from her, and they both made sounds of loss. He gathered her close, their damp bodies pressed tightly together. She felt both fragile and impossibly resilient.

She suddenly pulled back, her gaze alarmed. "Oh, God, we weren't thinking clearly. What if there's a child?"

His own apprehension eased. "Man O' Wars are sterile. Run too hot."

She relaxed back into his arms with a sigh of relief. Then yawned.

Smiling to himself, he carefully disentangled them from each other, and began to dress her. She struggled to help, but her movements were languid and sluggish. When she was clothed, he fastened his trousers and pulled on his waistcoat. Without its buttons, it simply hung open, but he didn't need it for warmth.

He helped guide her back down to the nest of blankets on the floor. Her head pillowed on her arm, she curled close to him. Gently, he brushed strands of hair off her forehead.

It had become more and more clear to him over the course of the night. She was lovely and courageous. She'd proven herself, and his doubts had receded. There was an inevitability about this, that they'd make love.

But now that passion had been temporarily sated,

those doubts flooded back into his mind. They both stood upon the deck of a rocking ship, direction uncertain, without a clear shore ahead. He saw a flicker of disquiet in her eyes, too, just before she dozed off.

With her asleep in his arms, he waited for the dawn.

DAWN HAZE KEPT everything in shades of purple and ash. The buildings were too crowded together to permit much morning light to touch the city's streets. Though men and women moved through the avenues and alleys, bringing their wares to market, Medinat al-Kadib remained hushed, as if afraid to make too much noise and wake a sleeping dragon.

Daphne felt as though she, also, should tread cautiously as she walked beside Mikhail toward their rendezvous with al-Zaman. Her sleep had been fitful, her dreams filled with images of her lying at the bottom of a pit of wires, electricity shooting through her body, with Mikhail standing at the edge of the pit, sneering at her agony. In her dream, she hadn't been able to call out for help, for she'd wrapped the wires to her own limbs, and had only herself to blame.

Jolting echoes of that pain shot through her now. Each step closer to the Café Ifrit only intensified them. A strange alchemy, to feel the wondrous afterglow of making love with Mikhail, and also the sharp stab of her conscience. When he learned the truth, the mistrust she'd overcome would rush back in gale force. She wouldn't blame him if he hated her.

He'd awakened her sweetly with a kiss. But they'd both been quiet since then.

They neared the café. Despite the earliness of the hour, men were already—or still—at tables, drawing on their hookahs and nursing tiny cups of coffee.

She couldn't be a coward any longer. "Mikhail," she rasped. "You need to know—"

Al-Zaman and his two hired Man O' Wars appeared at the entrance of the café. Though she wasn't holding Mikhail's hand, she could feel the tension coil within him when he spotted the Russian Man O' War. The hatred between them was thick as coal smoke, and just as choking.

Her parents weren't with al-Zaman. Ice frosted along her spine. Perhaps they were kept somewhere nearby.

"Ah, *Sayidati* Carlisle, and her gracious companion," al-Zaman called out cheerfully. He beckoned to her. "Join me inside, and we shall break our fast together."

She glanced at Mikhail as opportunity slipped away. *After I make the exchange with al-Zaman*, she promised herself. *I'll tell him then.*

Though she feared by then it would already be too late.

Much as she had no desire to eat, the trade couldn't be made on the street. She followed al-Zaman into the café, all the way back to the private curtained chamber in which they'd met the night before.

While al-Zaman took his seat, and his two Man O' Wars stood behind him, a boy came in with a tray of coffee, hot bread, and dates and set it on the table. She eyed the food, her stomach roiling. And as poorly as she'd slept, coffee would be ill advised. She couldn't even sit. All the while, Mikhail and the Russian Man O' War glowered at each other.

Al-Zaman either didn't notice or didn't care. Humming to himself, he took a cup of coffee and sipped at it, then smiled.

"They do know how to brew a proper cup of coffee here," he said contentedly.

Her patience snapped. "I don't give a damn if they serve cups of dung. Where are my parents?"

Al-Zaman maintained his infuriating geniality. "The terms of our agreement required that you provide something first. Though, the intelligence traversing the street is that you were successful in your endeavor."

Impossible that Khalida's guards would let slip word that the vault had been broken into. But doubtless that al-Zaman had spies all over the city, bringing him the latest information.

"If you know we've got the damned thing," Mikhail snarled, "then show us her parents."

"The astrolabe first," al-Zaman said, "if you please."

Daphne pulled the object from her satchel. As she did so, al-Zaman's eyes widened. A grin spread across his face. He made an impatient gesture for her to hand it to him. Still, she hesitated.

"The bastard's got us by the balls," Mikhail said lowly. "He won't make a move until he gets what he wants."

Slowly, she slid the astrolabe across the table. Al-Zaman snatched it up, cackling. He examined both sides, even going so far as to pull out a miniature optiscope to ensure its authenticity. Apparently, what he saw pleased him.

"Excellent. Most excellent. How delighted my master will be."

"We're pissing ourselves with glee," Mikhail answered.

"Now it's time for you to honor your end of the bargain," she snapped at al-Zaman. "My parents and their assistants. Immediately."

Tucking the astrolabe into a leather case, al-Zaman merely shook his head. "Oh, but my master wouldn't dream of conducting such delicate business here in Medinat al-Kadib. No, for this undertaking, we require the safety of the desert."

Rage filmed Daphne's eyes. "We did everything you asked—"

"And beautifully," interrupted al-Zaman. "Truly, no thief in known memory has ever gotten in or out of that vault alive. But my master insists that the final exchange for your parents will be made at his compound tomorrow. It lies a hundred miles south of the city. At the risk of redundancy, I must tell you that the defenses and fortifications of his compound are substantial. Even a Man O' War"—he fixed his gaze on Mikhail—"will find it impossible to breach. Who knows? In all the chaos of a battle, our guests might be hurt."

The warning was clear. *Don't try any acts of heroism. Play the game our way.*

Despair choked her. She had no choice. From the beginning, the reins had always been in al-Rahim's hands. No matter what she did, he was in control. And if she were to try to subvert this in any way . . . she'd never see her mother and father alive again.

"Tomorrow," she said through gritted teeth.

"Tomorrow." Al-Zaman took another sip of his coffee. "And do look a little more cheerful, *Sayidati* Carlisle. Soon, you and your parents will be united."

Without another word, Daphne strode from the chamber and from the café. She barely made it to an alley before her legs stopped working. She crouched down and dug her knuckles into her eyes. Every step forward only made the journey even longer. Naively, she'd believed she had only to follow the emissary's directions, and everything would right itself.

She heard Mikhail's hurried steps as he followed her into the alley. His hand upon her shoulder was meant to offer comfort, but it only shoved the knife deeper.

"What a black joke this life is," she said, hoarse. "There's nothing simple. Nothing direct."

She glanced up at his rasped laugh. "Oh, *professorsha*, if you ever believed that, you've been in the library for too long."

"Told you, I don't spend much time in libraries."

He carefully pulled her to her feet, the compassion in his gaze like acid. "Good. The lessons learned out here are harder, but they'll keep your arse in one piece."

A MESSENGER SCARAB was dispatched from one of the many kiosks offering the service. After they provided the clerk with the proper coordinates, the mechanical beetle whirred off toward the *Bielyi Voron*. The scarab carried the message that Daphne and Mikhail would meet the jolly boat outside the east city gates, and then they would return to the ship.

On their way out of the city, he purchased for them a bag of pastries redolent of cinnamon, but she couldn't manage a single bite. It took a considerable amount of assurance that she had no intention of eating. When she finally convinced him, he devoured every last one of the pastries, licking spices off his fingers. Just before they left the city, he also bought several pieces of roast lamb and devoured those, too. Dimly, she remembered hearing that Man O' Wars required more food than an average person to fuel them, which meant that he had to be starving, having eaten nothing since they'd arrived in Medinat al-Kadib.

She only hoped that the food he consumed as they strolled out of the gates left a sweet and savory taste in his mouth, because what she had to tell him would certainly be bitter.

The sun climbed higher into the sky, gilding the outer walls of the city, as she and Mikhail walked out to meet the jolly boat. Several vendors had set up stands outside, not wanting to pay the exorbitant taxes to sell within the gates, and they called out to her and Mikhail, offering dried fruit, clockwork toys and tools, sticks of incense. Though their cries quieted a little when they caught sight of Mikhail's intimidating figure.

She barely heard the vendors, too absorbed in her own thoughts.

The established rendezvous point was some half a mile outside the city, at a dry wadi where a lone shepherd boy tended his herd of goats. The animals nibbled at weedy plants growing in the shade, occasionally making their uncanny bleats, while the boy crouched at the edge of the ravine, more interested in the two Europeans than his herd.

"Do you speak English?" she asked him.

The boy only stared back.

Well, there was no risk that he'd go telling tales. This was as good a time as any to speak. Even so, she clambered down into the dry gulch and paced along its length. Mikhail kept pace beside her.

"Men with tiny cocks always boast about how massive they are," he said. "Al-Rahim's no different. He'll shake his shriveled prick at us, but we'll cut it off." He put his hand on her shoulder and turned her to face him. "Daphne, we'll get your parents back." Absolute conviction was in his voice, and she wished so fervently that she could simply sink into the certainty and comfort he offered.

"I lied," she said without preamble. "Not merely about the gold, but . . . something else."

He frowned at her, as if trying to decipher her words. Then, understanding dawned. His frown deepened into a scowl. "Muddying the damned waters. Again."

She had to speak quickly, purge the poison. "What I said to you the other day, that I would pay for my parents' release by leading al-Rahim to an ancient diamond mine—I wasn't speaking the truth. There is no mine. There's nothing."

He pulled away abruptly, taking several long strides as if to keep her out of his reach. Pain twisted his face, yet his words seemed almost offhand. "I could set a watch by your deception." Turning back to face her, he gave her a ghastly imitation of a smile. "Or maybe what's most reliable is the fact that you played me for a fool—again. And used your honeyed little body to clinch the deal." His gaze raked her, unforgiving.

"It wasn't like that. I wanted to tell you sooner—"

He stalked toward her. "What the hell were you planning on using as payment for your parents' release? No more lies."

For the briefest moment, she hesitated, and this made his expression darken even further. He'd never looked as fierce as he did at that moment.

When her fingers went to the buttons at the top of her blouse, he snorted. "Sweet as you were, *professorsha*, I'm not so drunk on your pussy that you can distract me."

His deliberate crudeness felt like a slap, but she continued undoing the buttons until she could reach inside her blouse. She tugged out the necklace, with its three large stone beads, and unfastened it.

Fumbling through her satchel, she produced two flasks, then crouched down. She set the necklace on the ground, opened the flasks, then poured their contents over the stone beads. An acrid froth bubbled over the surface of the beads. When the froth subsided, the dull stone casings were gone, revealing their true contents.

Mikhail cursed. Floridly.

She dug a kerchief out of her satchel, in case any of

the chemicals lingered, and used it to pick up her neck-lace. Sunlight gleamed off the three beads—only they weren't beads, but three dazzling star sapphires. They glittered like a constellation brought down from the heavens.

"These." She stood. "I planned to pay the ransom with these."

A muscle in his jaw twitched as he stared at the gems. A mercenary like him knew their value.

"Where'd you get them?"

"Liquefied all my assets, all my savings. I have nothing else. Not even my books."

He shot his hand out and snatched the necklace from her. Words of protest died on her lips.

"Give al-Rahim this," Mikhail growled, "and you'll just be paying for your own death."

"The terms of the agreement . . . his code of honor—"

"Means shit. He'll take the jewels, kill you, kill your parents, then pin it all on Khalida. Snap her ties with Britain completely and come out of the whole thing like a goddamn conqueror." He sneered at her. "Profit's the only carrot for scoundrels."

The cold in his eyes numbed her. "The sapphires are all I have. Without them, I've got no way to free my mother and father."

A shadow passed overhead. Glancing up, she saw the jolly boat circling for its approach and landing.

"Ah, now the *professorsha* speaks the truth," Mikhail sneered. "These gems *are* going to pay for your parents' release, except you won't be paying al-Rahim.

You're paying me. Finally." The precious stones disappeared into the grip of his massive hand. His smile was icy as the tundra. "And for that payment, *I'll* free your parents."

the jolly boat land, or Herrera
the company has acquainted himself, his attention was
was the time. "And for that persuasion, I deserve
prison.

Chapter Eleven

MIKHAIL BARELY NOTICED the jolly boat land, or Herrera
calling out a greeting. His attention was solely pinned on
Daphne, staring at him with a look of guilt and horror.

The necklace in his hand felt like a rope of fire. Another deception she'd used on him.

Hell—what was this sensation between his ribs? To
become a Man O' War, he'd had to endure an hours-long
implantation procedure, without benefit of anesthetic.
Until that point, he'd never experienced such pain, the
telumium filaments attaching to his heart felt as though
Hell itself ripped through his chest. But he'd known that
the pain of the procedure would be an agony.

Nothing prepared him for what he felt now.

He didn't understand it. Where this pain came from.
The first time he'd caught her in a lie, he'd been angry.

Oh, he was angry now. But this pain . . . didn't make any
damned sense. Like he was torn apart from the inside out.

Mercenary—that's what he was. Criminals and liars were as routine to him as typewriters and ledgers were to clerks. Yet somehow, coming from *her* . . . it made him want to howl like a wounded animal.

He'd been betrayed once by someone close to him, too, two years ago, making this agony all the sharper.

She licked her lips. "You'll free my parents?"

"For this"—he held up the sapphires—"I will."

"Or you could take the jewels and leave me here."

He barked out a laugh. "Mistrust from the woman who's played me false *twice*." His glance took in the dried and nearly barren ravine, a fitting place for them to have this argument. "Look around you. See many allies lining up to help? Don't see the British soldiers lining up in all their crimson glory. No Italian airships sweeping in out of the sky. And gallant knights on white horses only exist in books. Go it alone against al-Rahim. Or rely on me to get the job done."

She stood motionless, her face ashen. He didn't want to notice the suffering and regret in her eyes. Told himself he was seeing what he wanted to see. That her deceit had hurt her as much as it had him. More lies, but these were falsehoods he told himself, which made him even more of a fool.

He held the necklace out to her. "Take them. Find your own way to al-Rahim's compound, give him the jewels. See what happens. Or," he went on, merciless, "these pretty stones are mine, and I'm the one to get your parents free. Your choice, *professorsha*."

For a moment, she said nothing. Then, her words barely a whisper, "Mikhail—"

"Choose, goddamn it," he growled.

She tipped up her chin. "I choose you." Holding his gaze, she said, "I'm the one who's deceitful, but you've never been. Not once. You've always been honest ... about everything. Who you were. What you wanted, and how you'd get it. The whole time I've known you, you've only spoken the truth. And I knew I could rely on you."

He shoved the string of gems into the pocket of his coat. They felt cold and dead. "Get in the jolly boat."

It looked as though she meant to say something more, then changed her mind. Quickly, she strode to the waiting boat. When she stumbled a little climbing into the vessel, Herrera took her hand and steadied her.

Merely watching Herrera touch her made jealousy burn low in Mikhail's gut. He despised and resented this, too.

Just hate her, damn it. Clean and simple.

But damn him, he couldn't. She had faith in him, and it resonated like a longed-for sunrise. For years, he'd told himself he didn't give a cockroach's arse what anyone thought of him, and for the most part, he didn't. But *her* opinion mattered.

"Captain?" Herrera called.

He stalked over to the jolly boat and swung himself over the side. After fastening his harness, he gave Herrera a nod to signal it was time to leave. The vessel rose up into the air. Though Daphne's gaze never left him, he kept his own fixed pointedly at the rocky horizon.

It didn't make any goddamn sense—this hurt. He should be inured to this kind of deceit. And if it had been just about the money, all he'd have to do was toss her overboard or abandon her in the middle of the blasted desert, then take his profit.

Yet here she was, hands gripping the sides of the jolly boat, watching him with her green, remorseful eyes. Eyes he couldn't let himself stare into, or else he'd find something he didn't want, didn't need.

After several silent minutes flying in the jolly boat, the *Bielyi Voron* came into view. His weapon-laden ship. The purpose for which he was created. He had to remind himself: he was built for war, and whenever he tried for anything more, disaster struck.

They reached the ship, the jolly boat taking its usual place in the cargo hold. Hardly had the small vessel settled than he leapt out. Levkov waited for them. Mikhail tossed the necklace at the first mate, who caught it with one hand, then gaped at it.

"Put that in the strong room," Mikhail commanded.

At once, and without complaint or demand for explanation, Levkov hurried to put the jewels into safekeeping. Once, Mikhail had danced to Daphne's tune, letting her keep what he'd believed was a strongbox of gold in her cabin. But even that gesture had been hollow, because there hadn't been any gold. Just as there hadn't been any diamond mine. But the star sapphires—those were his now. His only recompense for this whole debacle of a mission.

After Levkov had gone, Mikhail strode out of the cargo bay. Daphne seemed to hesitate for a moment, but he heard the unmistakable sound of her boots on the planks, following him.

Instead of heading straight to his quarters, Mikhail took a different route. His crew seemed to sense his black mood, for they all scurried out of his way as he passed. Finally, he reached his destination. He flung open the door, stepped inside the long chamber, and studied the racks and racks of weapons there: ether pistols and rifles, filled ether tanks for replenishing the firearms, plasma grenades, cases of bullets.

He began pulling guns from the racks, stacking them up on the table in the center of the armory. Every weapon would have to be checked and rechecked by the crew. All of it had to function at peak capacity tomorrow. Hell, they might need some of this today.

Sensing Daphne's presence in the doorway, he said without looking up, "The *Bielyi Voron*'s strong. So's her crew. But I'm not going to doubt al-Zaman. Al-Rahim's compound is probably better fortified than the tsar's palace, and a rat couldn't breach that place's cellars."

"And al-Rahim has those two Man O' Wars working for him," she added.

He did glance up then, and she visibly restrained herself from stepping back from the heat of his glare. "I haven't forgotten about Olevski. Or that French rogue."

"One Man O' War against two, and an impenetrable fortress." She eyed the guns stacked up on the table, and the other weapons in the armory. "This might not be enough."

"It won't." He checked the sights on a rifle, then set it beside the others. "Which is why we need an ally."

"The British won't help us. But if not them, then who?"

He gave her a brutal smile. "Khalida."

FINDING A NOMADIC warlord wouldn't be difficult for a Man O' War and his airship. They had an advantage that earthbound men didn't have: the sky.

"Al-Rahim's compound is to the south of the city." In the pilot house, Mikhail, Daphne, and Levkov studied a chart of the area, showing Medinat al-Kadib and the wide stretches of desert surrounding it. "Here, where there are ridges and mountains to help with the defenses."

"If Khalida and he are enemies," Daphne said, "they'll keep far enough away from each other to maintain their territories. They'd use the city as neutral ground between them." She pointed to a region north of Medinat al-Kadib. "I'd wager my field compass she'll be found here."

Again, he didn't want to be impressed by her intelligence and tenacity, but the feeling rose up in him like an old illness. She hadn't even argued against the idea of going to Khalida, showing her trust in his judgment, in him. He wanted this uncomplicated. Instead, he got twists and turns, and a hell of a lot of conflicted emotion he didn't want.

Locating a warlord wasn't nearly as thorny. Mikhail had the helmsman steer the ship northward, and they passed over the minarets, towers, and crowded buildings of the city before reaching the broad expanse of the desert.

He stood on the forecastle, Daphne and Levkov flanking him. Hot, dry wind swept up from the desert floor, and everything looked as seared and barren as he felt. Colorless.

"Don't know how anyone or anything could live out here," grumbled Levkov.

"It's pure," Daphne countered. "Stark, but beautiful. Nothing extraneous. And there is life. It merely operates on a contained scale."

Mikhail's vision caught these details: snakes and lizards darting amongst the rocks, wheeling birds searching for prey, straight-horned antelope. All scrabbling for existence in a land that gave them little to work with. "Hard way to live, though."

"Every place has its threats," she murmured. "Home can be a rocky, barren plain, but if it's home, and all you know, you come to love it."

Levkov muttered something about philosophy not saving your arse if you're dying of thirst, but both Mikhail and Daphne ignored him. Each word from Daphne's mouth felt like the bitterest pleasure.

Better, and easier, to focus on the task before him. Bare and empty as the desert seemed, seeing it from the sky gave a different perspective. "There," he said, pointing to the ground. "Tracks in the earth. Looks like they were made by horses and camels, some tetrol-powered vehicles, too. People use these routes." Through the shipboard auditory device, he instructed the helmsman on altering the ship's course to follow the routes.

Soon, they spotted people riding in a small caravan. The sight of an airship's shadow made them all look up,

shielding their eyes, and watch the *Bielyi Voron* fly overhead. As the ship continued on its course, it passed watering holes and a small group of tents. The occupants
could be coming or going from Khalida's own encampment, but it meant that the ship was traveling in the right
direction.

"More caravans," Daphne noted. "They're approaching from different directions, but they're all converging
on the other side of that ridge."

The airship continued on its course, going over the
ridge, and there they found their destination. Khalida's
encampment. It formed its own small-scale city—a collection of over a hundred tents, some of them fabric,
while others were collapsible metal structures. Cattle
milled in pens, tended by both humans and automatons.
Smoke from cooking fires rose in columns. There were
men and women not only on horseback, but a few riding
mechanized camels, the iron-and-brass beasts adorned
as ornately with tasseled reins and blankets as their living
counterparts.

Gyrocopters buzzed in patrols around the
encampment—small craft made of wood, leather, and
canvas. When they spotted the airship, they formed a
protective line in front of the camp. The men flying the
gyrocopters brandished extremely long rifles he recognized as *jezails*. Only these *jezails* were equipped with
ether tanks. Courtesy of Khalida's British allies, no doubt.

Daphne stiffened in alarm when she spotted the gyrocopters. "They can't fly as high as an airship, can they?"

"But their ether-powered bullets can still hit us." He

strode from the forecastle, Daphne following, heading for the cargo bay and the jolly boat. "Time to head down there and practice our diplomacy."

"Or our sprinting."

"We talk fast." He went below decks. "But I never run from a fight like this."

OVER THE COURSE of her life, Daphne had walked directly into situations that weren't in and of themselves safe. The most recent having been setting foot in the tavern in Palermo, searching out a notorious rogue Man O' War to take her to the Arabian Peninsula. But circumstance had forced her to it. Safety meant staying curled up beneath her desk at the Accademia, hoping that the perils of the world might simply pass her by.

Safety also meant stasis. And the ceding of power. Neither option was acceptable.

Outrageous as Mikhail's gambit was, she knew it was their best hope for success. So, wordlessly, they took the jolly boat to the very edge of Khalida's encampment. The moment the vessel lowered to the ground, heavily armed men and women surrounded them. Sunlight danced across pistols, rifles, and swords, all of them pointed at her and Mikhail. The faces of the people encircling them were likewise hostile.

Both Daphne and Mikhail lifted their hands.

She said, "We've come—"

"Silence," a man in a blue headscarf barked. He jerked his sword and immediately, three men stepped forward and roughly removed all weapons from her and Mikhail's possession. There went her revolver, her knife, and Mikhail's ether pistol. Her satchel was searched, as well. They were now completely unarmed. Though Mikhail himself was a weapon, a fact revealed by the wary gazes of the encampment's guards whenever they glanced his way.

Much as she expected this reception, cold fear congealed in the pit of Daphne's stomach. When crossed, tribal warlords weren't quite known for their tolerance or sense of humor. She could only hope that Khalida proved the exception to this custom.

"Did you think you could walk into our camp and go unrecognized?" Blue Headscarf sneered. "Our guards spoke of an Englishwoman and a giant man who looked like a djinn." He grinned viciously. "I should present Khalida with your heads as a gift, *ferengis*."

"And deprive her of the pleasure of killing us herself," Mikhail answered.

"The man of metal talks sense, Hassan," said a woman wielding a curved *jambiya* knife. "You saw her last night when she learned the astrolabe had been stolen. She swore to cut their throats and drink their blood."

The grisly image turned Daphne's pulse into a frantic tattoo. Yet she said, "Think how angry Khalida would be if we haven't any blood left to drink."

Hassan didn't look pleased by this logic, but he was clearly more concerned about his chieftain's wrath than getting vengeance. "Bind their wrists," he commanded, and several of the guards hurried to obey.

Daphne bit back a curse as her arms were ruthlessly pulled back and her wrists manacled. Mikhail looked unimpressed as one of the men snapped fetters on him. Clearly, he could snap them as if they were made of pasteboard, but he seemed to be humoring his captors.

Awkwardly, Daphne was dragged out of the jolly boat by some of the guards, and she stumbled slightly before gaining her balance. Mikhail suffered no such indignities. He stepped easily out of the vessel, and as he stood to his full height, he dwarfed everyone around him. Mutters rose up from the guards. Bound as she was, Daphne still felt gratitude that Mikhail was on her side. More or less.

Escorted by their well-armed guards, they were led through the encampment. It was the largest of its type she'd ever encountered, blending the ancient and the technologically innovative in a complex fusion. The bleats of sheep mingled with the hiss of wheeled, steam-powered ovens tended by elderly women. A child watched them from atop a mechanized donkey. Some of the people hurled insults, while others simply stared with a mixture of curiosity and wariness.

They reached an enormous tent. Five guards were posted outside, and Hassan snapped at them to step aside so he might present their chieftain with a prize. The guards hurried to obey, one of them pulling back a gauzy curtain to permit them to enter.

It took several moments for Daphne's eyes to adjust from the brightness of outside, but when they did, she barely held back a gasp. She'd seen well-appointed, even sumptuous tents. Simply because one led a nomadic existence didn't mean that one couldn't have luxuries. But Khalida's tent far surpassed anything she'd witnessed before. Silks of every hue, shot through with gold, draped from the central support posts. Thick, ornate carpets covered the ground, and atop those were low couches strewn with pillows. A mechanized silver fountain, studded with jewels, stood to one side, and there were ornately inlaid tables heaped with every delicacy Daphne could name, from honey-soaked pastries to roast pigeons to ice cream in chilled goblets.

She and Mikhail were herded toward the far end of the tent, where a woman reclined upon a divan. Despite the fact that she'd never met the warlord, Daphne recognized Khalida at once. She appeared to be somewhere in her mid-forties, with henna designs painted on her cheeks and forehead. Silver embroidery richly covered her black robes, and her hair was covered by a dark wrap, held in place with a leather fillet. A jeweled, curved blade jutted from the silver sash at her waist, and bandoliers crossed each of her shoulders. Her kohl-rimmed eyes were sharp and merciless as a hawk's as she watched her visitors approach, a slight smile curving her mouth.

Half a dozen young, handsome men sprawled nearby, many of them with their robes partially open to reveal muscled chests. One of the men handed Khalida the stem of a hookah pipe, and she drew on it as she continued to study Daphne and Mikhail. It was not unlike being contemplated by a lioness, wondering when the predator would strike.

Daphne carefully kept her eyes trained on the ground, though she observed as best she could through her lowered lashes.

Hassan made a deep obeisance. "*Lalla*, I have brought you—"

"The Emperor and Empress of Japan." Khalida exhaled a cloud of smoke. "I know who they are, Hassan."

He flushed and bowed again. "Humblest apologies, *lalla*. Shall I fetch your goblet of gold and amber, that you might have a vessel to collect their blood?"

The warlord waved her ring-adorned hand. "Later. For now, I want to simply look at the two . . . lunatics? Imbeciles? I cannot decide what they are, only that it was decidedly foolish of them to steal from me. Most foolish, indeed." The softness of her tone instilled far more terror in Daphne than if Khalida had yelled and raged. "My gravest concern is how I will kill you, for I have so many ways that would be excruciating, and it is difficult to pick precisely the right one."

"We're here of our own free will," Mikhail said.

"Perhaps you *are* imbeciles," spat Hassan. "Or wish to spare yourself the agony of wondering when and how my chief will end your lives."

Mikhail barely spared Hassan a dismissive glance. "I've got an airship, Khalida. I could be halfway to Iceland by now."

"That would've been the wiser choice," the warlord said drily. "My assumption is that you did not come here to return my astrolabe."

"Al-Rahim has it now," Mikhail said.

At the mention of her rival's name, Khalida's face twisted, and she spat upon the ground. Fury blazed in her eyes as she shot to her feet. "You stole my prize for that camel's turd?" There was a hiss as she drew the knife from her sash. She strode to Mikhail and put the dagger to his throat. "Man of metal or not, you can still bleed."

"It'll take a stronger blade than that," he answered.

"Let us test that," Khalida snarled. She pressed the blade tight to his neck. At first, nothing happened, but she gave the dagger a hard shove, and a droplet of Mikhail's blood finally appeared. Khalida grinned brutally. "This may go slowly, but I'll enjoy it more."

Daphne could no longer keep silent. "Al-Rahim has my parents captive, and the only way I could secure their release was by stealing the astrolabe."

Without removing the blade from Mikhail's neck, the warlord asked, "And this concerns me how?"

"Because," Mikhail said calmly, "al-Rahim knew that you'd lose face with all the tribes if someone took the damn thing. And having a British citizen be the responsible party would strain the alliance you've got with those tea-drinking bastards. He gets the prize, comes out top dog, and you're left with the crumbs of former glory, alone with your useless playthings." He flicked a dismissive glance toward the handsome young men, who sulked in response.

"Hassan," Khalida said, "fetch me the sharpest scimitar. Let's see how much punishment this metal man's neck can take."

Hassan eagerly darted away in search of the weapon.

Was Mikhail deliberately goading Khalida? There was brash and confident, and then there was mad.

"Or," he continued, "you can finally cut al-Rahim's balls off and take your position as the rightful leader of this territory. The *only* leader of this territory."

Interest gleamed in Khalida's eyes, but she seemed to deliberately bank it. "Lovely idea—but in the desert, wadis are sometimes high with water, other times dry as bones. My own supply of water is ebbing away, and all because of an astrolabe. If I wanted to drown al-Rahim, I wouldn't be able to do so. Not now."

Mikhail's grin flashed. "But now you've got a Man O' War as an ally."

Slowly, Khalida lowered her dagger. She narrowed her eyes. "You?" Her voice dripped with skepticism. "So generous with your worthless declarations."

"We wouldn't have come here if we didn't mean it," Daphne said. When Khalida turned her piercing dark gaze on her, she continued, speaking quickly. "What did we gain by bringing ourselves to you? None of us are stupid, Khalida, especially not you. Captain Denisov spoke the truth. Consider it: had we wanted to, we could be on the other side of the globe by now. But we chose to come here, to you."

She glanced at Mikhail, who gave her a subtle nod of encouragement.

"The people need a leader, Khalida," she went on. "They need someone who will act swiftly, with a show of force the likes of which has never been seen in these lands. Join forces with us, and we'll take back the astro-labe and decimate al-Rahim."

Khalida frowned in contemplation, which Daphne decided to take as an encouraging sign. "Al-Rahim has two men of metal, whereas there is only this one." She nodded toward Mikhail.

"I know the Man O' Wars' weaknesses," he said. "And they haven't my skills in combat."

"One sage is far more valuable than two fools," added Daphne.

Khalida gave a soft snort. "You speak well, for a *ferengi*."

"She's damned intelligent," Mikhail said. "Between her brainpower and my strength, you're not going to find better allies."

Pleasure throbbed in Daphne's chest, hearing Mikhail's praise. Perhaps it was only meant to convince Khalida, yet it gratified Daphne just the same. She'd once feared his scorn because it meant that the mission to free her parents would be jeopardized. Now, his contempt wounded her deeply. His respect meant something to her.

Hassan ran back into the tent, carrying a large and wicked scimitar. Bowing, he presented it to Khalida. "As you requested, *lalla*."

"Today is a day of disappointments for you, Hassan." Khalida turned away and strode back to her divan. After tucking her dagger back into her sash, she stretched out on her couch. "I've decided to keep these two alive for a little longer."

Indeed, Hassan stifled his look of regret as he held on to the scimitar.

Khalida drew on her hookah again, then exhaled a cloud of fragrant smoke. "If we were to ally, there can be no room for hesitation, no ill-conceived plans for battle. And we must succeed. We have to strike against him once, and once only."

"Cut the head off the snake," Daphne said, which made the warlord nod with understanding.

"Only a fool takes to the sea without being able to read the stars," said Mikhail. "No one knows the sky better than me. And for this voyage," he added with a grin, "I've already plotted our course."

Khalida's laugh was low and throaty. "Are all men of metal as cocksure as you?"

"There's no one like him," Daphne said before he could speak.

He didn't look at her, but she saw the flex of muscle in his jaw.

"Let's hear these schemes of yours," the warlord said.

"Free her first," he answered, jerking his head toward Daphne.

Khalida held herself still for a moment, and Daphne wondered if Mikhail's commanding tone had pushed the warlord too far.

Then, at last, Khalida nodded. One of the guards stepped forward and undid the manacles around Daphne's wrists. It was difficult to resist a groan of relief when the fetters came off, and she rubbed her arms to soothe their ache.

"Don't you want to be freed?" Khalida asked Mikhail.

In answer, Mikhail simply flexed his arms. The manacles snapped off his wrists and fell to the carpeted floor. Mutters of shock circulated through the tent, and Khalida's entourage of handsome men shifted uncomfortably, surreptitiously testing their biceps.

Khalida took another contemplative pull of her hookah as she stared at him. "Yes, I can see why you might be useful."

"You won't regret joining forces with him," Daphne said to Khalida. She turned to Mikhail, her gaze meeting his. Nothing else existed in that moment, the warlord's tent fading away, the desert itself disappearing. It was only her and Mikhail. Together. And she let him see this, for she might not ever have another chance to do so. "I never have."

Chapter Twelve

ONCE THE MANACLES came off, they were treated to Khalida's hospitality. Allies now—though warily so—and the warlord seemed determined to show her generosity. Tea and roasts and bread and pilafs studded with dried fruit and cakes perfumed with rosewater.

Mikhail could be a good guest. He devoured everything, his hunger monstrous. It was a surprise that he hadn't much felt it until this morning, since it was with him always. But Daphne had kept him distracted from the needs of his body. *Certain* needs. Others had demanded satisfaction.

And they still did. He and Daphne sat upon cushions on the floor, eating, discussing plans for tomorrow's assault. He paid no attention to the women who would bring him more food, more tea, more curious and flirtatious glances. It was the *professorsha*, and only her, that drew his attention. He was always aware of Daphne, of the movement of her fingers to her mouth, the soft glow of silk-filtered light upon her skin.

Again, they'd worked well together, navigating the treacherous waters of Khalida to now find themselves her—somewhat—honored guests. Each anticipating the other's intent, taking the thread of persuasion and spinning it out, until the warlord had agreed to become their confederate. They made a damned fine team, he and Daphne, as colleagues. As lovers.

Like she'd said, it's a black joke. Nothing's simple. Everything has its twists, its dangers.

But he'd other concerns right now. Namely, the plotting and strategy for tomorrow's all-or-nothing battle.

The whole of the day they talked, making plans, deciding tactics. Khalida's generals joined in the discussion. Lamps were lit as darkness fell. More food and drink was brought, consumed mainly by him.

After hours and hours, they'd reached a final plan. Daphne looked exhausted but resolute. She hadn't been silent during the discussion, offering her own good suggestions, many of which they planned on using. But they had all reached the limits of planning. There came a time when words had to give way to action. Tomorrow would be that time.

He needed to get back to his ship before Levkov decided to send out a search party. Generous as Khalida had been, she wouldn't take kindly to her encampment being invaded by a party of mercenaries.

And Daphne did look ready to collapse from fatigue.

"Gather your warriors," Mikhail said to Khalida. "I'll give them transport to al-Rahim's compound."

The warlord only smiled. "A kindly offer, but unnecessary. We have our own means of flight."

"The gyrocopters," said Daphne.

"We call them *zawbaahs*."

"Whirlwinds."

Mikhail got to his feet, and Khalida and her generals immediately did the same, eyeing his great height when standing. Typical reaction. But no one was ever taller than Mikhail—except other Man O' Wars.

Another fire burned through his heart. Tomorrow, he'd face Olevski. Only one of them would survive the encounter.

"At the day's first light," Khalida said, "we will meet just beyond the ridge shielding al-Rahim's compound. But I warn you, if you fail to show—"

"We'll be there," Daphne said, rising to her feet.

From her sash, Khalida pulled her dagger. "More than words are needed to seal this alliance." She drew the blade across her palm. A line of blood welled, and the warlord offered her dagger to Daphne.

Without hesitation, she took the knife. Scored it over her hand, barely making a sound as she did so. Mikhail gritted his teeth as bright blood appeared.

Daphne held her cut hand out to Khalida, who clasped it against her own. The two women also locked gazes, making silent promises to each other. Satisfied with Daphne's demonstration of loyalty, Khalida turned to Mikhail.

"I'll need that scimitar," he said, glancing at the sharp blade that Hassan had produced earlier in the hopes of cutting his head off.

Hassan looked reluctant to give the deadly weapon to him, but Khalida nodded her approval. When the sword was given to Mikhail, he swiped it across his palm. The blade had indeed been honed to incredible sharpness, for it cut him right away. As soon as a line of blood appeared on his hand, he clasped palms with Khalida. The blood oath was sealed.

Everyone turned to leave, but Daphne stayed where she was. Instead, she held out her hand to Mikhail.

Though she tried to keep her gaze stoic, a yearning hope shone beneath the surface.

He stared at her hand for a moment, the cut that marred her skin, and the smeared crimson. Part of him wanted to turn away, ignore her offer of trust. Yet part of him demanded he take her hand and pull her to him, wrap her in his arms, forgive her anything.

Instead, he simply clasped their hands together. But he couldn't ignore the feel of her skin against his, couldn't pretend that his blood and hers didn't mix. Though he kept himself perfectly still, reverberations traveled through him, like a silent chant.

Doesn't mean anything, he told himself. *Blood is cheap, easily spilled.*

Not her blood. Not theirs together.

At last, they released each other. Khalida glanced back and forth between them, speculation sharp in her gaze, but she said nothing. Mikhail fought the urge to demand a bandage for Daphne's hand. She took care of it herself, removing a handkerchief from her satchel and wrapping it around her palm.

Mikhail said, "Dawn tomorrow." Then, after making sure Daphne would follow, he turned and left the tent. It was a measure of trust that only a few guards, including Hassan, accompanied them back to the jolly boat. Mikhail and Daphne climbed in.

After they had both fastened their harnesses, he brought them back up into the sky. From above, the encampment at night shone with cooking fires. Lamp and torchlight flickering against fabric and metal. Beyond the limits of the encampment was the broad desert, dark as the bottom of the sea. But the stars above glimmered, and that damned waning crescent moon hung overhead, reminding him of what he and Daphne had shared. It had been only last night, but lifetimes had been lived in the intervening hours.

They reached the *Bielyi Voron* quickly, and a council of war was called. All the senior members of the crew assembled in Mikhail's quarters, Daphne also in attendance, and the plans for tomorrow's battle were gone over.

"The jewels are already in our strong room, Captain," said Levkov. "No need for us to risk our necks."

"Fortunate we're not still in the navy, Piotr Romanovich," Mikhail growled. "Or else you'd get ten lashes for insubordination."

The first mate's mouth formed an obstinate line.

"Why *are* you going to fight?" Daphne asked quietly.

All eyes turned to her, then back to Mikhail.

"Two reasons," he said after a long pause. "First: Olevski's going to be there."

Several crewmen swore, knowing Mikhail's history with the bastard.

"Reason enough," said Levkov.

"What's the other?" asked Herrera.

Mikhail took a slow, deep breath. He tried not to look at Daphne, but his gaze clung to her despite his wishes. "I gave my word."

What was the word of a scoundrel worth? Only as much as he valued it himself. No one on this ship, including Daphne, would be at all surprised if he decided to fly the *Bielyi Voron* to some distant tropic shore, and leave kidnapped archaeologists and feuding warlords to sort their problems out on their own.

But he couldn't. He had to see this through.

"We'll be rendezvousing with Khalida and her warriors at dawn," he went on. "So if you aren't on watch tonight, get the hell to your bunks and get some rest."

The crew filed out, mumbling their good-nights. Akua was the last man to leave. He cast a glance back into Mikhail's stateroom, then shut the door firmly behind him.

Mikhail and Daphne were alone. The last time they'd been in his cabin, their kiss had set fire to the night. Since then, they'd made love with a passion that redrew every atlas. He knew her taste, her feel. Her wickedly clever mind. And her deceit.

She stood in front of the bank of windows, the night sky jeweled black velvet as it spread out behind her.

Hell, he thought, shaking his head at himself, *there I go, turning poetical again. Should change my name to Pushkin.*

He scrubbed his hand over his face. "Go to bed."

"And lie there sleepless, thinking of all the things I want to say to you?"

"Never cared for words. They're just sounds. Sounds that make everything damned complicated and messy." A shot of vodka sounded, however, like the most basic and essential thing in the world. He pulled the bottle from its chiller. Deciding to spare himself the pretense, he drank straight from the bottle. Cold slid down his throat, leaving a pleasant warmth in its wake.

"There's a reason I didn't become a professor of English," she said quietly. "It's much easier to simply watch how cultures and societies interacted. Actions hold more weight than words. And yet," she moved away from the windows, separating out from the night's shadows, "I can't think of the right thing to do to make you understand."

"Nothing to understand," he said, gruff. "You had an objective: free your parents. You did whatever it took to achieve that objective. Including lie to me. Twice." He hated the bitterness in his voice. Him—who couldn't be touched by anything. But that raw and bleeding part of him continued to throb.

"I confessed my second deception. That should count for something."

It did. It didn't. He gave her a noncommittal shrug, then took another drink.

She stepped in front of him, refusing to be shunted aside. "My parents were going to be killed if I didn't do something. Lying to you—I had no choice."

He snorted, and she glowered at him, continuing, "I didn't. And if put in the same situation again, I wouldn't change my actions. You said it yourself. My one goal was to get my parents out of al-Rahim's clutches. So I did what circumstance forced me to do." She made a strange, choking laugh. "Do you know what my biggest lie was before this? I told a colleague that I'd read and enjoyed her monograph about the agricultural economy of fourteenth-century Hamburg."

He couldn't stop himself from chuckling. Seems even the *professorsha* had her academic limits.

She looked encouraged by his laugh, stepping closer. "What you and I had—in the vault, when we made love— none of that was a lie. I can't counterfeit how I feel." She seemed to struggle with her words, as though she reached for them but they fought back. "I know how to make bars of clay look like gold, or jewels resemble worthless stones, but . . . I can't dissemble when it comes to my heart."

The safer thing would be to turn away from her, or even remove her from his quarters, so he wouldn't have to hear her, see her. Yet he stayed where he was, his gaze moving over her as if by sight alone he could know her every secret, and whether she spoke the truth or not.

Give him a map, any map, and he could read it. It'd always been that way with him. Learning terrain. Having an innate sense as to the how and why of a place, even before clapping eyes upon it. And when seeing the place in truth, no longer printed on a map, he had an ingrained sense of it, its topography already imprinted upon him.

A face was a map, too. He read hers now, his throat tight, surprising himself with how much he truly wanted to believe her.

In the curve of her lips, in the green and gold of her eyes, and the depths revealed there, he discovered the landscape of her inner self. And found . . . no deceit. Every word she spoke rang true, the certainty of it like the gleam of the approaching horizon promising the end of a long, rocky voyage.

He hungered for that shore, and he feared it. He could find safety, or he could founder and crash.

After another burning cold drink of vodka, he said, "Deceiving a mercenary, twice, is a hell of an accomplishment. Admirable, even."

This hadn't been what she'd expected, and she frowned slightly at his reply. "Not many would think so."

"Depends who you ask. People in my world—if they gave out medals, they'd give one to you. *Esteemed Achievement in Manipulation and Deception*. In fact, I'd be the one to pin it on you."

Hurt crossed her face. "Don't repay my honesty now with ridicule."

"All the things I am—rogue, mercenary, bastard—a liar isn't one of them." Instead of reaching for her, he ran his free hand over the crest of his hair, feeling its spikes against his palm. "Do I trust you? Not fully. Not yet."

She turned away, disappointed.

"But I respect the hell out of you," he said. "Not too

many earn my respect, but you did. Because I never saw your deviousness coming. No hint. No clue. As wily as a mercenary."

"Must admit," she said, rueful, "I surprised myself." A frown pleated her brows. "I don't know if I should be proud of that. Or how to interpret it."

"It means that you've got the sharpest brain of anyone I know." He'd seen her intelligence in action. Not simply with her deception, but throughout their whole voyage together, he'd witnessed the intricate machinery of her mind. "But you've also got a heart, so you won't make a good mercenary. Not like me."

She stepped even closer to him, so only a few inches separated them. Wariness shone in her eyes, and uncertainty. Slowly, she reached out, testing the distance.

Her hand pressed against his chest, causing his pulse to race, and she looked up at him with warmth and sadness. "Damn it, Mikhail," she sighed. "For someone who can spot treasure at a hundred feet, you're remarkably shortsighted when it comes to yourself."

With her other hand, she traced along the line of his jaw. "You *do* have a heart, one I'm helplessly drawn to, but you keep it protected behind something far stronger than telumium."

He felt his heart now, throbbing inside his chest, as if it was striving for something. For her.

"I don't know if I can ask for forgiveness for something I felt I had to do," she continued. "But I hate that I hurt you in the process. And put your life in danger many times. If I could take that back, I would."

These weren't palliative words, thrown carelessly to win him to her side. He heard the truth in her voice, read the honesty in her eyes. No one had ever offered him so much, and it shook him. Down to his core.

He ached with wanting more, and he feared it. Risks. He'd spent his life with them. In his youth, he hadn't cared about consequence, plowing ahead with regard for nothing and no one, least of all himself. But time and circumstance changed a man. He was far more wary now than he'd ever been . . . knowing the damage that could be done with a misstep. But if he stayed just as he was, incapable of movement, he'd rust like one of those useless ships in the harbor, a corroded carcass.

What she offered him now . . . They both knew it couldn't last. There'd be more wounds, more suffering. Yet to turn away would mean denying himself, and her, the bright world they created together. Even if only for a short while.

He leaned down, his hands curving around her waist. A flare of pleasure lit her eyes as she stretched up on the very tips of her toes, and slid her hands behind his neck. Their mouths came together.

The taste of her lips was sweet, the feel of her against him sweeter. He and Daphne clung close, taking and giving, their kisses open and demanding. He quickly undid her braid, letting her hair spill around her shoulders.

It had been only a day since last they'd kissed. Too long. She was silk and strength, his audacious scholar, and he wanted every part of her.

Sweeping her up in his arms, he carried her to his bunk.

Fortunately, he'd gotten rid of the narrow standard-issue naval bed, replacing it with something much larger and more accommodating. Only a few hours remained until the dawn. He was determined not to waste them.

But when he laid her down upon the bed and stretched out beside her, ready to touch her everywhere, he sensed something unexpected. Trembling. She actually shook, very slightly, but enough for him to sense.

She was afraid.

Her fear pierced him. He stroked gently along her cheek and down her neck. "I didn't hurt you before, and I swear I never will."

Her eyes widened. "God, no. That's not . . ." She shook her head, her hair rustling against the pillow. "It's tomorrow that worries me. If something happens to you ... I've lost and gained you so many times. What this is," she said, glancing down at their intertwined bodies, "is so much more real because of that. But I could lose you all over again tomorrow." Her fingers trailed along his neck.

He didn't want to point out that she was far more vulnerable than he would ever be. Yet at that moment, her words disarmed him. She was concerned about *him*. As more than the captain of an airship, or the means to secure her parents' freedom. Him, as a man. Apprehension and tenderness brimmed in her eyes. How long had it been since anyone looked at him that way? Maybe no one ever had.

"Takes a lot to bring down a Man O' War," he said. "We're built for battle."

"Maybe so, but the battle tomorrow is going to be

huge. Even with Khalida and her warriors helping us, the odds are so steep. We're facing not just al-Rahim and his hundreds of warriors, but two other Man O' Wars."

He felt his jaw tighten. "Don't worry about Olevski."

"Like you said, there's no such thing as an innocuous Man O' War."

"He's a dangerous bastard, that's certain. But I *will* defeat him."

Propping herself up on her elbows, she gazed intently at Mikhail. "You say his name like a curse."

"I used to curse him every day, with every breath." Mikhail felt his mouth twist into a cold smile. "He's the reason I went rogue."

THE BED SHIFTED as Mikhail rose from it. Daphne stared at the broad width of his back, feeling the tension pouring from him in cold, unseen waves.

"Olevski and I were at the naval academy together," he said, his voice flat. "Didn't like each other at first—we were both arrogant bastards—but soon we became close as brothers. He didn't have any family, so on holidays I used to bring him home with me. They welcomed him with open arms. He loved being a part of my family— teasing my mother, playing cards with my father. He truly became like a brother to me. And when he started courting my sister Irina, everyone was happy."

"Neither of you were Man O' Wars yet, I take it," she said quietly.

"No, but when Olevski and me were both selected for the transformation, everyone in my family was overjoyed. Irina was disappointed she wouldn't be a mother, but she was willing to sacrifice that for him. So, Olevski and I underwent the procedure, became Man O' Wars, and flew off for promised glory. Irina vowed to wait for him."

He strode to the cabinet and pulled out a cloth-wrapped bundle. Unfolding the cloth, he held up a military sash, medals arrayed like proud troops. When he spoke, his voice was edged, icy. "The fruits of my labors for the Russian Imperial Navy. Olevski has one just like it. We'd wear them to official functions, galas. They'd give us new medals like handing out candy, but we earned every one. *Fearless,* the Admiralty called us. Or maybe we were just stupid and arrogant." He shook his head. "Didn't matter. All that mattered was that we were the pride of the navy, so they sent us both to Italy, to see if we couldn't pummel the Italians into submission. It seemed perfect, that my adoptive brother and I should go into battle together."

He continued to study the sash, but he didn't seem to see the ribbons or bits of polished metal and enamel.

"We fought a few battles, knocked some enemies out of the sky. A grand old time. Then Olevski told me there was a cache of gold in the Italian Alps. The Hapsburgs were sending ground troops to retrieve the gold, but Olevski had a better idea. He and I would take the gold for ourselves. One half for me, one half for him and Irina."

"But the Hapsburgs are allied with Russia," she noted. "You would've been stealing from your own allies."

His wide shoulders lifted in a shrug, but he wouldn't look at her. "The Hapsburgs wouldn't know. An easy trick: Olevski planned to plant evidence, evidence that'd make it look as though Dr. Rossini and her rogue Man O' Wars took the gold. No one's ally, the mad doctor. So easy for anyone to believe she'd be the one stealing the gold. Olevski and I were going to be rich, and nobody'd be the wiser."

Dread settled in her stomach. It was clear that Mikhail hadn't rejected Olevski's scheme.

"Things didn't play out quite as you and Olevski had planned it, though," she surmised.

A humorless laugh rattled in Mikhail's chest. "They did—at first. Not difficult for two Man O' Wars to break through one Alpine fortress's defenses. He and I went in on foot, to keep it fast and keep it quiet. We slid in, knocked out the security, and grabbed the gold. I gathered up as much as I could carry, and that's when I heard it. A sharp clicking noise. The sound of an ether pistol being cocked. I turned around, and Olevski had an ether pistol pointed right between my eyes."

"Oh, God," she gulped. The story continued to get more and more ugly.

"He was practically my brother, was going to marry my sister, and that was how my trust was repaid," Mikhail said bitterly. "He even taunted me with it. Said he'd tell my family how I'd been killed in combat, and then he'd take over as favorite son. It's what he'd wanted all along."

Sickness choked her. Olevski's betrayal was horrifying, and it had to have been so much worse for Mikhail, who'd cared for his friend so deeply.

And when *she* had deceived him . . . no wonder he'd been enraged.

"What did you do?" she whispered.

"Threw a handful of coins at him." He smiled cruelly. "Olevski could always be distracted by something shiny. His eye was on the gold, and that's when I knocked the gun out of his hand. Then we did what all men do who betray each other. We brawled."

She could only imagine the awful spectacle of two Man O' Wars fighting each other. Like something out of ancient legend, or a fable used to terrify children and nonbelievers. She must have made some noise of distress, because he sent her a bleak glance over his shoulder.

"It got better," he said sardonically. "Instead of foot troops, a fifty-gun Hapsburg airship showed up. Caught me and Olevski in possession of the gold—never mind the fact that we were beating the hell out of each other. That Hapsburg Man O' War was surprised as hell. So-called allies were trying to steal the treasure out from under his telumium-enhanced nose. Pretty picture, isn't it?"

She wisely said nothing. Instead, she drew her legs up and wrapped her arms around them, as if to shield herself from Mikhail's sordid tale.

He went on, as if purging long-held poison from his system. "Olevski and I were fucked. That much was clear. Whatever you think of Hapsburgs, they're damned organized and follow the rules. The Hapsburg Man O' War was sure to report what we were trying to do. Mother

Russia would have to send their two *fearless* Man O' Wars to forced labor at a *katorga*. Better that loss than risk the Hapsburg alliance."

"What happened?"

"We fought the Hapsburg Man O' War. Hoped to keep him from notifying the navy of our treachery."

Lord, if two Man O' Wars in combat was a terrifying sight, she couldn't begin to fathom what it must be like to witness *three* of the mechanized men clashing. The Alps must have shaken with the force of their blows.

"Even with me and Olevski against the Hun," Mikhail continued, "I saw the direction of the tide. A crime like the one we'd committed—there'd be no hiding that evidence. The Admiralty would find out, and then I'd spend the rest of my life mining lead in Siberia. So while Olevski and the Hapsburg were distracted and brawling, I broke off from the fight. Left the gold behind and just got the hell out of there."

His arms flexed, the muscles bunching, and the sash he held tore apart like so much tissue paper. He dropped the shreds to the ground, the medals making soft, sad pinging noises at they hit the floorboards, like the worthless bits of metal he thought them to be.

"I consider that my third birthday. My first was when my mother pushed me out of her womb into this bitter world. The second, when my implants were grafted to me, turning me into a Man O' War. And my third—"

"The day you went rogue," she whispered. The day his closest friend betrayed him.

"Olevski survived the fight and turned rogue, too," he

said. "Took a year before I found out. My one solace was that he'd been as cast out from my family as I was. No marriage to Irina. No supplanting me as favorite son. And I hadn't laid eyes on him until Medinat al-Kadib. I will again. Tomorrow. When I do"—his voice was obsidian—"only one of us will survive. And it's not going to be him."

He turned back to face her, and the light from the quartz lamp carved him into unforgiving planes. "Think I still have a heart, *professorsha*?"

"Of course you do," she answered immediately.

His mouth twisted. "Then you must be deaf, and didn't hear a damned word I said. I'm not a virtuous, wronged hero." He stalked to the window. "Don't know much about chemistry, but someone like Olevski is called the *catalyst*. There's one real culprit here: my greed. If I hadn't agreed to steal the gold, none of this would have happened. But I did agree. It cost me everything. My position in the navy. My country. My friend." His voice roughened. "My family."

"Mikhail—"

He planted his hands on the window, coronas of heat forming where he touched the glass. "Greed's all I have now. It's the only thing I've got. My only motivation."

She rose up from the bed and approached him. Slowly. "What does your father do? As a profession."

He faced her, frowning slightly. "Paper shuffling. Works in the Ministry of Transportation."

"So, he never was in the navy?"

"God, no. Can't even watch the clockwork toy boats in the pond at the park without getting seasick."

"And any of your siblings? Were they ever sailors?"

"Only me." His brow lowered. "You're leading me down a road, *professorsha.*"

"I want to know why you joined the navy. Why you became a Man O' War in the first place. The procedure was excruciating, so you said, and I believe you. There were huge risks involved. Yet you did it, anyway. Why'd you do any of it?"

"Because . . ." He stared out at the sky and the dark sprawl of the desert beneath them, but it seemed as though he saw not this shadowy landscape, but the even more obscure one inside himself. "I wanted to help my country. Wanted to do good." His gaze turned inward. "But war's not what anyone expects. Not what I thought it would be. There's glory, and heroism and courage. There's blood, too," he said, his voice hoarse, "and cruelty. Good men killed for no reason. Decisions made by admirals and generals in far-off rooms, never thinking of the human cost. Or worse, not caring."

Absently, he rubbed at his chest, over the telumium implant. "It . . . deadens you. Inside. When I was in the navy, I couldn't remember what I was fighting for. Just moved from one battle to the next. One prize to the next. Rich English and Italian ships to capture and plunder. I was a mercenary before I even left the navy."

She saw it now, how the acquisition of things, of wealth, took the place of his idealism, and how that avarice ate away at him, transformed him. But not entirely.

"There wasn't much of a journey from decorated naval captain to actual rogue mercenary." The hollowness in his gaze chilled her. "Whatever heroic role you've cast me in, I'll never learn the lines. I can't fit the costume."

She stepped between him and the window, and rested her cheek against his chest. Heat seeped through her, soaking deep into her flesh, her bones, her heart. "And yet," she murmured, "you could've taken the star sapphires, left me to face al-Rahim on my own. But you didn't."

"Olevski—"

"A man motivated by revenge thinks of nothing else. You wouldn't have let years pass without trying to kill Olevski, if that's all that mattered to you. No," she said, gazing up at him, "there's far more to you than you're willing to admit, Mikhail Mikhailovich Denisov. I can see it. Why can't you?"

His gaze was bleak. "Imperfect machinery."

"We can only work with what we're given, but that doesn't mean hope is abandoned."

He growled a laugh. "Hope."

"A fragile thing, to be sure," she acknowledged. "But that's why I study different cultures. Always a hope that we'll survive. That we may, in truth, evolve into something better."

Yet they both seemed to understand that there'd be no time for evolution. All they had was that moment—the two of them, in his cabin, waiting for the morning and its promise of bloodshed.

Then he pressed his lips to hers, for words and thoughts of tomorrow were imperfect and clumsy. Bodies could speak with much more eloquence.

Chapter Thirteen

_____

FOR THE SECOND time in as many days, Daphne woke in the protective shelter of Mikhail's arms. He was solid and warm all around her, covered with acres of muscle. She inhaled his now-familiar scent of male flesh and hot metal. His weight was substantial but not crushing. Mostly, she realized, because he carefully kept his body angled so he didn't lie fully atop her.

Her mind drifted back to last night. Their kisses had grown more demanding, their hungers building, until they'd made love, using every surface in his quarters. It had been as good between them as it had been in the cupola. Better. For they knew the ways of each other now, what their bodies craved, and how to satisfy those cravings. As if they had developed an instinct for each other.

She ought to feel fragile and tiny, lying beside him, feeling against her own body the vast differences between them. She had no telumium implants to make her big and strong. Yet there was something within him that shored up her own strength. A belief in herself. For all the mistrust she'd cultivated between them, they'd actually grown more certain of each other. Last night, she'd tasted it in his kisses, in the way they'd made love with rough, confident urgency, each assured in themselves and each other.

Opening her eyes fully, she studied him in the pre-dawn light. He still slept, his full lips slightly parted. But sleep didn't soften him. A collection of sharp contours—cheekbones, nose, jaw—that outrageous crest of hair, and the rows of rings along his ears. Everything he could have done to himself to brand himself an outsider, he'd done. She knew the why of it now. The permanent exile he'd assigned himself, not just in distance, but in his heart.

Except she'd felt him drawing closer. Their bodies, yes—he had filled her to her utmost, and she still felt a pleasant soreness hours later. Yet there had been more. He'd revealed hidden parts of himself, his darkest thoughts and deeds. But if he'd thought to scare her away or repel her . . . he'd much to learn.

There wouldn't be any more time to learn anything. Every minute brought them closer to al-Rahim's compound, and to battle.

At the thought of what was to come, she shifted slightly. Mikhail's eyes immediately opened, sharp with full wakefulness. She tried to smile at him. He didn't return the smile, his gaze somber, and leaned down and kissed her, his fingers tangling in her hair. When he moved back, she felt his reluctance, and she resisted the impulse to grab him and pull him close. They couldn't pretend that this was just another morning.

"I'll have some breakfast brought," he said, voice gravelly.

"I couldn't possibly eat." She pressed her hand to her stomach, already fluttering with anxiety.

"Make yourself."

She bristled at his command, though she knew his intentions were good. Any words she had of complaint died, however, when he got up naked from the bed and stretched. In the cupola, and in the light of the dimmed lanterns last night, she hadn't seen him fully nude, and the sight of him now—telumium gleaming on his shoulder, body solid with ridged muscle, his cock, impressive even at rest—nearly made her forget her trepidation about the upcoming battle. He may have been created to be a weapon of war, but she'd never seen anything or anyone so beautiful.

Catching her staring, he finally smiled, that audacious grin of his. Utterly unconcerned with modesty—he might have been preening, in truth—he crossed his cabin and headed into the water closet. Seeing his naked body in motion, she appreciated his lack of shyness.

They took turns using the water closet and washing up. Then it was time to get dressed, making themselves ready for the day. After Daphne had pulled on her clothing, a crewman delivered a tray, utterly indifferent to the fact that she was in Mikhail's cabin. Once the crewman left, she forced herself to eat a roll and cheese, chasing it with a cup of bracing coffee. Even though she'd never been in battle before, she understood that growing faint from hunger in the middle of it would be a disaster.

Mikhail ate three loaves of bread, a whole roast chicken, and two nectarines. As he did so, he finished dressing and then engaged in the extensive process of arming himself. Not just his ether pistol on his thigh, but an ether rifle holstered on his back and a bandolier of plasma grenades. His actions were quick, practiced.

She started to tuck her revolver into her belt.

"Use this." He tossed her another belt, which held an ether pistol, two extra ether tanks, and pouches of ammunition.

She buckled the belt around her hips. "I've never shot one of these before."

"Works the same as a normal gun, but the kick can knock you on your arse. Whenever you fire, keep your legs braced, your breathing steady, and make sure to replace the tanks after twenty bullets, or you won't get the same power."

"I'll try to remember all that," she answered, wry. "Though I might be too busy recalling all your instructions to actually shoot someone."

Suddenly, he was in front of her, his expression severe. His large hands cupped her shoulders. "Shoot anyone who crosses your path, anyone who looks threatening. No hesitation. No uncertainty. Be as cold as the fucking tundra, and stay alive."

The intensity of his gaze and words made her heart seize. "You do the same."

He stared at her for a moment, then kissed her. Hard. She returned the kiss just as hard.

Such a painful pleasure, this moment. It had taken thousands of miles and a vault filled with deadly traps and negotiations with ruthless warlords, and here they were, she and Mikhail, as they were meant to be. But only for a short while.

She'd had one mission: to get her parents back. And she'd done everything, used every trick, to make sure she succeeded. But there were no more tricks. No more hiding. Not from him, or her heart.

Courage. She needed it now, more than ever.

A tap sounded at the door. "Captain," Levkov said.

She and Mikhail broke apart. The time for battle was here.

"I HATE WAITING," Mikhail grumbled.

Daphne, standing beside him on the forecastle, raised a brow. "I'm not an encyclopedia of military strategy, but isn't waiting rather important?"

He scowled, bracing his hands on the rail. The sky continued to shift, lighter and lighter, with the approach of morning.

"It's necessary," he conceded. "Doesn't mean I have to like it. At the naval academy, I'd been upbraided several times for rushing into the thick of a conflict, rather than holding back and waiting for the exact right moment to launch my own attack."

"Seems an unwise tactic," she said.

"Took me a while to learn that, but I did. I overcame my instinctive desire to dive into the heat of battle. A hasty captain puts not just himself in danger, but his ship and his crew." He rubbed the heel of his hand against his chest. "Harder to overcome that impulse after my telumium implants."

"But you did."

"For the sake of survival and strategy."

"Not much longer now," Levkov said, also standing nearby.

The *Bielyi Voron* was hidden behind one of the mountain ridges encircling al-Rahim's compound. The ship was flying extremely low—barely twenty feet off the ground—to ensure it remained hidden. Mikhail had memorized the detailed map Khalida had drawn yesterday, and though he couldn't see beyond the ridge, he knew what he'd find on the other side.

Al-Rahim's compound was a collection of buildings surrounded by a thick wall, topped with gun turrets and guards patrolling the parapets. A heavy central gate was the only way in or out. The compound itself lay in a plain, with another ridge running at a diagonal. Just as Mikhail's ship was hidden behind one of the mountain crests, so Olevski and the French rogue had their ships tucked behind a distant ridge, out of sight from anyone foolish enough to try to attack the compound, thinking it defended only by guns and men, not airships. But both Mikhail and Khalida were counting on that.

They'd planned their strategy well, yet it meant biding his time, being unable to make the first move.

He could hear the guards patrolling the perimeter of the compound, unaware of the attack moments away from happening. They only expected the arrival of Mikhail's airship, for what was supposed to be Daphne's delivery of a ransom.

"What is it?" she asked, when he turned away from the prow.

"They're coming. I can hear them." The sound was faint, but he'd picked it up long before the origin of the noise would become evident.

Her eyes widened as she finally heard it, too. And then, suddenly, gyrocopters sped past the airship, flowing around it like a tide. The *zawbaahs* resembled low, three-wheeled vehicles, with canvas stretched over a wooden frame, and four blades spinning atop the craft. Ether-powered guns were mounted on the front of each *zawbaah*. Robed men and women piloted the gyrocopters, their eyes shielded by goggles, and as they swept around the airship, all the pilots raised their fists in salute. Mikhail, Daphne, and the rest of the *Bielyi Voron*'s crew lifted their hands in response.

The gyrocopters raced over the crest of the ridge and then down into the plain, heading straight at al-Rahim's compound. As they did, thunder sounded from the ground. Riders mounted on horses galloped along the same path as the *zawbaahs* toward the compound, their animals churning up dust as they raced. Khalida was one of their number, and as she and her warriors stormed toward al-Rahim's fortress, she and her band lifted their voices in an ululating battle cry. They rode and shot their rifles without breaking stride, a flawless unity of human, animal, and technology.

It was too soon for the *Bielyi Voron* to make its appearance, but Mikhail's hearing allowed him to know everything that happened beyond their cover.

"Khalida and her warriors are firing on the compound," he narrated for Daphne and Levkov. "The guards are shooting back. Al-Rahim's men are massing along the parapets. There," he said, hearing several sharp whines. "Khalida's snipers were able to position themselves on the ridge closer to the compound without anyone seeing them. Now they're using their ether *jezails* to pick off guards, and the guards can't return fire, because they're too far away."

As he narrated, Daphne stood up on her tiptoes, as if she could strain to see what was happening. "Now?" she demanded.

"Not yet."

Then came the low double drone that he'd been anticipating. Olevski and the French Man O' War were coming out of hiding, their airships finally appearing to repel what they must have thought was merely a raid by Khalida. But they had no idea with whom she was allied. The sounds of more gunfire erupted across the plain, including the *rat-a-tat* of the airships' Gatling guns.

"Now!" Mikhail commanded.

At once, the *Bielyi Voron* rose up over the ridge.

A scene of chaos unfolded below: Khalida and her fighters against the guards protecting al-Rahim's compound, and the two enemy airships hovering above everything, unleashing their arsenals against the tribal warriors. The *Bielyi Voron* raced toward the other airships, its crew unleashing a barrage from ether cannons and ether rifles.

Neither Olevski's ship, the *Chyornyi Golub*, nor the French ship expected Mikhail. The two airships wheeled around in confusion, both scrambling to make sense of this new, unexpected foe.

"Full engagement, Levkov," Mikhail shouted at his first mate.

"Aye, Captain."

Daphne was already running along the deck of the ship with him, both heading for the jolly boat. She didn't look afraid—only determined. Heat and admiration spread through him at the sight.

They hurried below, and down through the ship, until they reached the cargo bay. Herrera waited by the release lever.

Mikhail put his hands on her shoulders as she headed toward the jolly boat, and turned her around. She stared up at him, confused and impatient.

"I can do the assault with one of my men," he said. "You'll stay behind here, on the ship."

She scowled at him. "Hide, you mean?" She made a sound of aggravation. "Those are *my* parents down there. This mission is *mine*." Her mouth firmed. "Those sapphires paid for my right to go into battle, and I'm determined to get my money's worth."

He resisted the impulse to grin. Much as he wanted her safe, he couldn't fault her logic, or deny her courage.

Instead, he nodded, and took the tiller, while Daphne

positioned herself at the front of the boat. Per Mikhail's instructions, Herrera had set up a harpoon gun at the stern. The moment that Mikhail and Daphne had harnessed themselves in, and he'd given Herrera the signal, the cargo doors opened. The jolly boat plunged downward. Into the heat of battle.

Mikhail steered the small ship as Daphne hefted her rifle and provided covering fire. They passed over Khalida and her warriors engaged in ground skirmishes, and flew past the *zabwaahs* as the gyrocopters combated gun turrets and guards shooting from atop the bulwarks. The flying craft couldn't gain headway against the barrage and penetrate into the fortress. As much as Khalida's warriors fought on the ground, they couldn't breach the compound's gate. It remained firmly closed to their assault.

Daphne continued to fire as Mikhail guided the jolly boat over the compound's walls, bullets whizzing all around them. Within the walls of the fortress were numerous buildings, some no more than sheds, others serving as stables or storage, with one larger structure adorned by columns and domes. This had to be al-Rahim's residence.

"I don't know where my parents and their assistants are being kept!" Daphne shouted above the chaos.

"Only one way to find out." And it wasn't from the air. The guards on the ramparts were too preoccupied with the gyrocopters to pay much attention to a lightly-armed boat. Mikhail banked the jolly boat sharply, then brought the craft down.

He barely had time to unstrap his harness and leap out of the boat before the guards suddenly realized that the jolly boat presented a very real threat. The enemy attacked. After all the waiting and pent-up frustration, it was a relief to unleash the fight within. His movements were all instinct. Yet throughout his continuing battles, he never lost sight of Daphne. She aimed the harpoon gun, then fired. The harpoon shot into the heavy door. The explosive mounted to the front of the harpoon detonated.

The force of the explosion knocked everyone off their feet—including Mikhail and Daphne. He lurched upright. Panic cut through him when he saw her lying on the bottom of the jolly boat. He'd never run faster as he sped to her. Carefully, he picked her up.

She blinked, slightly dazed. He scowled when he saw the thin trickle of blood running down from her forehead.

"Goddamn it, you're hurt."

She touched her fingertips to the wound. "Can't even feel it. The gate . . ."

They both turned to see that the gate had been knocked down, and Khalida and her warriors now flooded the interior of the compound. The guards turned their attention to this threat, and everywhere was the ring of steel against steel and the whine of gunfire. On horseback, scimitar in hand, Khalida herself looked like the incarnation of war, slashing mercilessly at anyone who dared approach her. She shouted encouragement at her warriors, who yelled back their willingness to fight.

There was still no sign of al-Rahim, but Mikhail had no doubt the warlord would make an appearance soon.

Sounds of gunfire thundered overhead—sounds he recognized. Looking up, Mikhail saw the *Bielyi Voron* engaged in heavy combat with the two Man O' War ships. The French airship was smaller than Mikhail's, but Olevski's *Chyornyi Golub* was the same class, with the same number of guns. An even match—had they been fighting only each other. Yet the *Bielyi Voron* had not one but two opponents. Leaving Mikhail and Daphne very little time to find and free her parents before they had to get back to the ship.

Moving deeper into the compound, with the fight all around them, they searched for her mother and father.

Al-Zaman suddenly stumbled out from the swirling chaos. Seeing them, the emissary's face twisted with rage.

"Where are my parents?" Daphne demanded.

Al-Zaman sneered. "It does not matter."

Mikhail took a threatening step forward. "Tell me where they are."

The emissary attempted a look of defiance, but gave himself away when his gaze flicked toward the main building.

Both Mikhail and Daphne ran toward the palace.

"Your haste is useless," al-Zaman shouted after them. "Their throats will be already cut by the time you reach them."

Neither Mikhail nor Daphne responded. They pushed their way through the battle as it swept deeper and deeper into the compound. Any men who got in his way were knocked aside like dolls. He breached the interior of the main building. It was only after he ran through a courtyard and then down several corridors that he realized Daphne was no longer with him. Somewhere along the way, she'd disappeared.

THE CONFUSION HAD spread into the main building, and she fought to keep with Mikhail as servants and others fled. It was like swimming upstream, the current of humanity pushing against her.

When the first burst of panicked people ebbed, she found herself lost in a maze of hallways. Mikhail was nowhere to be found.

Daphne hadn't taken more than a handful of steps before al-Zaman blocked her path. The veneer of affability he'd worn in Medinat al-Kadib had crumbled away, revealing the rot of hatred beneath. He pointed a revolver at her, and she realized that her own gun had been knocked out of her hand when she'd been thrown by the explosion. *Hell.*

She could try to call to Mikhail for help, but that might delay him from reaching her parents in time. No, she had to face al-Zaman on her own.

Talking the emissary out of shooting her was impossible. Hatred blazed in his eyes. She had to act—quickly.

Strong and fast, she reminded herself. Any missteps meant her death.

With her left hand, she grabbed the wrist of his gun hand. At the same time, she used her other hand to grip the barrel of the gun and push it back toward him. The revolver now faced al-Zaman, his wrist completely twisted, and he grimaced in pain and fury. She covered his trigger finger with her own.

They struggled for the gun. She prayed he would be smart and simply let go, but he refused. Her heels slid on the floor, fighting for balance. She couldn't let him regain control of the revolver.

Suddenly, there was a muffled bang. Al-Zaman's eyes went wide. Color drained from his face, and his hand slackened on the gun. He stumbled backward. Fell. Daphne stood with the revolver in her hand, gazing down at him as he sprawled on the ground. A red stain spread across his chest. He gaped up at her. Then his eyes turned glassy and his head lolled to the side.

She stared at the weapon in her hand. A brief wave of nausea rolled over her. She'd actually killed someone. Looked him in the eyes and pulled the trigger, then watched as he died. *God.*

The sickness passed quickly. This wasn't just combat, but a war. For her life, for her parents' lives. For Mikhail.

Mikhail. She raced down a corridor in search of him, without giving al-Zaman another thought.

The further she got into the building, the more she had quick impressions of additional guards running here and there, many fighting with Khalida's warriors. Servants hid beneath tables and behind silken wall hangings. The palace itself looked sumptuous, covered in mosaics and filled with potted palms, but she barely noted any of this. She needed to find Mikhail, and her parents.

As she hurried down another corridor, she just caught sight of him turning a corner, fighting deeper into the building. She sped after him. Even farther ahead were two giant guards, heading toward the wing of the palace where her parents must be kept. They held massive scimitars. These had to be the men al-Zaman had sent to kill her mother and father.

The guards reached a door at the end of a corridor, where two more men stood sentry, but before they could open it, Mikhail launched himself at them. He threw one of the guards against a wall. The man slammed into the tile-covered surface, then slumped to the ground. He struggled to rise, but Mikhail planted a fist in the guard's face. The man's head snapped back and he was instantly unconscious.

The second guard finished entering the combination into the lock on the door. Before Mikhail could grab him, Daphne aimed al-Zaman's gun and fired. The guard howled, clutching at his wounded shoulder. His yowls of pain stopped, however, when Mikhail punched him into insensibility.

He fought against the two remaining sentries, knocking their drawn swords from their hands. Spinning, he planted a kick right in the middle of a sentry's chest. Gasping for air, the man flew backward. He also slammed into a wall, then fell to the ground, dazed. The other sentry stared at Mikhail for a moment before running off with a panicked yelp.

Daphne dashed up to Mikhail, who was standing

beside the door. He pushed it open, and they both stepped into the chamber.

She recognized the room from the cinemagraph, but her gaze moved quickly past the details of the chamber. Where were her parents? The chamber seemed empty. Was this another of al-Zaman's cruel tricks?

"Mama?" she called. "Papa?"

Figures darted out from behind a wall hanging, straight at her. Mikhail instantly took a defensive posture, ready to unleash an attack. She hadn't words to tell him it was all right. Instead, the two figures embraced her, and he dropped his fists.

"Daphne!" her mother cried.

"My God," her father choked, "it's really you? Here?"

She couldn't speak. Instead, she clutched her parents close as they hugged her back. Tears leapt into her eyes. They seemed a little thinner, but everything else about them was familiar, from her father's white-and-ginger beard to the little smile creases bracketing her mother's mouth. Safe. They were safe.

From the corner of her eye, she saw her parents' assistants come out from their places of hiding.

"You shouldn't have come," her father said gruffly, pulling back a little. "Too dangerous."

"I couldn't leave you here, Papa." Daphne's tight throat made talking difficult. "And I had some assistance."

She glanced at Mikhail, and caught, very briefly, a look of bittersweet longing on his face as she held tight to her parents. The expression disappeared quickly, replaced by the sangfroid of a battle-hardened warrior.

Her father's gingery eyebrows climbed up toward his forehead, and her mother made a small, shocked sound. Daphne almost laughed. She'd forgotten how his extraordinary appearance could startle people.

"Mama, Papa, this is Captain Mikhail Mikhailovich Denisov. Mikhail, this is Edgar and Adelaide Carlisle." She felt a little ridiculous, making formal introductions in the middle of this madness, but she *was* English.

Both her parents mumbled stunned greetings as Mikhail tipped his head. Her mother's gaze strayed to the glimpse of telumium beneath Mikhail's waistcoat. "A Man O' War? I know our captivity has kept us a little out of current events, but are the Russians now our allies?"

Her father stared at Mikhail's outrageous hair, the rings in his ears, and his elaborately adorned and modified coat. "I think Captain Denisov is a rogue, my dear."

"I'm only allied with your daughter, Mrs. Carlisle," Mikhail answered.

"Oh . . ." her mother murmured, looking even more astonished. She glanced at Daphne with concern. "Is that . . . wise?"

Despite her joy at being reunited with her parents, she felt immediately indignant on Mikhail's behalf. "He's the reason why we're here now, freeing you."

"I'm sure it's a long and fascinating tale." Her father winced as the building shook from the sounds of gunfire and explosions. "Perhaps you can recount it later. Much later."

Mikhail was all business. "Everyone to the jolly boat. Now." He ushered everybody out of the chamber, including her parents. Their steps were cautious, but gradually grew in confidence as they realized that no one was going to stop them from leaving.

The last to leave the room, Daphne stood in front of Mikhail, and placed her hand on his forearm. She felt the burn of grateful tears as she gazed up at him.

His expression remained impassive. "It's not over yet."

"I know," she replied. "But even this is a gift."

Before he could answer, another explosion rattled the building—the sound of airships engaged in furious combat. He was right: many more obstacles lay ahead. No time for sighs of relief.

Together, she and Mikhail ran from the chamber and back into battle.

Chapter Fourteen

MIKHAIL NEVER ALLOWED himself a sense of triumph until the final shot had been fired. He'd seen too many victories unexpectedly collapse.

As Daphne, her parents, and their assistants kept pace behind him, running through the corridors of al-Rahim's palace, Mikhail kept vigilant, his thoughts and body focused on combat. He'd felt a stirring of happiness seeing Daphne's joy at being reunited with her parents, but he'd ruthlessly suppressed it. Complacency would get them all killed. And to see her have what he never could only roused his own longing. There'd be no tearful reunions with his family.

Guards charged at them from behind columns and doorways. But he beat them back without mercy. And when any of al-Rahim's men aimed guns in their direction, Mikhail dropped them with single blasts from his ether pistol.

He glanced back to see Daphne shepherding the freed captives. While some of them, including her parents, looked utterly terrified by all the violence and anarchy around them, her expression was determined, focused. Betraying not a hint of fear. Only fortitude.

Goddamn it, but she made him proud.

As he ran, he saw al-Zaman's body lying on the ground.

"He wasn't particularly enthusiastic about our plans to free my parents," Daphne said.

Mikhail smiled grimly to himself. His *professorsha* was as fierce in battle as she was with her wits.

With Mikhail in the lead, they burst out of al-Rahim's palace to spectacles of pure bedlam. Fighting warriors filled every open space, some on horseback, some on foot, and even a daring gyrocopter pilot zooming down to take on an enemy armed with a Gatling gun. All of this chaos lay between them and the jolly boat. Mikhail was just glad that the boat was still there.

Looking up, he saw the *Bielyi Voron* bravely holding its own against the two enemy airships. The sky was filled with gray smoke, as though made of steel. Yet the *Bielyi Voron* didn't seem to have sustained much damage. Levkov might be a stubborn and opinionated bastard, but he was a damned genius when it came to commanding a ship in combat.

"Everyone to the boat!" Mikhail roared to his charges.

Again, he served as the lead, carving a path through the madness to reach the vessel. He knocked aside attacking enemies without breaking stride.

"Mikhail!" Daphne nodded toward one side of the open yard.

He didn't slow his pace, but still admired the sight. Khalida fought against a bearded man with a scar across one eye. Not only did the man have sumptuous robes, but he held two elaborately ornamented scimitars, one in each hand, and used them like a whirlwind against Khalida, who also held two swords. Though Mikhail had never actually clapped eyes on the man, he recognized him at once: al-Rahim.

The two warlords battled each other on foot, rage blazing the air between them. Though Mikhail had seen more than his share of armed combat, he'd never seen two people fight each other with such hatred, both of them baring their teeth as they struck steel against steel.

"Should we help her?" Daphne asked. "Wouldn't mind having a go at him myself."

"It's their battle," he answered, though part of him wanted to gut al-Rahim from throat to belly simply for putting Daphne and her family through such hell.

While she looked a bit disappointed that she couldn't join the fight against al-Rahim, she hurried on, and helped her parents and their assistants into the jolly boat. Mikhail leapt in, threw Daphne his ether rifle, and took the tiller. Once everyone had been secured, he brought the vessel straight up into the air. Yelps of astonishment rose up from the Carlisles and their assistants, but he kept his focus on dodging enemy gunfire and making sure that Daphne was unharmed. Using his ether rifle, she continued to shoot back at anyone who dared fire on them.

As the jolly boat climbed higher into the air, the sounds of triumphant ululation rose up from below. Glancing down, he saw Khalida standing over the body of al-Rahim, her swords lifted in victory. She caught Mikhail and Daphne watching her, and gave another long, piercing cry of triumph. Daphne flawlessly returned the cry, as did her parents.

Despite al-Rahim's death, the conflict was far from over.

Someone on *Bielyi Voron* must have seen the approaching jolly boat, because the ship beat a slight retreat from fighting the other airships, allowing the smaller vessel room to come closer. Mikhail brought the boat up into the *Bielyi Voron*'s cargo bay, and the doors swung shut beneath them.

"Stay below decks," he commanded his newest passengers. Everyone looked too stunned to argue. Except, as Mikhail headed topside, Daphne followed, still holding the ether rifle.

He rounded on her.

She spoke before he could. "If you think I'm going to cower in my cabin while you're up there risking your goddamn life," she said hotly, lifting her chin, "then you haven't been paying attention."

He swore, but she didn't blink. A shudder rattled the ship. Capable as Levkov was, the *Bielyi Voron* was still Mikhail's, and no one commanded her better in combat than he did. He had to get topside. And Daphne was determined to join him there.

Much as he wanted her safe, one of the things he

respected so deeply about her was her strength of will. Locking her in her cabin would only deny a part of her he admired.

"Keep low," he said quickly, "fire at anyone who looks threatening, and for God's sake, don't try to take on either of the Man O' Wars."

A corner of her mouth lifted. "There's only one Man O' War I'd ever take on."

He kissed her, quick and hard. Seemed the only fitting response. She kissed him back with bruising force. Neither of them seemed to care that the passageways were filled with crew members. All that mattered at that moment was the feel of each other, their shared heat and strength. But the kiss had to be brief, and they broke apart as the ship shook again.

Together, they leapt up the companionway, emerging onto the top deck, and the elegant brutality of aerial combat.

DAPHNE COUGHED AS smoke wreathed the deck of the airship. Crew members were everywhere, shooting ether cannons at the two other ships. She felt the concussion of the ether cannons thundering in her chest. Shouts and explosions, the whine of gunfire, and the world spinning as the three airships dove and wheeled in combat. She had never known anything like this.

She was grateful she'd gained her air legs as she staggered after Mikhail. It felt as though she'd fallen into a bellicose dream, where flight and combat interlaced. Half a mile below stretched the desert, dotted with the figures of Khalida's and al-Rahim's warriors still fighting, and all around her was the sky, scented by cordite, streaked with smoke.

The enemy ships had positioned themselves on both sides of the *Bielyi Voron*, so the ship was taking fire from all angles. It seemed impossible that they could survive such bombardment.

Levkov looked relieved when Mikhail appeared beside him. "Doing what I can, Captain, but two against one doesn't make for a nice dinner party."

"Then we disinvite one of the guests," Mikhail answered. "Target the French ship. Give it everything."

Though it made little sense to her that Mikhail would want to go after the smaller and less threatening of the two enemy airships—particularly given his hatred of Olevski—Levkov seemed to understand his strategy. "Aye, Captain," he said, then hurried off to spread the word to the crew.

Once the message reached the crew, the ship spun about to face the French airship. Every cannon and ether gun on board the *Bielyi Voron* was unleashed. The enemy ship shuddered and quaked, pieces of its hull shattering and crew falling to the deck, wounded. In response, the French airship began to retreat, drawing closer to Olevski's ship as if seeking protection.

"If the French Man O' War does that," she said above the sound of gunfire, "he'll crowd Olevski. Give him no way to maneuver." Her eyes widened as she understood the strategy.

"We get you some telumium implants," Mikhail answered with a ferocious grin, "you might make a damned fine airship captain."

Indeed, as the French ship tried to find cover, it nearly collided with the Russian airship. Several moments passed as the two vessels awkwardly attempted to position themselves. Olevski seemed to want to bring his ship around to launch a broadside against the *Bielyi Voron*, but the French ship kept getting in the way.

"Bring us closer to the *Chyornyi Golub*," Mikhail roared to the helmsman. He turned to other crew members. "Golovkin, Cheng, Simonov, Alvarez—grappling hooks on the starboard side!"

As the ship flew nearer to the Russian ship, four of the *Bielyi Voron*'s crew members appeared at the rail, each carrying gramophone-sized devices. The brass-cased devices were open on one side, and she could just make out what looked like a steel claw within. A small tetrol-powered engine was attached to each device, as well. The crew clamped the devices onto the rail, with the open side facing outward.

She held her breath as the *Bielyi Voron* drew up only thirty feet from the side of the Russian ship. At this distance, she could see the battle-enraged faces of the other ship's crew, and Olevski striding up and down the deck, bellowing orders.

"Fire!" Mikhail commanded.

The four crewmen pulled handles on the side of the devices fixed to the rails. Four hooks shot from the devices, with stout iron chains attached to them. The hooks latched onto the rail of the enemy ship. Golovkin, Cheng, Simonov, and Alvarez then flipped levers on the engines, and winches inside the devices began to draw in the chains and their attached hooks. The grappling devices pulled the two airships ever closer together, shortening the distance foot by foot.

Both crews massed at the railings, everyone bristling with weapons of all varieties, from cutlasses to revolvers to ether pistols. Though a crewman on the enemy ship worked frantically to saw at the chains binding the two airships, he couldn't work fast enough. The distance continued to narrow. Twenty five feet, twenty.

Mikhail jumped up onto the rail. In each hand, he held a long, wicked sword. His face was a mask of determined fury, his hate-filled gaze fixed solely on Olevski, who glared back with equal loathing. A distance of over fifteen feet separated the ships. Then Mikhail leapt, and Daphne forgot how to breathe.

He seemed suspended in the air, half a mile above the ground, for an eternity. Yet he jumped over the heads and raised weapons of Olevski's crew. Mikhail landed in a crouch right in front of Olevski. For a moment, the two Man O' Wars simply stared at each other. And then they bellowed in rage and charged each other.

As the two ships continued to draw closer, Mikhail and Olevski launched into furious combat. They moved with superhuman speed and strength, their blades moving so quickly as to be steel blurs carving through the air. Their swords clashed together with enough force to draw sparks.

The hulls of the airships ground together as the grappling hooks reeled the Russian ship close. The massed crew members stood at the rail, swinging blades and shooting guns, each struggling to board the others' ship. Daphne stood just behind this melee, trying to see the progress of Mikhail's fight with his most hated enemy. Goddamn it, she *needed* to do something.

A roar rose up from Mikhail's crew as they gained the upper hand, surging over the rail to board the enemy ship. The fight continued onto the upper deck of the Russian airship, rogue crew against rogue crew. But the crew of the *Bielyi Voron* seemed to fight as a cohesive unit rather than in a disorganized jumble. Two of the enemy crew had enough organization to realize that the main threat came from Mikhail, and aimed their ether guns at him.

Instinct took over. Daphne stood atop the railing, getting above the fight. From her vantage, she clearly saw two of the enemy crewmen preparing to shoot Mikhail. She lifted her rifle, taking aim. Despite the chaos around her, she made sure her breathing stayed level. Then squeezed the trigger. She turned and fired on the other gunman. Both men went down instantly.

If Mikhail noticed, he gave no sign. He fought against Olevski with a terrifying viciousness. Cuts covered the faces, arms, and hands of both Man O' Wars, but neither seemed to show any sign of slowing down. Mikhail thrust one of his swords at Olevski, and the other Man O' War slipped aside a split second before getting skewered. But the sword was jammed hard into the wooden deck.

Rather than try to wrest it out, Mikhail left it. Mikhail kicked one of Olevski's hands, and his foe's sword flew from his grasp. Now he and Olevski faced each other with one blade each.

Roaring, they rushed each other again. Their swords collided. And shattered from the force of the strike. Neither Man O' War seemed to care that they were now both unarmed. They continued to fight, throwing punches so hard that when their fists connected with the deck or bulwarks, wood shattered into splinters.

She leapt down from the rail, joining Mikhail's crew pushing further onto the enemy ship. She tried to aim her ether rifle at Olevski, hoping at least to wound him. But as she lined him up in her sights, someone grabbed her from behind, his arms wrapping around her and squeezing the rifle from her grip. She struggled against him, twisting and kicking.

"Heard Denisov had himself a little English piece." The crewman's breath was hot and foul in her ear. "You wouldn't turn my head, but I could have some fun with you, and let him watch."

Mikhail, seeing her struggle, tried to break away from Olevski to come to her aid. But the other Man O' War blocked his path. Olevski seemed to taunt Mikhail, glancing over his shoulder at her and sneering, as though her presence weakened Mikhail.

No—she wouldn't let herself be a liability. She shoved her feet against the deck, pushing against her attacker. She managed to wriggle enough space between them to lash backward, catching him in the eye with her thumb.

The man released her at once, crying out. She spun around. With all her might, she punched him in his jaw.

The crewman stumbled backward, toward the rail. This side of the enemy airship was not hooked to the *Bielyi Voron*. The only thing that lay beyond the rail was open air. The crewman hit the rail, throwing off his balance. His eyes widened in horror as he toppled over the railing.

His scream faded as he fell the half mile to the ground.

She refused to go to the railing to look. It was enough that the man's threats wouldn't come to pass. Whirling around, she searched for Mikhail. It didn't take long to find him.

The battle between him and Olevski raged on.

RELIEF POURED THROUGH Mikhail as the crewman assaulting Daphne fell to his death. It would've been more satisfying if he'd been able to kill the bastard himself, but he was damned impressed by her, sending that son of a bitch to his doom all on her own. For now, she was safe.

He, however, wasn't. Mikhail had never been so injured, his every bone and muscle aching with each thrown punch, each absorbed blow. But he wouldn't let up. Either he or Olevski had to die today.

Olevski swung at Mikhail, who ducked the attack. "Blaming me. But the blame's on you, too. You were eager for that gold. Panting for it."

"Carry that like an anchor around my neck." He slammed a boot into Olevski's thigh, causing him to stagger. "Same way I blame myself for ever introducing you to my family. For letting them love you. But the gun pointed at my head—that was your doing. Cost us time. Cost us everything." He swung a fist, connecting with Olevski's jaw. It made a satisfying crack.

"Damn fool." Olevski spat blood and a tooth onto the deck. "Rushing into a fight when I had you cornered. I should still be in the navy. Be a rich admiral. Married to your sister and carving the roast for the Denisov Christmas dinner." His bloodstained mouth curled. "Blame's all yours, Mikhail Mikhailovich. The damn thief of my life."

They threw themselves at each other again, grappling and punching. Back at the Admiralty, during training, Man O' Wars had faced each other in the gymnasium, but they'd never gone full out like this. With the intent to kill. Olevski pushed Mikhail against the bulkhead of the pilot house, then locked his forearm across his neck, trying to crush his windpipe. Mikhail shoved his knee into Olevski's stomach, throwing him back.

"I'll kill you," Olevski vowed hoarsely, "kill your crew. Break your ship into scrap. Sell that Englishwoman to al-Rahim—"

"Al-Rahim's dead."

Olevski shrugged, unconcerned over the death of his employer. "Plenty of warlords from here to Oceania. Rich warlords who'll pay good money for her. It won't be a total loss of profit for me."

Smoke-colored fury clouded Mikhail's eyes. Rage unlike anything he'd ever felt turned his veins to fire.

Olevski could say anything he wanted about Mikhail, but *no one* threatened Daphne.

The ship juddered from all the damage it had taken from the *Bielyi Voron*'s ether cannons. A thick metal support beam, jagged at one end, swung loose from where it had held up an ether tank.

Mikhail raced toward the beam.

Olevski saw his intent, and tried to beat him to the thick piece of metal. But Mikhail was faster, motivated by far more than revenge or greed.

Snarling, he snapped the beam free. He swung around to face Olevski. His enemy pointed an ether rifle at his face. If Mikhail took a step, Olevski would shoot. A standoff.

Olevski fired. Mikhail rolled under the shot, narrowly avoiding it. He leapt up and swung the beam against the rifle, and the gun broke apart in Olevski's hands.

Wasting no time, Mikhail slammed his boot into Olevski's knee. The other Man O' War fell to the deck.

Mikhail lunged.

The jagged metal slammed into Olevski's chest, impaling him. Mikhail shoved hard, and the beam went all the way through, emerging from Olevski's back. Blood covered the metal as Mikhail, roaring, plunged the beam into the deck, pinning Olevski to his ship.

Mikhail stepped back, watching as Olevski clawed at the metal sticking up from his chest.

"Changes nothing," Olevski wheezed. "Never have . . . your family back. Always be . . . an outcast. Even to . . .

her . . ." His glassy gaze slid toward Daphne, who looked on grimly.

Saying nothing, Mikhail watched as Olevski's blood dripped down the beam, forming a large, dark pool on the deck. Olevski gave one final, rattling gasp. Then stilled.

The crew of Olevski's ship saw this. Panic spread like a disease, from one crewman to another. Without Olevski, they had no more source of ether. If they didn't have enough ether stored, the ship could crash in a matter of hours. In a rush, the crew sped below decks, pushing each other aside in their haste to get to the parachutes and sailcraft stored in the cargo bay.

Mikhail didn't notice or care. He only knew that Daphne was suddenly beside him, her arm wrapped around his waist. It stunned him how unstable his legs were—he, who seldom felt any pain, any weakness. But now he could barely find anything left to support his weight. Daphne did her best to keep him upright, though she struggled beneath his bulk. Levkov appeared on his other side, and with Daphne's help, they guided him toward the rail and back to his ship.

By the time he reached the rail, he had regained enough strength to walk on his own. He climbed over the rail without any assistance, then reached over and lifted Daphne across. The rest of his crew also leapt back over the rail . Some had been wounded, and were immediately taken down to the sick bay to be tended by Dr. Marlowe. Once everyone had gotten back on board the *Bielyi Voron*, the grappling hooks were disengaged. The two airships moved apart.

Members of Olevski's crew used parachutes and sailcraft to abandon ship, floating down to the ground like dead leaves shaken from an autumn tree. No one remained on the deck of the drifting *Chyornyi Golub*— except Olevski, who gazed up at the smoky sky with vacant, lifeless eyes.

The French airship lost no time in retreating. It came about quickly, then sped off toward the horizon.

"Should we pursue, Captain?" asked Levkov.

Mikhail glanced down at Daphne as she leaned her head against his chest, her arm around his waist, watching the lifeless airship float away like so much flotsam. She looked exhausted, with dried blood caked along her forehead, her hair falling out of its braid. Her gaze turned from the *Chyornyi Golub* to the shattered ruin of al-Rahim's compound below. With their leader dead, al-Rahim's tribe had surrendered to Khalida, and he was gratified to see that none of the surrendered fighters were being killed or hurt. But bodies from the fight littered the ground. It would take a long while for either tribe to fully recover.

He shook his head. "Let the Frenchman go. This battle is finally over."

INJURIES NEEDED TO be tended. Daphne had to spend a good thirty minutes with her parents, all of them reassuring one another that they were fine. She gave them as brief an account as possible of what had happened since their kidnapping, leaving out nearly everything between her and Mikhail. Fortunately, they didn't press her for details. She wasn't certain what she would tell them, anyway. They'd won this fight, yet everything remained as uncertain as a half-finished map. No way to know where the path led.

Once the situation on the *Bielyi Voron* had been settled, Daphne and Mikhail took the jolly boat back down to the scarred plain that held the broken walls and half-razed buildings of al-Rahim's compound.

Khalida met them outside the destroyed gate, a contingent of warriors flanking her. The warlord limped slightly, but there was no denying the triumph in her gaze.

"I had no idea that working with *ferengis* could be so advantageous." She held up the astrolabe. "This is mine again, as is this territory." She eyed the groups of people who had once followed al-Rahim. "We'll have more stability now."

"You aren't the only tribal leader in the area," Mikhail noted.

"Will there be more war?" asked Daphne.

Khalida lifted her gaze heavenward. "That is for destiny to decide."

"You're a stronger force than destiny," Daphne said. "And can do more for this region than fate ever could."

"Sounds as though you've got a plan," the warlord noted.

"She always does," Mikhail said.

Much as his words pleased her, Daphne continued, level. "Join forces with the other tribal leaders."

Khalida looked appalled. "Each tribe is unique. We are not some place like England or the United States where we pretend to be alike and ignore our differences."

"All you need is to present the *appearance* of a cohesive front to the *ferengi*—I mean, European factions," Daphne explained. For some time, she'd been pondering a solution to the unrest that plagued the region since the discovery of telumium. When the smoke cleared, there'd be more uncertainty. "If they think they'll have a united power block to contend with, they'll be less likely to cause trouble, and you and the people of the Peninsula won't be as vulnerable."

Raising a brow, Khalida asked, "But we won't actually form a coalition?"

"You can retain as much of your diversity and autonomy as you like. It's only to fool the Europeans."

"A deception," said Khalida.

The word made Daphne's cheeks heat. She couldn't exactly regret the lies she'd told, considering what they'd gotten her: her parents freed, the Man O' War beside her. Yet did she truly have him? Certainties gave way to more ambiguity. "Well—"

"I like it." The warlord grinned, and she turned to Mikhail. "Very devious, this one."

He smiled down at Daphne. "In the best way."

Chapter Fifteen

DAPHNE FELT A profound sense of disquiet to see her parents in Mikhail's quarters. It was as though they existed in two separate realms—the rogue Man O' War who had become her lover, and her parents with their achingly familiar faces and voices, their clothes and mannerisms. Not only that, but only hours earlier, she and Mikhail had made love atop the table where her parents now drank their tea. Daphne sat in a nearby chair, unsure where to look.

Afternoon sunlight poured through the bank of windows, and the sounds of the ship being repaired reverberated everywhere. In their way, the sounds were comforting. Reminding her that they had survived. Her parents and their assistants were alive. A kind of order had been restored to the region.

Yet she couldn't feel easy. She glanced over at Mikhail, who leaned against a far bulkhead, arms crossed over his chest, expression distant. Their time together was almost over, and the thought felt as though her heart was being slowly, slowly crushed within her chest by some unseen vise.

"We've been discussing taking university positions, your father and I," Daphne's mother said. "Getting out of the field."

"But you love being in the field," she protested.

Her father coughed. "We're not spry youths anymore. This . . . ordeal . . . has proved it, rather painfully. It might do us good to settle in one place for a while."

"King's College has been rather dogged in their pursuit of us," added her mother. She turned a pointed look at Daphne. "I daresay they'd welcome someone with your qualifications, too."

"I have a position at the Accademia. With a budget that allows me plenty of fieldwork of my own."

"I'm sure they value your presence there, darling," her father said quickly. "But we, that is, Adelaide and I, thought it might be best—"

"Safer—" her mother threw in.

Her father continued, "Yes, safer. While this dreadful Mechanical War continues, you might find it best to stay in England. Where you can be secure and protected."

Silent up until that point, Mikhail said tonelessly, "I can fly you part way there. It'll be faster and less dangerous than taking a seafaring ship. Or you could sail. It's little difference to me."

She stared at him. Ever since they'd returned from meeting with Khalida, he'd become more and more detached, until he seemed completely uninterested in her presence. Was this how it was to be, then, with the heat they'd shared turning to frost?

"Mama, Papa, perhaps you ought to take Captain Denisov up on his offer. The seas are dangerous, and his ship is fast."

"I couldn't help but notice that you made no reference to yourself, dearest," her mother noted. "You won't be coming with us to England. Will you find another way back to Florence?"

She took a breath. What she had to say wouldn't be well received—by anyone—but it had to be spoken. Rising up from her chair, she said, "I'm not returning to Florence, or the Accademia."

"Where will you go?" her father asked.

"Nowhere. I'm staying right here in Arabia."

Both her parents made sounds of shock, each sputtering about the danger of remaining in the area, even with Khalida's attempts to create stability.

Mikhail said nothing, but his crystal gaze burned her from across the stateroom. A muscle in his jaw tightened. She knew all the signs of his emotions now, his thoughts now. Even when he tried to keep them hidden, she knew.

"I've seen the effects of war here," she said. "There are countless people caught in the middle, and they're suffering. Hell," she went on, "all over the globe, the war's taking its toll. I can't bury myself in my studies and pretend that it's not happening. Maybe something can be done to make it better. Maybe I'm someone who can help."

"You can't play savior to these people," Mikhail said, voice like iron.

"I never claimed that I could," she fired back. "They didn't ask for my help, and they might not want it. But I can offer it, at least."

"But . . . you're only an anthropologist," her father protested. "They don't need you to analyze societal structures and write monographs."

"Yet I do know the warring sides." She strode to the window, but kept a distance between herself and Mikhail. Though the people moving around below looked very tiny from this height, she'd never mistake them for toys or dolls to be manipulated as she desired. They had their own needs, their own wants. They were not extensions of herself. All she could do was offer them her help, and, if they wanted it, do what she could.

"Perhaps better than the locals might," she went on. "I can suggest to Khalida and the other tribal leaders how to interact with Europeans to get the best possible results." She smiled ruefully. "Studying how societies function can be very useful in the middle of a war."

Her parents continued to protest her decision, but she did not try to answer their every objection.

Mikhail, in a voice so low only she could hear, said, "I'm not going to leave you here, *professorsha*."

She turned to him. There, beneath the frost in his eyes, she saw it. Genuine concern, and loss. They both knew what her answer meant. By her staying here, in this hotbed of political unrest, they'd never see each other again.

A web of fractures spread through her heart. It would take just the tiniest tap against it to shatter completely.

She'd always believed that the process of coming to care for someone would take months, or years. That there could be no true feeling between two people without the long passage of time. She couldn't tally the number of days she'd known Mikhail, only that—with his scoundrel's smile and wounded heart—he'd become as integral to her as sunlight. Her world would be very dark without him. Dark and cold.

She might be cold and alone here in Arabia, but she could try to make someone's life better, even if it wasn't her own.

"What could we have together?" she whispered. "Stolen moments in Palermo, in between my academic work and your life as a mercenary?" She shook her head. "It couldn't be enough."

"We'd make it enough," he said, low and fierce.

"For how long? Until we each wanted more, and couldn't give it."

She stared at his profile, bold and sharply defined, and saw the tight tension along his jaw, down his throat.

"I'm not ashamed of you, Mikhail," she said quietly, and the flare of his nostrils told her that she'd hit close to his fears. "This isn't me turning my back on you. I've found a purpose here that I can't ignore, and you've got the freedom of the skies. We know that we can never fit into each other's worlds."

Pain blazed in his eyes. He glanced away, then reached into his coat pocket and pulled out three dazzling blue gems. The star sapphires.

He held them out to her. "Keep 'em."

"But your payment—"

"There's plenty left in al-Rahim's hoard. And I've got a feeling you'll need them more than I will."

Carefully, she took the necklace from him. Unconcerned that her parents were there in the stateroom, she leaned close and kissed Mikhail. She needed to feel his lips against hers one last time.

He drank of her, bringing his hand up to cup her face, then forcibly pulled himself away. His chest rose and fell as if he'd run a great distance.

"Send me telegrams in Medinat al-Kadib," she said quietly. "I promise I'll answer them."

His gaze flashed, and then he strode from the cabin without another word.

THE DAMNED PROBLEM with an airship was that privacy came at a premium. Mikhail had taken himself off to the armory, and now cleaned the rows and rows of weapons after they'd been used in battle.

"Don't we have crew to take care of this?" asked Levkov, standing in the door.

Mikhail didn't look up from disassembling an ether rifle and scrubbing its bore with a solvent-soaked brush. He was the captain of the damned ship. No need to explain himself to anyone.

Cleaning the guns stopped his mind from thinking thoughts he didn't want to have, kept his hands busy, reminded him that this was the life he'd forged for himself.

A life that now seemed as empty as a spent ether canister. He'd been on the *Bielyi Voron* for years. It had a crew of nearly fifty. Yet it seemed to echo with her absence.

They'd be flying on to Siam soon. Plenty of opportunities for profit in Siam.

Levkov stepped into the armory. "Herrera's dropped them off, her and her parents." No need to explain who *her* was. "The Carlisles wanted some more time with their daughter before they headed back to England. In about a week, some of Khalida's warriors are going to escort the Carlisles to Alexandria, and they'll take a seafaring ship home to Britain."

Mikhail didn't answer, only continued to disassemble and clean gun after gun. They made orderly rows on the table in front of him, their parts laid out, ready to be put back together again. It was easy with guns. Break them apart. Give them a cleaning. Reassemble them. Good as new. Reliable.

"She'll be staying with Khalida for a while," Levkov continued. "They'll be working with al-Rahim's people to get the tribes to cooperate with each other together."

Already, Daphne was committing herself to her new role. She never did anything by inches. All or nothing with his *professorsha*. But she wasn't his *professorsha* anymore. He'd half a mind to send her a telegraph from Bangkok, just to see if she'd keep true to her word and answer. But he wouldn't. No use trying to survive on a diet of crumbs when he'd be satisfied only with the feast. All it would do was remind him of what he couldn't have, what he'd lost.

"How soon can we leave?" Mikhail asked, rubbing oil into the bolt of a rifle.

A brief silence from Levkov. Then, "Now, if you want it. The ship's good for a few hundred miles before we'll need to make bigger repairs."

"No sense lingering. Tell the helm and crew to make ready for departure." He checked the rifle. It was ready once again for use. He looked up when Levkov didn't move. "That was an order, Piotr Romanovich."

His old friend gave his customary scowl. "You didn't ask her to stay."

Mikhail barked out a humorless laugh. "A scholar on a mercenary's ship. Perfect combination."

"Won't know until you try."

With fast, sharp movements, Mikhail took apart another rifle. "She wouldn't be happy here. Got her grand ambitions for doing good."

A stab of envy cut through him, that she'd found a cause she believed in, and wanted to make the world a better place. As he'd once wanted.

"That's it, then?" asked Levkov.

"That's it."

The first mate opened his mouth as if to say something more, then snapped it shut. *Thank God.* Mikhail had no desire to continue to dwell on all the reasons why he and Daphne had nothing holding them together. Nothing but desire, and affection, and respect. But it wouldn't be enough, just as she'd said.

Without another word, Levkov left the armory. A few moments later, the ship hummed as its turbines spun to life. The airship came about, heading toward its newest destination, and Mikhail continued to take apart guns, pretending he cared that one rifle stock would need some extra polishing to buff out a gouge along the wood. A little extra work, and it would be as good as new. And only he'd know the damage it had taken.

DAPHNE COULDN'T BEAR the sorrowful looks her parents kept directing at her. Painful enough to feel her own misery at Mikhail's departure, but the way her mother kept saying, "Darling, we've all undergone trials. If you ever want to talk . . ."

Daphne didn't want to talk. She wanted solitude. So as the sun dipped lower to the horizon, she climbed one of the remaining towers in al-Rahim's compound. It offered an uninterrupted view of the desert, and the hills turning to ash with the approach of dusk. The enemy rogue airship had drifted away. Either someone in its crew would fly it as far as it could go without its power source, or it already rested on the desert floor, abandoned. If that were the case, doubtlessly scavengers would be along to pick it clean.

There was no sign of the *Bielyi Voron*. It had flown on half an hour ago.

Her chest ached, thinking of how she and Mikhail had said goodbye. Or rather, how they hadn't said goodbye. He'd paced from his quarters and vanished, making no appearance as Daphne, her parents, and their assistants had all boarded the jolly boat. Herrera had waited for nearly fifteen minutes, glancing toward the companionway that led to the cargo bay. At last, she'd had to say, "We ought to get going." So they did, and she wondered now if the hurt would ever lessen, if she might one day wake up and find herself, at last, numb. She couldn't hope for happiness.

Where would he go next? The whole world was his. She might picture him anywhere—flying above jagged Chinese limestone mountains, or above the smokestack-crowned cities of the United States. She'd hold that tightly, like a sharp-edged gem that cut her even as she clutched it close. And she hoped that, when she did next go to Medinat al-Kadib, a telegram would be waiting for her.

Though she stood atop a tower, she could still hear the hum of human conversation below as the wounded received medical attention, tents were pitched, and evening meals were made ready. Despite the fierce battle that had been fought hours before, life resumed its normal rhythms. She would have to go down there . . . eventually.

But as she looked out at the western horizon, watching the descent of the sun and hearing the drone of mundane life, another sound caught her attention. A kind of whooshing sound. Very much like . . . an airship's turbines.

Suddenly, directly above her, was the *Bielyi Voron*. She started, and a great cry arose from the people around the compound. It seemed to appear out of nowhere. She actually rubbed at her eyes, trying to dispel what had to be an illusion. But no, the ship still hovered fifty feet above her.

Her heart pounded in her chest as the cargo doors

opened, and a thirty-foot rope tumbled down. And then there was Mikhail, sliding down the rope, his long coat flying around him, looking like a bird of prey swooping from the sky. The rope didn't extend far enough, but he didn't slow or stop, merely let go, and jumped the rest of the way.

He landed in a crouch right in front of her, shaking the tower. Then he straightened to his full height.

He was terrifying. And thrilling. And wonderful.

And she couldn't move a muscle. Not toward him, not away. Only stood and stared, as though caught in the throes of a dream.

"The night sky missing the North Star," he said without preface. "No guidance, no direction. That's what it's like, in here." He slapped his hand in the center of his chest. "You never would've found me crying into my atlas, though. I didn't much care. Those old dreams—making a difference, protecting my country—all long dead. War and my own greed killed 'em. Turned me rogue. It made me drift like flotsam from one job to the next. Steered by the lure of profit. I thought it was all I needed." He shook his head. "I was wrong. So damned wrong."

He stepped closer to her, and her pulse beat so hard she felt as though the earth itself shook.

"It's all changed," he continued, his gaze holding hers. "Because of you. You've given me back my North Star." He reached down between them and took her hands between his own, engulfing her with his size and heat. Yet she felt his tremors.

"I want . . ." His voice roughened, and he had to start

again. "I want to join your fight. Protecting those caught in the middle of the war."

"The fight brought you back," she said quietly.

"Not *the* fight," he answered hotly. "*Your* fight. I want it to be mine, too."

"There's much to be done. Not just here, but all over the world. Lives torn apart by the war."

"Then we fix them," he said with complete confidence that the two of them could do just that.

She felt compelled to say, "Not an easy prospect." Because she wanted no more illusions or deception between them, and what lay ahead would be a continual challenge.

"Nothing worth doing, or having, is simple." His grin made everything inside her heat and soften. "A *professor-sha* taught me that. Besides," he added, "if there's any two people who can take on impossible tasks, it's you and me. An unbeatable armada of two."

She liked the sound of that.

"And will your crew be satisfied with this arrangement?"

"To hell with them if they aren't. There are plenty of nefarious ways an airship crewman can make a living." He raised a brow. "Trying to talk me out of this?"

"God, no," she answered at once, appalled by the very notion.

His expression grew tight, focused. "Whatever you need of me, I'll give it to you. My ship, my strength." He swallowed hard. "My heart. They're all yours. For as long as you want them." The trepidation in his eyes nearly undid her. This nearly indestructible man feared what she might say.

She struggled to catch her breath. "And if I want them forever?"

It took him a moment to fully understand her answer. His eyes narrowed. "Honestly?"

"When it comes to you and me," she said, her throat aching, "I'll always be honest. And I honestly want and need you, Mikhail. For now. For always."

A grin spread across his face. He pulled her close, wrapping his arms around her. "Then I accept your terms, *professorsha*."

They kissed, sealing their vow, and the sky darkened with evening, and the world seemed to open with infinite possibility and limitless direction.

EXPLORE THE
ETHER CHRONICLES

If you loved SKIES OF STEEL,
don't miss the rest of Zoë Archer
and Nico Rosso's smart,
sexy Ether Chronicles collaboration

Coming in November 2012

NIGHTS OF STEEL
by Nico Rosso

Bounty hunter Anna Blue always finds her fugitive. But her latest mission is filled with mystery—a high price for an eccentric inventor. A twisted trail. And a man tracking her every step. Her biggest competitor in the Western territories, Jack Hawkins, is also hunting the bounty. Two of the best at what they do, neither is willing to back off.

When a rogue Man O' War flies his airship out of the coastal fog, guns blazing, Anna and Jack are forced to team up, or die. But it isn't the danger that has them ready to flare like gunpowder. For years they'd circled around each other, but never said a word, thinking their interest was just rivalry. Deeper, though, a hot passion draws them together. Fighters and outsiders, they never thought they'd find a kindred soul. Can they survive this mission long enough to track the most elusive fugitive—their hearts?

Available Now

NIGHT OF FIRE
by Nico Rosso

Night of fire, night of passion

US Army Upland Ranger Tom Knox always knew going home wouldn't be easy. Three years ago, he skipped town leaving behind the one woman who ever mattered; now that he's seen the front lines of war, he's ready to do what he must to win her back.

Rosa Campos is long past wasting tears on Tom Knox, and now that she's sheriff of Thornville she has more than enough to do. Especially when a three-story rock-eating mining machine barrels toward the town she's sworn to protect.

Tom's the last person Rosa expects to see riding to her aid on his ether-borne mechanical horse. She may not be ready to forgive, but Rosa can't deny that having him at her side brings back blissful memories . . . even as it reignites a flame more dangerous than the enemy threatening to destroy them both.

SKIES OF FIRE
by Zoë Archer

Man made of metal and flesh

Captain Christopher Redmond has just one weakness:
the alluring spy who loved and left him years before . . .
when he was still just a man. Now superhuman, a Man
O' War, made as part of the British Navy's weapons pro-
gram, his responsibility is to protect the skies of Europe.
If only he could forget Louisa Shaw.

A most inconvenient desire

Louisa, a British Naval Intelligence Agent, has never left
a job undone. But when her assignment is compromised,
the one man who can help her complete her mission
is also the only man ever to tempt her body and heart.
As burning skies loom and passion ignites, Louisa and
Christopher must slip behind enemy lines if they are to
deliver a devastating strike against their foe . . . and still
get out alive.

Give in to your impulses . . .
Read on for a sneak peek at two brand-new
e-book original tales of romance
from Avon Books.
Available now wherever e-books are sold.

THE FORBIDDEN LADY
By Kerrelyn Sparks

TURN TO DARKNESS
By Jaime Rush

An Excerpt from

THE FORBIDDEN LADY

by Kerrelyn Sparks

(Originally published under
the title *For Love or Country*)

Before *New York Times* bestselling author Kerrelyn Sparks
created a world of vampires, there was another world of spies
and romance . . .

Keep reading for a look at her very first novel.

CHAPTER ONE

Tuesday, August 29, 1769

"I say, dear gel, how much do *you* cost?"

Virginia's mouth dropped open. "I—I beg your pardon?"

The bewigged, bejeweled, and bedeviling man who faced her spoke again. "You're a fetching sight and quite sweet-smelling for a wench who has traveled for weeks, imprisoned on this godforsaken ship. I say, what *is* your price?"

She opened her mouth, but nothing came out. The rolling motion of the ship caught her off guard, and she stumbled, widening her stance to keep her balance. This man thought she was for sale? Even though they were on board *The North Star*, a brigantine newly arrived in Boston Harbor with a fresh supply of indentured servants, could he actually mistake her for one of the poor wretched criminals huddled near the front of the ship?

Her first reaction of shock was quickly replaced with anger. It swelled in her chest, heated to a quick boil, and soared past her ruffled neckline to her face, scorching her cheeks 'til she fully expected steam, instead of words, to escape her mouth.

"How . . . how *dare* you!" With gloved hands, she twisted the silken cords of her drawstring purse. "Pray, be gone with you, sir."

"Ah, a saucy one." The gentleman plucked a silver snuffbox from his lavender silk coat. He kept his tall frame erect to avoid flipping his wig, which was powdered with a lavender tint to match his coat. "Tsk, tsk, dear gel, such impertinence is sure to lower your price."

Her mouth fell open again.

Seizing the opportunity, he raised his quizzing glass and examined the conveniently opened orifice. "Hmm, but you do have excellent teeth."

She huffed. "And a sharp tongue to match."

"*Mon Dieu*, a very saucy mouth, indeed." He smiled, displaying straight, white teeth.

A perfectly bright smile, Virginia thought. What a pity his mental faculties were so dim in comparison. But she refrained from responding with an insulting remark. No good could come from stooping to his level of ill manners. She stepped back, intending to leave, but hesitated when he spoke again.

"I do so like your nose. Very becoming and—" He opened his silver box, removed a pinch of snuff with his gloved fingers and sniffed.

She waited for him to finish the sentence. He was a buffoon, to be sure, but she couldn't help but wonder—did he actually like her nose? Over the years, she had endured a great deal of teasing because of the way it turned up on the end.

He snapped his snuffbox shut with a click. "Ah, yes, where was I, becoming and . . . disdainfully haughty. Yes, that's it."

Heat pulsed to her face once more. "I daresay it is not surprising for *you* to admire something *disdainfully haughty*, but regardless of your opinion, it is improper for you to address me so rudely. For that matter, it is highly improper for you to speak to me at all, for need I remind you, sir, we have not been introduced."

He dropped his snuffbox back into his pocket. "Definitely disdainful. And haughty." His mouth curled up, revealing two dimples beneath the rouge on his cheeks.

She glared at the offensive fop. Somehow, she would give him the cut he deserved.

A short man in a brown buckram coat and breeches scurried toward them. "Mr. Stanton! The criminals for sale are over there, sir, near the forecastle. You see the ones in chains?"

Raising his quizzing glass, the lavender dandy pivoted on his high heels and perused the line of shackled prisoners. He shrugged his silk-clad shoulders and glanced back at Virginia with a look of feigned horror. "Oh, dear, what a delightful little *faux pas*. I suppose you're not for sale after all?"

"No, of course not."

"I do beg your pardon." He flipped a lacy, monogrammed handkerchief out of his chest pocket and made a poor attempt to conceal the wide grin on his face.

A heavy, flowery scent emanated from his handkerchief, nearly bowling her over. He was probably one of those people who never bathed, just poured on more perfume. She covered her mouth with a gloved hand and gently coughed.

"Well, no harm done." He waved his handkerchief in the

air. "*C'est la vie* and all that. Would you care for some snuff? 'Tis my own special blend from London, don't you know. We call it *Grey Mouton*."

"Gray sheep?"

"Why, yes. Sink me! You *parlez français*? How utterly charming for one of your class."

Narrowing her eyes, she considered strangling him with the drawstrings of her purse.

He removed the silver engraved box from his pocket and flicked it open. "A pinch, in the interest of peace?" His mouth twitched with amusement.

"No, thank you."

He lifted a pinch to his nose and sniffed. "What did I tell you, Johnson?" he asked the short man in brown buckram at his side. "These Colonials are a stubborn lot, far too eager to take offense"—he sneezed delicately into his lacy handkerchief—"and far too unappreciative of the efforts the mother country makes on their behalf." He slid his closed snuffbox back into his pocket.

Virginia planted her hands on her hips. "You speak, perhaps, of Britain's kindness in providing us with a steady stream of slaves?"

"Slaves?"

She gestured toward the raised platform of the forecastle, where Britain's latest human offering stood in front, chained at the ankles and waiting to be sold.

"Oh." He waved his scented handkerchief in dismissal. "You mean the indentured servants. They're not slaves, my dear, only criminals paying their dues to society. 'Tis the mother country's fervent hope they will be reformed by their experience in America."

"I see. Perhaps we should send the mother country a boat-load of American wolves to see if they can be reformed by their experience in Britain?"

His chuckle was surprisingly deep. "*Touché.*"

The deep timbre of his voice reverberated through her skin, striking a chord that hummed from her chest down to her belly. She caught her breath and looked at him more closely. When his eyes met hers, his smile faded away. Time seemed to hold still for a moment as he held her gaze, quietly studying her.

The man in brown cleared his throat.

Virginia blinked and looked away. She breathed deeply to calm her racing heart. Once more, she became aware of the murmur of voices and the screech of sea gulls overhead. What had happened? It must have been the thrill of putting the man in his place that had affected her. Strange, though, that he had happily acknowledged her small victory.

Mr. Stanton gave the man in brown a mildly irritated look, then smiled at her once more. "American wolves, you say? Really, my dear, these people's crimes are too petty to compare them to murderous beasts. Why, Johnson, here, was an indentured servant before becoming my secretary. Were you not, Johnson?"

"Aye, Mr. Stanton," the older man answered. "But I came voluntarily. Not all these people are prisoners. The group to the right doesn't wear chains. They're selling themselves out of desperation."

"There, you see." The dandy spread his gloved hands, palms up, in a gesture of conciliation. "No hard feelings. In fact, I quite trust Johnson here with all my affairs in spite of his criminal background. You know the Colonials are quite wrong in thinking we British are a cold, callous lot."

Virginia gave Mr. Johnson a small, sympathetic smile, letting him know she understood his indenture had not been due to a criminal past. Her own father, faced with starvation and British cruelty, had left his beloved Scottish Highlands as an indentured servant. Her sympathy seemed unnecessary, however, for Mr. Johnson appeared unperturbed by his employer's rudeness. No doubt the poor man had grown accustomed to it.

She gave Mr. Stanton her stoniest of looks. "Thank you for enlightening me."

"My pleasure, dear gel. Now I must take my leave." Without further ado, he ambled toward the group of gaunt, shackled humans, his high-heeled shoes clunking on the ship's wooden deck and his short secretary tagging along behind.

Virginia scowled at his back. The British needed to go home, and the sooner, the better.

"I say, old man." She heard his voice filter back as he addressed his servant. "I do wish the pretty wench were for sale. A bit too saucy, perhaps, but I do so like a challenge. *Quel dommage*, a real pity, don't you know."

A vision of herself tackling the dandy and stuffing his lavender-tinted wig down his throat brought a smile to her lips. She could do it. Sometimes she pinned down her brother when he tormented her. Of course, such behavior might be frowned upon in Boston. This was not the hilly region of North Carolina that the Munro family called home.

And the dandy might prove difficult to knock down. Watching him from the back, she realized how large he was. She grimaced at the lavender bows on his high-heeled pumps. Why would a man that tall need to wear heels? Another pair of lavender bows served as garters, tied over the tabs of his silk knee breeches. His silken hose were too sheer to hide padding, so those calves were truly that muscular. *How odd*.

He didn't mince his steps like one would expect from a fopdoodle, but covered the deck with long, powerful strides, the walk of a man confident in his strength and masculinity.

She found herself examining every inch of him, calculating the amount of hard muscle hidden beneath the silken exterior. What color was his hair under that hideous tinted wig? Probably black, like his eyebrows. His eyes had gleamed like polished pewter, pale against his tanned face.

Her breath caught in her throat. A tanned face? A fop would not spend the necessary hours toiling in the sun that resulted in a bronzed complexion.

This Mr. Stanton was a puzzle.

She shook her head, determined to forget the perplexing man. Yet, if he dressed more like the men back home—tight buckskin breeches, boots, no wig, no lace . . .

The sun bore down with increasing heat, and she pulled her hand-painted fan from her purse and flicked it open. She breathed deeply as she fanned herself. Her face tingled with a mist of salty air and the lingering scent of Mr. Stanton's handkerchief.

She watched with growing suspicion as the man in question postured in front of the women prisoners with his quizzing glass, assessing them with a practiced eye. Oh, dear, what were the horrible man's intentions? She slipped her fan back into her purse and hastened to her father's side.

Jamie Munro was speaking quietly to a fettered youth who appeared a good five years younger than her one and twenty years. "All I ask, young man, is honesty and a good day's work. In exchange, ye'll have food, clean clothes, and a clean pallet."

The spindly boy's eyes lit up, and he licked his dry, chapped lips. "Food?"

Virginia's father nodded. "Aye. Mind you, ye willna be working for me, lad, but for my widowed sister, here, in Boston. Do ye have any experience as a servant?"

The boy lowered his head and shook it. He shuffled his feet, the scrape of his chains on the deck grating at Virginia's heart.

"Papa," she whispered.

Jamie held up a hand. "Doona fash yerself, lass. I'll be taking the boy."

As the boy looked up, his wide grin cracked the dried dirt on his cheeks. "Thank you, my lord."

Jamie winced. "Mr. Munro, it is. We'll have none of that lordy talk aboot here. Welcome to America." He extended a hand, which the boy timidly accepted. "What is yer name, lad?"

"George Peeper, sir."

"Father." Virginia tugged at the sleeve of his blue serge coat. "Can we afford any more?"

Jamie Munro's eyes widened and he blinked at his daughter. "More? Just an hour ago, ye upbraided me aboot the evils of purchasing people, and now ye want more? 'Tis no' like buying ribbons for yer bonny red hair."

"I know, but this is important." She leaned toward him. "Do you see the tall man in lavender silk?"

Jamie's nose wrinkled. "Aye. Who could miss him?"

"Well, he wanted to purchase me—"

"*What?*"

She pressed the palms of her hands against her father's broad chest as he moved to confront the dandy. "'Twas a misunderstanding. Please."

His blue eyes glittering with anger, Jamie clenched his fists. "Let me punch him for you, lass."

"No, listen to me. I fear he means to buy one of those ladies for . . . immoral purposes."

Jamie frowned at her. "And what would ye be knowing of a man's immoral purposes?"

"Father, I grew up on a farm. I can make certain deductions, and I know from the way he looked at me, the man is not looking for someone to scrub his pots."

"What can I do aboot it?"

"If he decides he wants one, you could outbid him."

"He would just buy another, Ginny. I canna be buying the whole ship. I can scarcely afford this one here."

She bit her lip, considering. "You could buy one more if Aunt Mary pays for George. She can afford it much more than we."

"Nay." Jamie shook his head. "I willna have my sister paying. This is the least I can do to help Mary before we leave.

Besides, I seriously doubt I could outbid the dandy even once. Look at the rich way he's dressed, though I havena stet clue why a man would spend good coin to look like that."

The ship rocked suddenly, and Virginia held fast to her father's arm. A breeze wafted past her, carrying the scent of unwashed bodies. She wrinkled her nose. She should have displayed the foresight to bring a scented handkerchief, though not as overpowering as the one sported by the lavender popinjay.

Having completed his leisurely perusal of the women, Mr. Stanton was now conversing quietly with a young boy.

"Look, Father, that boy is so young to be all alone. He cannot be more than ten."

"Aye," Jamie replied. "We can only hope a good family will be taking him in."

"How much for the boy?" Mr. Stanton demanded in a loud voice.

The captain answered, "You'll be thinking twice before taking that one. He's an expensive little wretch."

Mr. Stanton lowered his voice. "Why is that?"

"I'll be needing payment for his passage *and* his mother's. The silly tart died on the voyage, so the boy owes you fourteen years of labor."

The boy swung around and shook a fist at the captain. "Me mum was not a tart, ye bloody old bugger!"

The captain yelled back, "And he has a foul mouth, as you can see. You'll be taking the strap to him before the day is out."

Virginia squeezed her father's arm. "The boy is responsible for his mother's debt?"

"Aye." Jamie nodded. "'Tis how it works."

Mr. Stanton adjusted the lace on his sleeves. "I have a fancy to be extravagant today. Name your price."

"At least the poor boy will have a roof over his head and food to eat." Virginia grimaced. "I only hope the dandy will not dress him in lavender silk."

Jamie Munro frowned. "Oh, dear."

"What is it, Father?"

"Ye say the man was interested in you, Ginny?"

"Aye, he seemed to like me in his own horrid way."

"Hmm. Perhaps the lad will be all right. At any rate, 'tis too late now. Let me pay for George, and we'll be on our way."

An Excerpt from

TURN TO DARKNESS

by Jaime Rush

Enter the world of the Offspring with this latest novella in Jaime Rush's fabulous paranormal series.

CHAPTER ONE

When Shea Baker pulled into her driveway, the sight of Darius's black coupe in front of her little rented house annoyed her. That it wasn't Greer's Jeep, and that she was disappointed it wasn't, annoyed the hell out of her.

Darius pulled out his partially dismantled wheelchair from inside the car and put it together within a few seconds. His slide from the driver's seat into his wheelchair was so practiced it was almost fluid. He waved, oblivious to her frown, and wheeled over to her truck. "As pale as you looked after hearing what Tucker, Del, and I went through, I thought you'd go right home." He wore his dark blond hair in a James Dean style, his waves gelled to stand up.

She *had* been freaked. Two men trying to kill them, men who would kill them all if they knew about their existence. She yanked her baseball cap lower on her head, a nervous habit. "I had a couple of jobs to check on. What brings you by?" She hoped it was something quick he could tell her right there and leave.

"Tucker kicked me out. I think he feels threatened by me,

because I had to take charge. I saved the day, and he won't even admit it."

None of the guys were comfortable with Darius. His mercurial mood shifts and oversized ego were irritating, but the shadows in his eyes hinted at an affinity for violence. In the two years he'd lived with them, though, he'd mostly kept to himself. She'd had no problem with him because he remained aloof, never revealing his emotions, even when he talked about the car accident that had taken his mobility. Unfortunately, when he thought she was reaching out to him, that aloofness had changed to romantic interest.

"Sounded like you went off the rails." She crossed her arms in front of her. "Look, if you're here to get me on your side, I won't—"

"I'd never ask you to do that." His upper lip lifted in a sneer. "I know you're loyal only to Tucker."

She narrowed her eyes, her body stiffening. "Tuck's like a big brother to me. He gave me a home when I was on the streets, told me why I have extraordinary powers." That she'd inherited DNA from another dimension was crazy-wild, but it made as much sense as, say, being able to move objects with her mind. "I'd take his side over anyone's."

"Wish someone would feel that kind of loyalty to me," Darius muttered under his breath, making her wonder if he was trying to elicit her sympathy. "I get that you're brotherly/sisterly." He let those words settle for a second. "But something happened with you and Greer, didn't it? What did he do, grope you?"

"Don't be ridiculous. Greer would never do something like that."

"Something happened, because all of a sudden the way you looked at each other changed. Like he was way interested in you, and you were way uncomfortable around him. Then you sat all close to me, and I know you felt the same electricity I did."

She shook her head, sending her curly ponytail swinging over her shoulder. "There was no electricity. Greer and I had a . . . disagreement. I needed to put some space between us, but when you live in a house with four other people, there isn't a lot of room. When I sat next to you, I was just moving away from him."

Darius's shoulders, wide and muscular, stiffened. "You might think that, Shea. You might even believe it. But someday you're going to realize you want me. And when you do, I want you to know I can satisfy you. When I'm in Darkness, I'm a whole man." That dark glint in his eyes hinted at his arrogance. "I'm capable of anything."

Those words shivered through her, but not in the way he'd intended. In that moment, she knew somehow that he *was* capable of anything. Darius might be confined to a wheelchair, but only a fool would underestimate him, and she was no fool. Especially where Darkness was concerned. The guys possessed it, yet didn't know exactly what it was. All they knew was that they'd probably inherited it, along with the DNA that gave them extraordinary powers, from the men who'd gotten their mothers pregnant. It allowed them to Become something far from human.

"Please, Darius, don't talk to me about that kind of thing. I'm not interested in having sex with anyone."

The corner of his mouth twisted cruelly. "Don't you like

sex? Maybe you've never been with someone who could do it well."

For a long time the thought of sex had coated her in shame and disgust. Until that little incident with Greer, when she'd had a totally different—and surprising—reaction.

"Look, I'm sorry Tuck kicked you out, but I don't have a guest bedroom."

"I'll sleep on the couch. You won't even know I'm here." His face transformed from darkly sexual to a happy little boy's. "I don't have any other place to stay," he added, building his case. "You just said how grateful you are to Tuck for taking you in. I'm only asking for the same thing."

Damn, he had her. As much as she wanted to squash her feelings, some things did reach right under her shields. And some people . . . like Greer. Now, Darius's manipulation did. "All right," she spat out, feeling pinned.

Her phone rang from where she'd left it inside her truck.

"Thanks, Shea," Darius said, wheeling to his car and popping the trunk. "You're a doll."

She got into her truck, grabbing up the phone and eyeing the screen. Greer. She'd been trying to avoid him since moving out three months before. But with the weirdness going on lately, she needed to stay in the loop.

"Hey," she answered. "What's up?"

"Tuck and Darius had it out a while ago. Darius has this idea about being the alpha male, which is just stupid, and Tuck kicked him out. I wanted to let you know in case he shows up on your doorstep pulling his 'poor me' act."

"Too late," she said in a singsong voice. "Act pulled—very well, I might add. He's staying for a few days."

"Bad idea." Always the protective one. He made no apologies for it either.

She watched Darius lift his suitcase onto his lap and wheel toward the ramp he'd installed for wheelchair access to her front door. "Well, what was I supposed to do, turn him away? I don't like it either."

"I'm coming over."

"There's no need . . ." She looked at the screen, blinking to indicate he'd ended the call. ". . . to come over," she finished anyway.

She got out, feeling like her feet weighed fifty pounds each, and trudged to the door. All she wanted was to be alone, a quiet evening trimming her bonsai to clear her mind.

There would be no mind-clearing tonight. There'd be friction between Greer and Darius, just like there had been before she'd moved out. Tuck had eased her into the reality of Darkness, he and Greer morphing into black beasts only after she'd accepted the idea. Tuck told her it also made them fiercely, and insanely, territorial about their so-called mates. She hadn't thought twice about that until Darius and Greer both took a different kind of liking to her. She was afraid they'd tear each other's throats out, and she wasn't either of their mates.

"Two days," she said, unlocking her front door. "I like living on my own. Being alone." Most of the time. It was strange, but she'd sit at her table in the mornings having coffee (not as strong as Greer's k iller brew) and be happy about being alone. Then she'd get hit with a wave of sadness about being alone.

See how messed up you are.

"You might like having me around," he said. "If that guy

who's been creeping around makes an appearance, I'll kick his ass."

"Well, he's too much of a coward to knock on the door." She didn't want to think about her stalker. He hadn't left any of his icky letters or "gifts" in a few days.

She figured out where Darius could stash his suitcases and was hunting down extra sheets and a blanket when the doorbell rang. Before she could even set the extra pillow down to answer, she heard Darius's voice: "Well, look who's here. What a nice surprise."

Not by the tone in his voice. Damn, this was so not cool having them both here. They'd been like snarling dogs the day everyone had helped her move in here. She hadn't had them over since.

She walked out holding the pillow to her chest like a shield. Greer's eyes went right to her, giving her a clear *Is everything all right?* look.

She wasn't in danger. That's as far as she'd commit.

Greer closed the door and sauntered in, as though he always stopped by. "Thought I'd check in on you. After what happened, figured you might be on edge." There he went again, sinking her into the depths of his eyes. They were rimmed in gray, brown in the middle, the most unusual eyes she'd ever seen. And they were assessing her.

"She's fine," Darius answered as she opened her mouth. "I'm staying here for a couple of days, which will work out nicely . . . in case she's on edge." His unspoken *So you can go now* was clear.

Greer moved closer to her, putting himself physically between her and Darius. He was a damned wall of a man, too, way tall, wide shoulders, and just big. He purposely blocked Darius's view of her.

She'd done this, sparked them into hostile territory. Which was laughable, considering what she looked like: baggy pants and shirt, cap over her head, no makeup. She'd done everything she could for the last six years to squash every bit of her femininity. Her sexuality. Then Greer had blown that to bits.

He hadn't knocked, just barged into the bathroom, a towel loosely held in front of his naked body. She was drying her hair and suddenly he was standing there gaping at her.

"Jesus, Shea, you're beautiful," he'd said, obviously in shock.

She couldn't move, spellbound herself, which was ridiculous because she wasn't interested in anyone sexually. But there stood six feet four of olive-skinned Apache with muscled thighs and a scant bit of towel covering him. And the way he'd said those words, with his typical passion, and his looking at her like she *was* beautiful and he wanted her, woke up something inside her.

Breaking out of the spell and wrapping her towel around her, she'd yelled at him for barging in, stepping up close to him and jabbing her finger at his chest.

And what had he done? Lifted her damp hair from her shoulders, hair she never left loose, his fingers brushing her bare shoulders. "Why do you hide yourself from us?" he'd asked.

"Don't say anything about this to anyone." Would he tell them how oversized her breasts were? Would they wonder why she hid her curves, talking behind her back, speculating? "Leave. Now."

He'd shrugged, his dark brown eyebrows furrowing. "No

need to get mad or freaked out. It was an accident. We're friends."

He left, finally, and she looked in the steamy reflection. She didn't see beautiful. But she did see hunger, and even worse, felt it.

"How's your big job coming?" Greer asked now, pulling her out of the memory. He was leaning against the back of the couch, which inadvertently flexed the muscles in his arms.

He remembered, which touched her even if she didn't want to be touched. Still, she found herself smiling. "Great. We're putting the finishing touches now that the hard-scaping and most of the planting is finished. This is my biggest job yet. My business has kept me sane through all this. Gotta keep working on the customer's jobs." She glanced to the window. If the sun weren't going to be setting soon, she'd come up with some job she had to zip off to right then.

Dammit, she missed Greer. Hated having to shut him out. Now, things were odd between them. He looked at her differently, heat in his eyes, and hurt, too, because he didn't understand why she'd pushed him away. Like he'd said, it was an accident that he'd walked in on her.

"Do you want to stay for dinner?" she asked, not sure whether having them both there would be better than being alone with Darius.

Greer glanced at his watch. "Wish I could. My shift starts in an hour."

Darius wheeled up. "Yeah, the big bad firefighter, off to save lives." He made a superhero arm motion, pumping one fist in the air.

Greer's mouth twisted in a snarl. "I'd rather do that than tinker with computer parts all day."

"Boys," she said, sounding like a teacher.

Another knock on the door. Hopefully it was Tucker. He was good at stepping in. But it wasn't Tucker. Two men stood there, their badges at the ready. "Cheyenne Baker?" one of them asked.

She nodded, feeling Greer step up behind her.

"Detective Dan Marshall, and Detective Paul Marron. May we come in?"

"What's this about?" Greer asked before she could say anything.

"We have some questions about a recent incident." The man, in his forties, waited patiently for someone to invite them inside.

Greer inspected the badge, nodded to her. It was legit.

Shea checked it, too, then stepped back, bumping into Greer. "These are friends of mine," she said, waving to Greer and Darius.

Marshall closed the door behind them, taking in both men as though noting their appearance. He focused on her. "You've heard about the man who was mauled two nights ago?"

Her mouth went dry. How had they connected that to her? Bad enough that it triggered two men from the other dimension to hunt down their offspring. "Yes, it sounded horrible." She shuddered, and didn't have to fake it. "Wild animals attacking people in their own home."

"We don't think it was a wild animal. Do you know Fred Callahan, the victim?"

"No, I—" Her words jammed in her throat when she saw the picture he held up, a driver's license photo probably. All the blood drained from her face. "I knew him as Frankie C." She cleared the fuzz from her voice. "I haven't seen him for six years." She wanted the cops to go, or for Greer and Darius to leave. "I'm sorry, I can't help you."

Marshall's eyes flicked to Greer and Darius before returning to her. "We found pictures and notes about you on his computer. There was a letter in his desk drawer addressed to you, indicating he'd written to you before. It wasn't a very nice letter."

Her knees went weak. Greer somehow sensed it and clamped his hands on her shoulders. "What are you insinuating?" His hands started warming her, one of his psychic abilities.

Darius wheeled closer. "You can't possibly think this slip of a girl could tear a man apart."

"I've been getting letters, creepy gifts," she said. "But I didn't know who they were from." Frankie. She had wondered, yes, but how had he found her? And why after all these years?

"May I see them?" Marshall asked.

She'd wanted to throw them away, but thought they might be evidence if things escalated. She went to the file cabinet in her office and returned with the letters, and the box.

Marshall frowned when he opened it and saw the dildo, the flavored lube creams. "Can I take these?"

"Please." *And go. Say no more.*

He looked at Greer and Darius. "Did either of you know who was harassing her?"

Darius snorted. "No, but I'm glad the sick fu—the guy is dead. It's wrong to harass a woman like that."

Greer shook his head, but his gaze was on her.

Marshall turned to her again. "Callahan worked at the phone company. That's probably how he found you. You haven't heard from him at all in the six years since you filed charges against him and the other two men?"

"No, nothing," she said quickly. "I'd rather not—"

"I'm sure the detective you spoke to talked you out of going forward with the charges. I read the file and agree that it was a long shot to prosecute the case successfully. Still, I wish we had. One of those other men raped a teenaged girl a couple of years back. He's in prison now. The other's been jailed a few times on battery charges."

She felt Greer's questioning stare on her. "I'm sorry to hear that." Her words sounded shaky. *Leave, dammit.*

Marshall glanced in the box, then her. "But Callahan hasn't had another brush with the law. We did find some rather disturbing items in his home, including sex toys I presume he intended to send to you. One was a pair of handcuffs, and they weren't the fuzzy kind. It's the sort of thing that makes me uncomfortable about where he was going with this. So if you"—he looked at her friends—"or anyone had something to do with his death, it may have saved your life. But still, we have to investigate. It's a crime to tear a man apart, no matter how much of a scumbag he is."

"Son of a bitch," Greer said. His hands tightened on her as she slumped against the couch, and then he pulled her against his body, his arms like a shield over her collarbone.

Oh, God. Had Frankie been planning to rape her again? That overshadowed anything else in her mind at the moment.

Marshall seemed to be giving them time to fess up.

"We didn't know who the guy sending that stuff was," Shea said. "You can see from the letters that he never signed them." They'd been crude letters, detailing what he wanted to do to her body, and she'd forced herself to read them because she needed to know how much he knew about her. Or if they contained an explicit threat.

"Was it because of your earlier experience that you didn't report the stalking?" Marshall asked.

She shrugged, though it felt as though she wore an armored suit that smelled of a citrus cologne. "I didn't see it as threatening. Only gross and annoying."

Wrapped in Greer's embrace, she felt safe in a sea of chaos.

Marshall gave her his business card. "If there's anything else you know or remember, please give me a call." He took a step toward the door but turned back to her. "Ms. Baker, if anyone ever hurts you like that again, call me."

As soon as he left, Darius wheeled in front of her. "The guy's dead, Shea. You don't have to worry about him anymore. Isn't that great?"

Thank God Darius hadn't asked for more information. If only Greer would let it go.

He turned her to face him. "What happened? What was he talking about, if you're hurt 'again'?" His concern turned her to mush, and then his expression changed. He cradled her face, and as much as she wanted to push away, she couldn't. "Oh, Shea."

She heard it all in his voice—that he'd figured it out from

the detective's words. Raped "another" woman. She felt her expression crumple even though she tried to hold strong.

He pulled her against him, stroking her back. Her cap's brim bumped against him and it fell to the floor.

No, she had to push away. She would fall apart right here, and he would continue to hold her and soothe her, and it felt so good because no one had done that afterward. Not even her mother, who had the same opinion the cops did: that she deserved it.

She managed to move out of his embrace by reaching for her cap. She shoved it onto her head, pulling down the brim. "I'm fine. It was a long time ago."

"What are you two talking about?" Darius asked. At least he hadn't gotten it.

That was the difference between them, one of many. She wondered if Darius just had no emotions, nothing to squash or tuck away.

"You'd better go," she said to Greer, her voice thick. "You don't want to be late for your shift."

He was looking at her, probably giving her the same look he'd been giving her since the bathroom incident. The *Why are you shutting me out?* one. She couldn't tell, thankfully, because the brim of her cap blocked his eyes from view. At least he'd also pushed back after the bathroom incident and gone on, continued dating. He'd been cool to her afterward. That's what she wanted. Even if it stuck a knife in her chest.

"I do have to go. Walk me out." He took her hand, giving her no choice but to be dragged along with him.

The air was even more chilling now that the sun was setting. He paused by his Jeep, turning her to face him. "Shea, that's why you hide yourself, isn't it? Why you freaked when I accidentally saw you naked." He pulled off her cap. "*Three* of them?" His agony at the thought wracked his face.

"I don't want to discuss this. I freaked because I don't want people to see me naked."

"Because you've got curves—"

She pressed her hand over his mouth, feeling the full softness of it. "I am not interested in discussing my curves or my past."

"You're hurting, Shea. It's why you shut down on me. I lost a friend once, because he was hurting, too. Holding in a painful secret. I left for a while, doing construction out of town, and when I came back, he'd taken his life. He couldn't take the pain anymore."

"I'm not going to take my life. I've survived, gotten over it—"

"You haven't gotten over it." He tugged at her oversized shirt. "You hide your body. All those years you lived with us, you hid yourself. Did you think we'd hurt you? Attack you?"

He had no idea. "Of course not."

"That's why you were so pissed about me seeing you. Your secret was out."

That he had right. "That's ridiculous." She took the opportunity to look down at her attire, to escape those assessing eyes. "This is just how I like to dress."

He took his finger and lifted her chin. "I suddenly saw you as a woman and not just the girl who's lived with us for the past few years. Seeing you as a woman changed everything."

She smacked his arm, which probably hurt her more than him. "Then change it back. I don't want you like that."

He slowly blinked at her statement. "Is it because of what happened to you? We can work through that."

"Is he bothering you?" Darius called from the front step.

Greer muttered something very impolite under his breath, and then said, louder, "Go back in the house. We're talking."

Darius started to wheel down the ramp. "Whatever concerns Shea concerns me, too."

"I'm going in now," she said, dashing off before Darius could get close. As she suspected, he turned around and followed her back to the front step. Greer stayed by his vehicle, giving Darius a pissed look. She was glad Darius had stopped that conversation. Way too close for comfort on many levels.

"I'm fine, Greer," she called to him. "Thanks for caring. Get to work."

"Did I interrupt a tense moment?" Darius asked once he'd caught up to her, watching Greer's yellow Jeep back out. "Looked like he was harassing you. It had to do with whatever he did to you, didn't it? Tell me, and I'll make sure—"

"It's none of your business." She stalked into the house to find something for dinner, anything to get her mind off what just transpired.

It was hard to think about spaghetti or leftover steak when one question dominated her mind: how could it be a coincidence that the man who had been mauled was her rapist?